The Jesus Nut

The Jesus Nut

A novel by
John Prather

atmosphere press

Published by Atmosphere Press

Cover design by Kevin Stone

The characters in this novel are fictional—most of them, anyway. A few are real, and their well-documented beliefs may be reflected (with certain literary license) herein. But what happens in this story is most definitely fictional. This is, after all, only a novel.

atmospherepress.com

To Reverend James Pennington, a man who embodies αγάπη (*agape*) every day. And to all who have suffered injustice under the guise of religion.

PROLOGUE

By the fourth century after Christ, the biblical canon was nearly complete. The first five books of the Bible, known as the Pentateuch and often believed to have been written by Moses, were canonized—accepted as sacrosanct—in roughly 400 B.C. This was followed over the next three centuries by the authorization of the remainder of the Old Testament, the finished product containing a total of twenty-four distinct books according to Jewish tradition or thirty-nine in the Christian version. Then, in the years following Jesus' death, the accumulation of the New Testament began, a process which took three additional centuries. This much is known for sure.

Yet, even as the Bible took shape, its core beliefs were far from universal.

That changed in the year 325 A.D., when Constantine the Great summoned representatives from the three factions of Christianity to Nicaea, at the time a Greek city but now part of modern Turkey. As the new ruler of the entire Roman Empire, Constantine directed these representatives to establish the true nature of the Christ: Was He a mortal touched by God, or was He God incarnate? Constantine himself did not care what they decided; he only envisioned the process as a means to unite the people under his rule. Bishops from throughout the Western world, 318 in total, heeded his call.

This diverse assembly somehow managed to find

common ground, whether through consensus or coercion, and expressed their agreed-upon philosophical position in a construct known as the Holy Trinity and an affirmation of faith called the Nicene Creed. Constantine's unified empire became the most vast and powerful on earth, covering much of Western Europe, the Middle East, and the entirety of North Africa. This, too, is known for sure.

Not much is understood of the exact process, though, only that the bishops at Nicaea were among the most formidable men in the Christian world, dedicated to and bound by their collective obligation to God. Nevertheless, a basic understanding of human nature suggests Constantine's directive was no simple task. Skeptics might contend the Council was a veritable melting pot of human shortcoming—a delicate balance of ego, self-interest, and imperfection upended on regular occasions when strong personalities clashed with one another over differences both principled and petty.

Did the Macedonian bishop actually threaten to vivisect the gentleman from Gaul for his audacity in suggesting the Psalms were "ponderous and depressing"? Did the imposing bishop from Heidelberg attack his diminutive counterpart from Antioch with a lute, as rumors suggest? Was the Sicilian paying the Vatican to keep his sexual appetite a secret? Was the Iberian's belligerence the result of his arduous journey, or the two bota bags of red wine he consumed daily? Did the Danish bishop repudiate Christianity, frustrated by his inability to convince others of the legitimacy of Paul's letter to the Skjöldungar? Was there really a movement by the Roman bishops, under the direct orders of Pope Sylvester's teenage grandniece, to change the name of the Old

Testament to *The Totally Righteous Gazette*?

There is, however, power in the collective, and the smartest or most ambitious of these men recognized the political capital to be gained from their acquiescence to the group. Some Christian leaders of the day continued to use alternative texts, but teachings which denied the Holy Trinity were branded as profanation. Constantine ordered these men exiled and their works burned. In 367 A.D., a letter written by Bishop Athanasius of Alexandria outlined the twenty-seven books of the New Testament, and the Holy Bible was deemed complete—the true revealed word of the Lord.

Still, the absolute nature of such a pronouncement continues to haunt scholars, who painstakingly scour antiquity in their attempt to answer one particularly vexatious question: *What secrets are contained in the rejected texts?*

One
HALEY BERKSHIRE

Ό κύριος εισήλθε τήν πόλη καί ἤρξατο διδάσκειν, όμως κανείς δέν ἄν άκουσοιεν ὅτι οἱ σκέψεις τού ασυνήθιστες είς αρχές. Ο ἱ γυναίκες έγιναν απασχολημένες μετ' τίς δουλειές καί οἱ άνδρες έγιναν επιμελείς μετά τὰ ἔργα αὐτῶν, καί όλοι περιφρονόταν τά λόγια τού.

The Lord entered the city and began to teach, yet none would hear Him because His thoughts were unusual to the authorities. The women made themselves busy with chores and the men became diligent with their work, and all were contemptuous of His words.

(The Gospel According to Trevor, chapter 7, verses 36–37)

Dr. Haley Berkshire was a tenured professor of Religious Studies who did not believe in God.

Her natural cynicism—born of a zealot mother and an alcoholic father and refined through the belittling dictates of the nuns at Saint Mary Margaret of Grace Elementary School in Houston, Texas—led her to reject Catholicism, as she quickly tired of allegedly celibate old men sprinkling incense and rebranded water and singing in off-key Latin.

In high school, her contempt spread to all Judeo-Christian faiths and their fantastic stories about spontaneously combusting shrubbery, a 900-year-old man, a sailor's three-day weekend in the digestive system of a whale, a floating zoo, and of course a carpenter's restorative and self-levitational powers. Old Testament or New, she decided it was all hogwash.

During her undergraduate program in History, she rejected Islam, Hinduism, Buddhism, and Confucianism. As a grad student in Anthropology, her disdain grew to encompass the belief systems of Sikhs, Wiccans, Druids, Bahá'ís, Shintoists, and Jains. Finally, while earning her Ph.D. in Religious Studies, she rejected African diasporic faiths, Native American spiritual beliefs, mysticism, shamanism, Zoroastrianism, agnosticism, atheism, and her first husband, who was a Lutheran.

Her colleagues at the University of Utah did not typically invite her to church on Sunday or, for that matter, to lunch during the week. They were not jealous of her conservatively styled blonde hair or resentful of the loose-fitting clothes which, they correctly suspected, were meant to hide the fifteen pounds she added over the past decade. They just thought she was a couple volumes short of a complete set—an appraisal which did not bother her one damn bit.

As a tenured professor at a major university, she was expected to do research, and not just when she felt like it. She was required to have a research *agenda*. And unfortunately, as much as she would have preferred her agenda to be combing through Pinterest in search of cute cat pictures, her bastard of a department chair had more nefarious expectations. "Research is vital to our standing as a major institution," he preached. "Research is tantamount to our reputation," he pontificated. "Research brings funding," he confessed. And so, as if by holy writ, Dr. Ronald S. Wexford, Chairman of the University of Utah's Department of Religious Studies, demanded that Dr. Berkshire's research be about religion.

Berkshire was thus in the process of outlining a book about cats throughout religious history—"in the process of outlining a book" being academic-speak for "I haven't even a vague idea of something which might interest me (and I'm not especially motivated to figure it out), so I hope this buys me some time." Even that process stalled when she discovered there were several hundred subreddits devoted to cats.

Nine years earlier, her first research effort described the astounding lack of building codes and safety procedures at such hallowed sites as Machu Picchu, Angkor Wat, and the Walls of Jericho. She worked on this project for more than a year, sweating its every detail because Wexford promised a promotion to Associate Professor when it was published. But as the months rolled past and the rejection letters rolled in, she grew disheartened. Finally, three days before she was set to move home to Houston, she received a letter from *The American Journal of Construction Management*, which agreed to publish her work. From this, she gained both her promotion and her second husband, a local building contractor who served as technical advisor on the paper. Months later, the winter edition of *The American Journal of Construction Management* included a heavily edited version of her research in its humor section, page 78, in the lower right-hand corner.

Unfortunately, she was unable to rest on her laurels, such as they were. Instead, Associate Professor Berkshire was challenged to do still more research, to continue to be productive. To advance her goddamned agenda.

It took her three years, but she finally produced an astonishing work about the Shroud of Turin, the sacred burial cloth of Jesus Christ. Her methodology drew on her academic background in history and anthropology, and employed historiography, iconography, carbon dating, forensic textile analysis, weather extrapolations, and review of primary source documents including maps, city records, letters, journals, and of course the Holy Bible. Her conclusion: The Shroud of Turin was actually a beach towel, acquired by the apostle Paul when he stopped at a resort in Sidon on a hot day and decided to take a dip in the Mediterranean.

This paper was rejected by every English-speaking professional journal of religious studies, plus both *The American Journal of Construction Management* and *Travel + Leisure* magazine. When she finally self-published through Amazon, Dr. Berkshire and the University of Utah became the laughing stock of the religious community. Priests and pastors criticized her heresy. Academics mocked her irrationality. Colleagues laughed at her lunacy. Even her neighbors in the Liberty Wells neighborhood of Salt Lake City, already wary of her idiosyncrasies, now rushed inside their homes when she came out to get the morning newspaper. Meanwhile, her second husband escaped with his secretary and became a realtor in Denver.

But her contract merely said "publish," not where or how, so on the strength of this loophole she became

Professor Haley Berkshire, tenured full professor of Religious Studies at the University of Utah. As an added bonus, she also earned $148.12 in royalties from the sale of forty-six copies of her book. Now, safe in her academic cocoon, she could utilize the exact same lecture notes, test questions, and poorly timed jokes semester after semester, year after year. Her classes were among the University's most popular—especially with the fraternity and sorority types, who maintained years of old exams, notes, and research papers they kept hidden in a file cabinet in a secret closet in the basement of the Interfraternity Council offices. Indeed, according to chapter bylaws, any member of Lambda Chi Alpha who could not pull at least a B+ in Dr. Berkshire's Introduction to World Religions class was immediately placed on academic probation.

By 2019, eleven years into her professorial career and six years since earning tenure, her evaluations had slipped and her research had become more sporadic.

So, too, had her love life. The good news was that her absolute denunciation of all religious dogma eliminated any moral compunctions regarding premarital sex. She felt no guilt, no shame, no remorse. The bad news was that she had been on maybe half a dozen dates since the end of marriage number two, and had gotten laid only once during that time—by a pudgy Professor of Economics from Brigham Young University, who informed her post-coitus that he was married. That was just as well, anyway, since his vanilla lovemaking technique left her far less satisfied than did her DiddleBang DeluXX, the pink silicone "friend" she kept in her nightstand.

Nevertheless, with the occasional need for human touch—but mostly to placate her relentless cousin Jolene—

Berkshire finally sat down at the computer one Thursday evening and created a Match.com account, username DocBerk.

Less than two minutes later, she received her first response, from JfromWyo:

Yo DocBerk. Whazzup?

Nothing. How are you?

Chillin. I like your name, DocBerk. Its like Berserk. Did you know thats a Viking word?

Yes. They were elite warriors who wore animal pelts into battle instead of armor.

GD, your smart. My favorite video game is Berserk and the Band of the Hawk. I fuckin crushhhh that game. Thats why I swiped right on you.

Lucky me. Do you ever use apostrophes?

Yeah I use apostrophe's. See?

How old are you?

Im 27.
What are you wearing?

Sweatpants and a T-shirt. Why do you want to know?

I was hoping you were wearing animal pelts and a Viking helmet LOL

Sorry to disappoint. My animal pelts are at the cleaners.

Thats a joke right?
So are you DTF or what?

The acronym confused her, but a quick consult of Urban Dictionary provided its meaning and the motivation to forego the grammatical skills and seductive charms of JfromWyo.

Three days later, she began an online chat with an engineer from Ogden. His picture was a little blurry, but he was well educated and seemed nice. After the usual innocuous small talk, the conversation drifted to her work.

Why is the Bible the Bible?

What do you mean?

I mean, by what right did a handful of
men get to decide what was the word
of God …

They were chosen by the church.

and what wasn't? Maybe there was some
other stuff that was better.

Maybe.

Then why isn't it in the Bible?

A simple question, really, and certainly not a new one among academics, but for some reason it piqued her interest. Two weeks later, by which time the engineer from Ogden had long since moved on to other prospects, the professor had a plan.

"I want to thank you all for your willingness to help on this important research project," Dr. Berkshire told half a dozen University of Utah undergraduates and one guy who worked at Home Depot and took night classes at Salt Lake Community College. She assumed half of them would disappear at some point, but with Wexford breathing down her neck and the cat book stuck in the mud, she could not afford to be choosy. "As you may know," she continued, "a bunch of bishops got together at Nicaea in 325 A.D. and decided upon the Holy Trinity. In doing so, they also rejected some religious texts, which essentially nailed down what went in the Bible and what didn't. Our objective—"

A hand shot up. "You mean God didn't write the Bible?" one student asked.

"Correct," Berkshire replied, stifling a laugh. "Although it is believed ... by some ... that the Bible is divinely inspired," adding air quotes to this last part. "Anyway, our objective with this project is to identify texts which were not included in the Bible, locate them and, if we're lucky, uncover some new shit ... stuff."

While the students yammered amongst themselves, Berkshire smiled at her success. After a moment, she added, "We'll start on Monday, three p.m., right here. I'll give you some direction on how to research this and exactly what we're looking for, but you guys are way more tech-savvy than I am, so use whatever resources you can. The dark web and social media and whatnot. We'll see what archaeologists and historians and biblical scholars are working on, and figure out where we go from there. Are there any questions?"

Home Depot guy raised his hand. "What happens if we don't find anything interesting? I mean, will we still get paid?"

"I have funding for this project so, yes, you will get paid either way," Berkshire answered. "Although it would certainly be better if you find something. And the money only goes through the end of the spring semester, so whatever you find, please find it fairly quickly."

Because, she thought to herself as she smiled insincerely, *this is my only chance to get a break from that bastard Wexford and his bullshit research agenda.*

Two

JESSE MORALES

Έκείνοι πιστεύουν ελοιοποιηθήσονται καί βασανιστήσονται από τούς απίστους, γὰρ δέ μετά ψευδαισθήσεις καί περιφρόνηση βρεθήσονται αντιμέτωποι, καί βρόσουσι μοναξιά μόνο ανάμεσα εξωστρεφείς. Ναί, ἀμὴν λέγω ὑμῖν, ή αχαλίνωτη εμφάνισή αύτους κρύβει τήν αληθινή τούς μεγαλοπρέπεια.

Those who believe will be ridiculed and tormented by the unbelievers. They will be confronted with mockery and scorn, and will find solace only among the outcasts. Yea, verily I say unto thee, their unkempt appearance hides their true splendor.

(The Gospel According to Trevor, chapter 1, verses 28–29)

Jesse Morales had forgotten how to walk on water.

It had been a long time—two thousand years, more or less—but he was growing ever more frustrated at his inability to do something he once did so effortlessly.

Not that he really needed to walk on water at this moment. What he really needed was to walk *in* water. He needed a shower or a bath, maybe even a complete delousing, since it had been at least a week, or maybe two, since soap and water last touched his coarse olive skin and ran through his bedraggled dark hair. However long the public showers at Venice Beach had been broken. And the spring had been unusually dry, no rain for the last month. Occasionally the Lord provided him a working sprinkler, but the current drought conditions in southern California made even that a rare pleasure.

Sure, he could have gone into the ocean, but Jesse Morales did not like the taste of saltwater, the thought of being eaten by sharks, the possibility that seaweed might irritate his skin, the annoyance of children on boogie boards, the occasional grain of sand in his eye, or the prospect of drowning. Despite being the Son of God, Jesse Morales was consumed by self-doubt.

Jesse also had not eaten in days—whether two or three, he could not recall. Not a piece of leftover hamburger from the garbage can outside Sea Side Burgers on Ocean Front Walk, not an overripe peach or nectarine from the dumpster behind Windward Market, not even a sliver of stale bread from the bakery on Venice Boulevard. Feeding the multitudes was, at best, only a vague aspiration to him these days. Feeding himself was a more pressing and immediate concern.

I must remain humble before God, he said to himself, often, *if I am to teach my flock*. But as his stomach rumbled with anger, such reassurances often seemed hollow and the idea of preaching his message of hope grew more challenging by the day. He despised his lack of spiritual wherewithal.

Then there was the prospect of summer, its official start only days away even as the thermometer declared it long since arrived. Its crowds and traffic made him anxious, and its oppressive heat drained him.

Most of all, he hated the rancid smells of summer. Tourists flocked to the trendy beachside bars, drank to excess, and culminated their frolicsome night by pissing in the alley or puking in the flower beds. The rich people off Abbot Kinney brought their annoying yappy dogs to the Boardwalk, allowed the miserable creatures to shit anywhere and everywhere, and left the unsanitary pile of excrement behind like it was beneath their dignity. Uneaten food from neighborhood restaurants was discarded in the dumpsters, and what Jesse and his unfortunate comrades could not or would not scavenge spent hours or often days marinating in the hot sun, haute cuisine eventually transformed into a fetid mess even flies were loath to experience. Then, finally, when the Waste Management truck made its rounds, it belched malodorous diesel fumes into the pristine ocean air, often at ungodly early morning hours. And fuck, was that thing loud.

Venice Beach may have looked Edenic, but it was Jesse Morales' idea of perdition.

On top of everything else, his groin throbbed. He did not know why. He could summon nothing from his limited memory, but he could not recall a time when it didn't hurt down there. He vaguely remembered a place called Afghanistan, some other guys, an explosion, and a lot of blood and screams, as well as some papers he had been given when he returned home. He remembered nothing before. And when someone stole his backpack, the papers disappeared along with it.

Jesse pulled off his tattered adidas sweatshirt and rolled his mat around it. He secured the mat with a fraying bungee cord and stashed the whole package behind a dumpster. This, plus the clothes on his back and a plastic bucket he now carried, represented the sum total of his worldly possessions.

Smoothing his orange polo shirt, Jesse emerged from the alley into the noontime glare, the morning mist all but burned off and the sun reflecting brightly off the water. He liked the orange polo shirt, a gift from his friends Tommy and Jeong at stall number forty-three along the Venice Beach marketplace. Venice Beach is famous for peddling authentic brand-name garments to tourists and bargain hunters at absurdly discounted prices, a process made profitable only by the fact that the legal teams at Izod, Nike, and Tommy Hilfiger are too busy to worry about these particular knock-offs. If you looked closely at Jesse's shirt, you could see the indistinct lines of the Izod alligator logo, and you knew the sweatshop in whatever remote area of China had not yet perfected its counterfeiting. Jesse liked the shirt, though, so he forgave them their sin of shoddy workmanship and hoped the new tariffs on Chinese goods he heard about did not force Tommy and Jeong out of business.

As he crossed toward the Venice Rec Center, he came upon a young boy, perhaps seven. "Bless you, my child," he said, placing his hand upon the child's forehead. "Just as you followed me to the temple, follow me again today. For while the adults may turn away, the children will lead us to salvation."

The boy kicked Jesse in the shin and fled. "Stranger danger!" he cried. "Mommy!"

"The time of the Lord is at hand," Jesse shouted after him. He watched as the boy anxiously explained to his mother what happened, pointing at Jesse as he spoke.

The woman's stare grew more withering until she finally spoke her mind. "You sleaze," she called to him. "You dirty, disgusting slimeball. You filthy pervert! Why isn't there a cop around when you need one?"

The boy pulled her sleeve. "Can we go now, Mommy?" he asked.

She looked at the boy, then at Jesse, then spun away, stopping for one final comment. "You can go to hell!" In a moment, mother and child disappeared.

"I come to save you from hell," Jesse whispered. "And if my Father in Heaven commands me go to hell in order to save you, I will most assuredly obey." He examined his shin, which was already bruising, and his stomach rumbled again.

"Just another day in Venice Beach, baby," said the man everyone knew as Jimi Hendrix on Roller Skates. He called himself the Kama Kosmic Krusader but, to tourists who encountered him only briefly, he was Jimi. For more than forty years, the black man in the flowing white robe and turban had skated thousands of miles, electric guitar in hand and amplifier on his back, playing improvised ballads to pretty girls and testosterone-charged anthems to the men who paraded from one end of Ocean Front Walk to the other. While some acts in the human freak show of Venice Beach were new and others had been plying their trade for years, Jimi was an institution. Many speculated an institution might also have been his last previous address.

"No better place to do the Lord's work," Jesse said to Jimi. Jesse squinted viciously against the ocean's glare, wrinkling his thin, dark face so it resembled the Nile River

Delta. "I am come, as promised," he continued, his hand over his eyes to block the sun. "All the signs have been laid before man, yet they will not see."

"I'm with you, J," said Jimi.

"I know you are, my friend. And one day you will join me in the kingdom of the Lord."

"That's right," Jimi answered. "Where I will jam with Hendrix, Lennon, Joplin, and Ray fucking Charles." He played a few licks on his guitar for emphasis.

"Amen," said Jesse, as Jimi skated away.

A young man walked by, a hipster-looking guy who probably worked at the Google office on Main Street. The massive cinnamon roll the hipster was eating made Jesse's mouth water.

The hipster stopped, took one final bite of his cinnamon roll, and tossed its substantial remnants into a trash can.

Jesse could not believe his luck. He looked to his left, then his right, then his left again. For some reason, even when ravenous with hunger, he thought daylight trash scavenging might be perceived as undignified, certainly beneath the Son of God. But with nobody looking, the leftover cinnamon roll was his for the taking.

But as he hastened toward the trash can, a squirrel with no qualms about dignity scurried up the side and emerged with the pastry treasure, defiantly eating it right in front of Jesse.

Jesse sighed deeply and sat down on a concrete bench. He placed the plastic bucket at his feet and pulled a sign from inside: *Homeless. Hungry. Please help the Son of God.*

Just then, a skateboarder whizzed past. Things had sure gotten more perilous since the city built the skate park last year (or maybe ten years ago, he couldn't be sure), and the noise and danger conspired to drive him away from his favorite spot, across from the Chinese massage place, where he always seemed to make a few extra dollars.

These days the panhandling business was slower, or maybe the competition was more robust. An average day on Ocean Front Walk used to generate at least ten bucks, a good Sunday close to twenty. Now it yielded only a fraction of that. He wondered if the old guy in the clown suit, who looked straight out of a cheesy horror movie as he wandered Ocean Front Walk, might be bad for business.

A pair of fat joggers now jiggled their way toward him, earbuds connected to their phones to protect against any interaction. Joggers were the worst, since they never carried any money but flung sweat indiscriminately when they passed. Jesse seemed to remember once being able to run a long way.

As he struggled with that memory, a man and woman swaggered past. The man's hand cradled the woman's ass, and she reached her hand inside his unbuttoned shirt to caress his muscular chest.

"The unrighteous man who dwells in earthly pleasures shall never see the house of God," Jesse said. The couple would not look him in the eye. "Dwell instead in the pleasures of the spirit."

Mister Chest turned and flipped a bird.

"Forgive them, Lord," he sighed, "for they know not what they do."

Three

BRIAN WILLIAM CALLUM ROBERT O'SHEA

Μήν είστε πάνω από τούς πειρασμούς τού κόσμου, αλλά πηγαίνετε ανάμεσα τούς αμαρτωλούς ώστε καταλάβήσοιτε τά πολλά βάσανα τού ανθρώπου.

Be not above the temptations of the world, but go amongst the sinners so that you may understand the many sufferings of man.

(The Gospel According to Trevor, chapter 3, verse 7)

Father Brian William Callum Robert O'Shea of the North Seattle Diocese knew a thing or two about sin.

He learned about it as a child in Boise, Idaho, pledged to avoid it while in seminary at Saint Thomas University in Miami, meditated about it during a year at a monastery in the Pyrenees mountains, and heard all about its many forms during confessions as part of his pastoral duties stretching from Pennsylvania to the Pacific Northwest.

He also knew that saying a few "Our Fathers" and "Hail Marys" could not keep sin away, his congregants and himself being human. But as the available tools at his parish and the groundwork of his faith, he dispensed them liberally. He understood they were more than salves, more than Band-Aids; they represented the very substance of Catholicism, words meant to cause sinners to reflect upon their transgressions and then reconnect with a powerful and forgiving God. Yet every week, the same people were back in the confessional booth, acknowledging both the same sins and more lurid ones, saying more "Hail Marys" in hopes of another seven days of absolution. O'Shea always listened intently to their confessions, scratching his stubbly brown beard and running his fingers through his wavy hair while he contemplated the sin, the sinner, and an article he recently read about alarmingly higher obesity rates among clergy. Fortunately he was still reasonably fit, trusting his daily fiber intake and occasional exercise to protect him from the fate of his colleagues.

Protecting his soul was of equal concern, so in recognition of his own humanity, Father O'Shea routinely said twenty "Our Fathers" every morning just to start his day on the safe side, and twenty "Hail Marys" every night so he could fall asleep with a clear conscience. Each morning he awoke refreshed, recited his "Our Fathers" over his morning oatmeal, and spent another day leading his flock to God.

He had been assigned to his current post at Saint Helen of Mercy Catholic Church after the previous cleric, a decrepit and nearly deaf old crust named Father Hugh Watt (but known amongst the Sunday school kids as Father Huh? What?), was asked to retire when he could no longer hear confessions. In contrast, Father O'Shea was a breath of spring. His congregants responded to his lively homilies far more than they did to Father Watt's parched monotone of yore. O'Shea smiled more often, occasionally threw in witty observations or a funny story, and limited his remarks to fifteen minutes. Lifelong Catholics especially appreciated his relative brevity and the fact that they could, most of the time, stay awake until after Holy Communion.

Tithes increased, and Father O'Shea's parish became the wealthiest in King County. The North Seattle Diocese, pleased with his work, created for him a discretionary fund, which he accepted as the groundwork for a community outreach program he called "Bringing the Collar to the Crowd." His five-week series on the clergy as traveling messengers of the Lord was a highlight of the Epiphany season.

The Epiphany season was also when he first discovered the Starlight Gentlemen's Club.

One Tuesday night, with the reflections of Epiphany, the sacrifice of Lent, and the celebration of Easter now past and the church into what it called Ordinary Time, Father O'Shea hurried from his weekly visit with Mrs. Skinner at the Evergreen Retirement Village and drove his Toyota Camry eleven blocks to the Starlight. The Club was sandwiched between a furniture reupholstering shop and a discount shoe outlet, a flashing neon sign providing the dark parking lot's only illumination. It was almost unwelcoming outside, but nobody went for the exterior aesthetics. The good stuff was inside. So Father O'Shea adjusted his collar, checked his pockets, and strolled toward the door.

"Good evening, Father," said the bouncer. He wore a T-shirt, sleeves straining to contain enormous arms. A tattoo of a devil's pitchfork peeked above the neckline. "Another night with the sinners?"

"How you doing, Scotty?" answered Father O'Shea. He turned and handed a five to the cashier, cover charge paid for by his sinful parishioners via the parish discretionary fund.

"Ten dollar cover," said the cashier. She was mid-forties, her low-cut shirt revealing breasts which were likely once on display at just this sort of place. "Not five."

Father O'Shea reached into his pocket and nonchalantly pulled out a card, which he handed to her.

"Oh, sorry," she said. "Five dollars for VIP members."

O'Shea turned to the bouncer. "She's new, huh?" The bouncer smiled and patted down the priest.

"Have a good time, Father," he said when satisfied.

"I always do," replied O'Shea.

Twenty minutes later, now on his second Bud Light, Father O'Shea watched a patron three tables away enjoying the services of one of the dancers, whose butt ended up in the patron's crotch just as the last notes of "Sweet Child O' Mine" blasted through the speakers. She stroked his hair and sat down next to him, and a cocktail waitress descended upon them within seconds. Father O'Shea chuckled to himself, knowing there would soon be a bottle of champagne on the man's table, a bottle which hours before might have been on the shelf at the Dollar Tree. And he knew that an hour from now, this man would be a hundred dollars poorer than when he first walked in, having earned only regret, humiliation, and a raging headache the next morning in exchange for his time and money.

Father O'Shea felt pride in his own self-control, as Tuesday was two-for-one night at the Starlight so his bar tab never exceeded twenty bucks plus tip. He began the habit of visiting only on Tuesdays as part of his Lenten self-denial, but felt it proper to continue the practice post-Lent as a testament to his inviolability. He congratulated himself for being a good steward of the discretionary fund.

Until he noticed *her* on the other side of the room.

She moved like a gossamer angel barely contained within an eighth of a yard of chiffon, lace, and Lycra. Her ass was as round as a Communion wafer and as firm as Abraham's devotion. Her breasts could fill the Holy Grail and her legs could part the Red Sea and erect the Tower of Babel.

Father O'Shea felt a slight stirring in his trousers, and as he ordered his second round of two-for-one draft beers, his eyes never left her. When the beverages arrived, he asked that she be sent over.

"Hi," she said when she arrived a few moments later. Her wavy brown hair fell to her shoulders in caramel ribbons. "I heard you asked for me."

"I did."

"How can I help you?" She noticed his collar and scrunched up her nose, so cute it made him shiver. "Are you a priest?"

"I am, indeed. Father Brian William Callum Robert O'Shea of the North Seattle Diocese, at your service."

"I don't go to church anymore, but thanks," she said, and turned to move away.

"Wait," said O'Shea, and she stopped. "Just let me stare at you for a while, my child. Please. You are heavenly."

She giggled. "I'm on stage next. You can stare at me there for three songs."

"Next up on stage," the disc jockey boomed. It sounded more like "Ex uppa stays," but Father O'Shea had now spent enough time at the Starlight Gentlemen's Club to decipher. Places like the Starlight Gentlemen's Club were never known for either their subtlety or their acoustics, unless one's idea of a good sound system involved only volume and excessive bass. *But hey,* he thought, *if I learned to translate Greek, Latin, and ancient Aramaic in divinity school, I can surely translate Starlight Gentlemen's Club distortion into recognizable English.*

"Puh yo hansto gedder fo du luffly Simone."

Simone, thought Father O'Shea. *What a lyrical name.* He figured her real name was probably far less exotic, like Margaret Jones, but he clapped vigorously nonetheless.

Three songs later, her purple G-string exploding with currency (much of it courtesy of the Saint Helen of Mercy discretionary fund) and her matching chiffon crop top draped over the good Father's head, she left the stage and sat next to him.

"Did you like?" she asked, touching his hand while making no effort to retrieve her clothes. Her breasts glistened with sweat thanks to her exertion under the hot lights. O'Shea thought of the words of Jeremiah, chapter thirty-two, which commanded him to "behold the mounds"—and thought it best to obey.

"I was entranced," he managed to say. Even as the next dancer took the stage, his eyes never left Simone.

"Should we get some champagne?" she continued and, before he could process, she summoned a nearby waitress.

The hook now set, she retrieved her top from O'Shea's head. "I guess I should put this on. Unless you don't want me to."

"I ... uh ... no ... yes, I mean ... If you want." O'Shea, ever-eloquent before his congregation, could manage only that. He was pretty sure his heartbeat was now approaching infinity.

"Will you excuse me for just a moment?" she asked, fastening her miniature top. "I need to use the bathroom."

"Of course," he stumbled, knowing at this moment he would have agreed to anything.

She winked at him and promised, "I'll be right back."

As he watched her divine wafer-like ass glide away, he knew the moment of reckoning was at hand. His "Hail Marys" came rapidly, and he completed twelve of them before she returned. She smelled of lavender, and her dark eyes reflected the garish neon lighting like a fire opal. As she sat, she gently touched his arm once again.

"I'm Simone," she said.

An hour later, an empty bottle of cheap champagne sat on the table and Simone sat on O'Shea's lap. He was a hundred dollars poorer than when he first walked in, and connected with the sinful thoughts of his parishioners in a most tangible way. Yet he felt neither regret nor humiliation, and only a touch of a headache which he felt sure could be eradicated by his morning "Our Fathers" combined with a long walk. For now, it mattered none.

"Ex uppa stays, less heerit fo du luffly Simone," reverberated through the Club, breaking his reverie.

"I've got to go," she said. "I'm up on stage again."

"I've got to go, too," he answered as he checked his watch, remembering an eight a.m. pastoral visit and knowing he was out of cash anyway. Her pout, offered in response, somehow emboldened him.

"When do you work next?" he asked.

"Thursday," she said over her shoulder before jumping onstage as the amplified drumbeat intro to "Rock the

Cradle of Love" vibrated their empty champagne glasses.

On the drive home, Father Brian William Callum Robert O'Shea nearly rubbed the finish off his rosary and needed to drive a couple of extra laps around the block so he could complete five times the requisite number of "Hail Marys." Yet he still fell asleep with the faint smell of lavender on his skin.

Four
THE REVELATION

Οΰτως γὰρ αποκαλυφθήσοιντο μεγάλες αλήθειες, πού λίγοι είναι έτοιμοι ΐν' ακούειν.

And so shall be revealed great truths, which few are prepared to hear.

(The Gospel According to Trevor, chapter 2, verse 29)

The North American Society of Religious Scholars meets annually, at garish hotels located in fantastic tourist destinations, for a three-day conference featuring religious academics from throughout the western hemisphere. The purpose of this conference is for college professors of religion to share the findings of their research, network with peers, and drink to excess. Thus, organizers always scheduled the conference for Memorial Day weekend, right after most professors turned in their final spring grades. Those oddball universities on the quarter system, which were not yet finished with classes at the time of the conference, dealt with the inconvenience as best they could, usually by springing for the more expensive vodka.

When the conference was held in Pigeon Forge, Tennessee two years prior, scholars learned about topics such as "Legal, Ethical, and Moral Challenges Associated With the Emergence of LGBTQ Clergy in Progressive Churches," "Religious Extremism and Its Impact on Global Security," and "A Pantheistic View of the Creation Story," and were treated to a day at Dollywood Theme Park and a performance by the Great Smoky Mountains Fighting Lumberjacks, featuring Bobby Joe and Joey Bob (aka the Axe-Throwing Twins). Conference-goers returned home exhausted yet informed, many hopeful of securing tenure because of the success of their juried presentations in Tennessee. The conference also brought additional change to a number of Religious Studies departments around the country as, beginning in September, seventeen schools created faculty axe-throwing leagues.

Last year, with the conference in Toronto, topics included "Government Restrictions on Religion: Comparing Western Europe to the Third World," "Religious Media and Their Impact on Belief Systems," and "An Analysis of Religious Symbols Worldwide Using the Principles of Transformational Geometry." But the most popular presentation was the visit to the Hockey Hall of Fame, followed by a tour of the Molson brewery—a tour made substantially more educational because the taps stayed open for the rest of the evening.

Because Dr. Haley Berkshire was terrified of flying, she had never before attended the North American Society of Religious Scholars annual conference. But with the 2019 edition scheduled for the Palms Casino Resort in Las Vegas—an easy six-hour drive from Salt Lake City—she determined she would finally make an appearance. Come

February, as her research project got off the ground, she decided upon an even more audacious approach. A week later she submitted an abstract of her project, albeit deliberately vague because she could not predict if her student researchers would actually find anything.

As it turned out, there were far fewer submissions than usual. So, to her great surprise, Berkshire's presentation, entitled "New Scholarship About Old Books: What Happened at Nicaea?", was accepted.

When she received notification in early April, her excitement was necessarily tempered with apprehension, since she still had no idea where her research would stand come late May. If her team discovered some obscure, long-forgotten document, she could put together a summary of their process and a brief interpretation of the significance of this new text. If, on the other hand, they hit a brick wall, she would have to cobble together a paper which described how their research methodology produced no results, perhaps concluding with an affirmation of the sanctity of the Holy Bible. Prepared to go in either direction, she only hoped her answer came with enough time to craft her paper. And, as April turned to May, the brick wall drew ever closer.

She arrived at the conference four weeks later to find she had been scheduled for the second afternoon. All of it.

Scheduled immediately after lunch and taking place in the hotel's main ballroom, her presentation was envisioned as a featured highlight of the conference—a series of papers followed by a panel discussion with three other experts, under the general title of "Religious Discoveries and Antiquities." With no other presentations opposite this one, her hopes for a small turnout now hinged entirely upon whether most of the attendees were too drunk to find the room or too busy chatting up cocktail waitresses to care. Unfortunately, the events staff at the Palms placed directional signs throughout the banquet facilities, and as it turns out their cocktail waitresses were more impressed by gratuities than by customers' ability to recite the *Bhagavad Gita* in its original Sanskrit. All possible circumvention now disposed of, the ballroom's hundreds of chairs were rapidly filling with the nation's preeminent religious scholars.

Seeing this, Dr. Haley Berkshire began to sweat.

She was the third of four panelists to speak, so she was compelled to sit, while her anxiety built, through an hour of presentations before her own. During this time she could barely focus, and although she occasionally made out terms like "canonical Semitism" or "ethno-archaeological exegesis," her mind was mostly blank. She chewed her lower lip, a nervous habit dating to preschool, and calmed herself by scrolling through Pinterest on her iPhone in search of cat pictures.

Finally she heard herself being introduced. "Dr. Haley Berkshire is a tenured professor of Religious Studies at the University of Utah. Her scholarship, which is always provocative ..."

I like the word 'provocative,' she told herself. Then, *Don't fuck this up.*

"... has appeared in a wide variety of publications. Let's give a warm welcome to Dr. Haley Berkshire."

The applause was enthusiastic, although for some reason it did not necessarily sound genuine. But with that introduction, she approached the podium.

"Thank you for being here today," she began. "I'm

honored to be part of this program."

A wizened professor from New York University, sitting in the third row, clicked open his pen and grumbled, "You mean you're *lucky* to be part of this program."

One chair over, a colleague from Harvard spooned ranch dressing into his eager mouth with a stalk of celery. "Interesting choice of speakers. The University of Utah is definitely not a hotbed for religious scholarship." He wiped a dribble of ranch from his chin.

"How do you think she got tenure?" replied the NYU man, and they both chuckled.

Berkshire noticed. She tried not to betray it, but those sitting toward the front definitely detected her wince.

She continued, "Over the past several months, I have led a team of students ..."

She turned toward the screen behind her and pressed a button on the small remote control she held. The screen showed a photograph of Berkshire with several students, one wearing his Home Depot apron.

"... in the exploration of an important question: What happened to the texts that were rejected by the Council at Nicaea and by the early church?"

She pressed the button to bring up the next slide, a random painting of religious figures in conference.

"And today," she continued, "I am pleased to report the discovery of perhaps the most important relic of ancient Christendom ..."

She paused for dramatic effect, there being actual murmurs of interest from the crowd. Unaccustomed to this reaction, she allowed the dramatic pause to go just a moment too long.

Next slide, showing the poster for *Raiders of the Lost Ark*.

"... at least since Indiana Jones found the Ark of the Covenant."

The laughter from the crowd was guarded, polite at best, her reputation for peculiarity and outright preposterousness well known among her peers.

She smiled at her attempt at humor, then continued. "My team and I have located a new text, rejected at Nicaea for its depiction of Christ and, as far as we can tell, never before studied."

Many in the audience actually sat up, genuinely attentive. This could be interesting stuff—although whether in a scholarly sense or more like a train wreck, it remained to be seen.

Next slide, showing clip art of an old book with a blank cover.

"This text is known as ..." She again drew it out, trying to emulate Bob Barker building anticipation on *The Price is Right*.

"... The Gospel According to Trevor."

She pressed the button and the words "Gospel According to Trevor" floated onto the cover of the book so her 'most important relic of ancient Christendom' looked as if it were created by a fourth-grader who just learned Photoshop.

"And I daresay it contains rare insight into the life, work, personality, and suffering of the Christ. Including his mortality. Christ as mortal man."

The professor from NYU turned to his Harvard colleague. "Oh, for the love of God, here we go again," NYU said. The Harvard man's laugh caused him to cough, and he spilled his ranch dressing on his pants.

Berkshire continued, "Most notable in the text is Trevor's description of the crucifixion, which diverges from those of the other Gospels."

She advanced to the next slide, showing Christ on the cross.

"We know, of course, that a Roman centurion, now commonly known as Longinus, drove his spear into Christ's side while He anguished on the cross."

Next slide, depicting Christ with his side pierced.

"But according to Trevor, this was not the most egregious suffering inflicted by the Romans. Trevor goes into great detail of their cruelty as he describes *khatzot eshekha meshicha*, as it would be called in the Aramaic." She paused to watch as some translated while others less schooled in ancient languages asked their neighbors what the term meant. There were many shrugs but also lots of hushed conversations.

"In the ancient Greek–the Koine–it would be *ho horchis tou Christou*. Or if you prefer, in Latin, *testiculus Christi*."

The crowd now buzzed. Most were familiar with at least one of these languages, plus the Latin translation was simple enough. This was some weird shit.

"The Testicle of Christ," she continued. "As described in the Gospel According to Trevor, one Roman soldier cut off Christ's left ... um ... ball."

The crowd noise continued to grow, louder and more antagonistic.

"As a souvenir ..."

Several male scholars squirmed and instinctively crossed their legs. Others offered rebuttal, their opinions that she was a crank and this just one more of her bizarre and worthless 'academic' findings. But now she was rolling.

"A souvenir which has never been recovered ..."

One professor grabbed his own crotch and offered, "Hey, sweetheart, you can recover my balls." He raised his glass of cheap Vegas scotch to toast his negligible wit.

"... but which, according to Trevor, may very well still exist."

By now, the crowd noise, a mixture of commentary and laughter, was almost so loud as to completely drown her out. But she pressed onward.

"I am hopeful I will be allowed to take a sabbatical next year in a quest to find this remarkable religious relic." Shouting, she added, "Yes, as God is my witness, I vow to you that I will discover the Testicle of Christ!"

Harvard, shaking his head in disbelief, turned to NYU. "The Jesus Nut."

"The testicle," NYU answered, "or her?"

Five

THE GOOD NEWS

Άποδεχτείτε όλα τά δώρα όπως αυτά προορίζονται, ώς δώρα από τού κύριου ΐνα χρησιμοποιήθειν όταν είναι σωστός ό χρόνος.

Accept all gifts, then, as they are intended—as gifts from the Lord to be used when the time is right.

(The Gospel According to Trevor, chapter 4, verse 22)

A week into the month of June, Jesse's life at Venice Beach could adequately be described as too many skateboarders, too much heat, too little food, and too many unbelievers. He was tired, dirty, hungry, and cranky. But one can safely assume it would be considered poor form for the son of God to be seen bitching at others. So, conscious of both his malaise and his propriety, Jesse spent much of his time out of sight, where he could suffer his privation and his dual aches—stomach and scrotum—in ascetic silence.

He often retreated into the darkness of Venice homelessness as soon as the sky grew dim. The city would stay awake for several more hours, but that was no great imposition. Jesse had long since grown accustomed to the chatter and laughter of animated drunks, to car doors slamming and car alarms chirping, to sirens blaring in the distance and horns honking around the corner. Besides, he had a vague feeling that at some point in his life, his nighttimes were far louder, far more immediate, far more visceral and ominous.

Eight hours later, as the sun began to warm the California sky, he would wake, an isolated figure alone amongst the scattered destitute. He longed for companionship but savored his solitude, a paradox which made both companionship and solitude equally impossible to enjoy.

As he woke, he ran his hands through his stringy, dark hair. A second time, and his hands paused. *My face is getting especially thin*, he noticed. And then his stomach growled, a caged bear in a desperate cry for freedom.

Just like he did every day, Jesse rolled his adidas sweatshirt inside his mat, secured it with his bungee cord, and tucked it behind a nearby dumpster. He climbed up the dumpster and peered inside, finding a worn desk chair, a couple of ratty blankets, several empty motor oil containers, and a dozen or so black plastic garbage bags stuffed with the flotsam and jetsam of daily living. He examined one of the blankets and decided it might be worth keeping, then climbed down with his new prize. As he did so he felt wobbly, and could not ignore the sobering fact that, at his current rate of decline, he might not be around come winter to even need the blanket.

While it was his job to provide others with their daily bread, he needed some for himself, and he needed it post-haste. He detested his weakness, and his sigh finally opened the door to his anguish. For several minutes he sat in the alley, back against a dirty wall, fighting vainly against the tears. Passersby ignored the weeping man, the image too painful for them to interrupt.

His tears exhausted, Jesse struggled to his feet. He sighed again, but this an act of resolve rather than hopelessness. *Pride goeth before a fall,* he said to himself, and while he knew that might be only a rationalization, he refused to allow his pride to starve him. He smoothed his orange fake Izod polo shirt and staggered into the light. Had such an empathetic man as himself seen his own reflection in a mirror, he surely would have cried yet again.

He stopped to rummage through a garbage can on Ocean Front Walk, but found not a single morsel. As he replaced the contents of the garbage can, he paused to look at a fresh newspaper. *Wednesday*, he noticed.

Wednesday, he knew, was the day the Church on Pearl fed the homeless. The church was in Santa Monica, about two-and-one-half miles away, but he heard the food was good and abundant and the people were kind. And while Pearl Street seemed a long way right now, he felt certain he had prevailed against greater adversity in the past.

So Jesse set his face and began the trek northward.

The walk took him almost two hours in his weakened condition, yet he still arrived long before the distribution. Forced to wait another couple of hours in the thin shade of a mulberry tree in front of the church, he used the time to consider his ministry.

Philosophically, Jesse believed food banks to be among the greatest manifestations of the essential religious tenets of love and compassion, but they were problematic for him in a practical sense. On the one hand, he often found that others like him—poor, meek, beyond the fringes of society—were more willing to believe. Perhaps they were the most uncorrupted by modern life and its vast array of people, tools, and messages whose only purpose seemed to be distracting humanity from its holy destiny and imposing more soot upon an already blackened collective soul. Or perhaps they were simply in the greatest despair, the most in need of hope in any form.

On the other hand, these people were dreadfully hungry, and Jesse found that once they received their bowl of cream of broccoli soup or their turkey sandwich, they approached the meal with absolute focus. Not even The Sermon on the Mount could stir them.

Nevertheless, once the food line opened, Jesse greeted others with a smile and a kind word, sometimes reciprocated but other times answered with blank, desperate stares. After getting his meal, he found a seat beside a dark-skinned man, probably Hispanic, probably a day laborer struggling for work and for his own minuscule piece of the American dream. On each of their trays sat a hearty bowl of beef stew, a salad, a roll, an apple, and a carton of milk. "Will you join me in a word of prayer to my Father, the one true God?" he asked his neighbor.

"Qué?" was the only reply.

Jesse prayed by himself and ate in silence, left half an hour later with three apples in a brown paper bag, and began the two-and-one-half-mile march back to Venice Beach. He arrived in time to panhandle a couple of dollars and immerse himself in God's splendor when the setting sun bathed the Pacific sky in orange, and to discover the public shower had been newly repaired. It was, all in all, a glorious day, and by the time he slinked into the alley to find his bedroll, his shower made him almost presentable.

But, as sure as joy and misery are constant earthly cohorts, his feeling of contentment would prove fleeting.

Oh, shit, he screamed to himself as he looked behind his dumpster. *Oh, motherfucking shit!*

His bedroll and his new blanket had vanished.

His mind whirled and his anxiety skyrocketed. He looked underneath the dumpster, climbed up to look inside it, then desperately repeated the process even though he knew it would be fruitless. He scurried to the end of the street to examine the street sign. *Am I in the right alley?* he wondered. Even though he knew he was, his instinctive reaction was still a thorough search of the entire sector to address the iota of possibility that this was all just a miscalculation.

He checked the next three alleys to the north, and then three to the south. He did it even though he knew what he would find there—the vestiges of other homeless and the detritus of a life lived in the shadows. But not that of his own. *My God, my God*, he asked, silently but no less urgently, *why hast thou forsaken me?*

And now, for the second time that day, Jesse Morales sat down in the alley and wept.

He might have cried for an hour, his petition to the Lord apparently unanswered. Exhausted from the physical and emotional exertions of the day, he pulled a newspaper from the dumpster, covered himself with it, and fell asleep.

It was a fitful sleep, filled with disturbing images of sand and fire, of desperate children and women in white, of flying across the desert and lying amidst a jumble of plastic tubes. With the first sounds of morning, mercifully, he woke.

Sleep provided no answers and little rest. He had no inkling what new miseries the day would bring, nor if he could withstand even one more. As he gathered the newspaper which served as his blanket on his darkest of nights, something caught his eye.

The story was buried in the *Los Angeles Times*, next to an item about a serial car thief apprehended in Gardena. The editors apparently thought it of little value. Jesse, it was fair to say, would not have agreed with the editors. He began to read:

NEW BOOK OF THE BIBLE FOUND

LAS VEGAS—A long-lost biblical text entitled the Gospel According to Trevor has recently been found by a team of students, a professor of Religious Studies claimed last week.

The professor, Dr. Haley Berkshire of the University of Utah, made the announcement at the North American Society of Religious Scholars annual convention, held Memorial Day weekend in Las Vegas.

Dr. Berkshire's announcement was met with skepticism among the religious community. Many of those present noted that the professor's previous scholarly articles have been dismissed for their bizarre conclusions.

"She's a nutcase, pure and simple," said Dr. Horace Gardiner, Professor of Religion at New York University.

Most notably, Dr. Berkshire claimed the Gospel According to Trevor describes Roman soldiers cutting

> off some of Jesus Christ's genitalia while he was on the cross.
>
> In making the announcement, Dr. Berkshire revealed plans to take a sabbatical in order to pursue what she called "the Testicle of Christ."

His hands shaking with emotion, Jesse folded the newspaper, then rubbed his pubic region and gazed heavenward. "Thank you, my Father," he exclaimed.

By late morning, Jesse was hunched over a computer at the Abbot Kinney Memorial Branch Public Library on Venice Boulevard. Despite his shower the previous evening, Jesse still smelled a bit ripe, so the computers on either side of him remained vacant. That was fine with Jesse, for it minimized the possibility of distraction. A helpful librarian, whose head cold and stuffy nose made her the only person in the library impervious to his aroma, helped Jesse locate Dr. Berkshire's paper on her website at www.utah.edu. Fortunately, Berkshire had been kind enough to translate the text from its original Greek. With no money to print any documents, Jesse read the professor's article and transcribed the entire text of the Gospel According to Trevor onto four-by-six sheets of scratch paper using a golf pencil he borrowed from the information desk. Three hours later, having completed the transcription, he realized he had been so focused on his work that he forgot to eat the apple he brought for lunch.

The next morning, he sunned himself after a long dip in the ocean's waters. Jimi Hendrix on Roller Skates approached, surprised. "Dude, you went in the ocean? I thought you hated the ocean."

"No time for hate," Jesse smiled. "God is calling me

home."

"I'm so sorry to hear that, brother." Jimi's arms went slack. "What's wrong with you?"

But Jesse only laughed. "No, no, not like that," he said. "Just the opposite. I have new life!"

Off Jimi's puzzled look, he continued. "Two nights ago, I was a beaten man. I was hungry and tired. Somebody stole my bedroll. I cried myself to sleep and slept under a newspaper."

"Oh, man, that sucks," said Jimi.

"But that night, my Heavenly Father touched me, and I woke to great news. They just found a missing book of the Bible. I knew there was more! I just knew it! It's called the Gospel According to Trevor, and it hasn't been seen since the fourth century. A council of bishops didn't like what it said, so they burned it. But someone saved a copy, and a university professor just found it."

"And?"

"And so I copied down the whole thing yesterday, then read it three times last night." Jesse's speech grew more rapid. "It makes my life clear. I am truly the Son of God."

"What you keep tellin' me."

"But now there's proof," Jesse continued. "It talks about the Testicle of Christ. How it was cut off by the Romans when Christ was on the cross."

"What the fuck?" said Jimi, recoiling unconsciously.

"Don't you see? That's *my* testicle."

"Again, what the fuck?"

"My injury. I have only one ball. The Roman soldier took the other one. And it's never been found."

Jimi eyed him suspiciously. "Maybe it ain't been found because it don't exist."

"Oh, it exists all right," Jesse responded. "I can feel it in my ... down there. And there are clues. It says, 'In the great metropolis of the modern world, a place both west and east, in a gathering place used by many.' I think it means New York City. Central Park, maybe."

Jimi shook his head at the preposterous story. "They didn't even have New York City in the fourth century."

"But the men who wrote the Bible were touched by God. Trevor didn't know about it, but God would."

"OK, let's say your family jewels ain't all there," Jimi said, taking a deep breath. "For the sake of argument. One of 'em's in New York City. Some squirrel buried the Testicle of Christ underneath a tree or some shit. What are you gonna do, invent a nugget detector and search the whole goddamn city?"

"If I need to," Jesse affirmed. "I want to be whole again. I want to fulfill my destiny. I'm leaving in a few hours."

"At least it won't take you long to pack," said Jimi. He began to skate away, then stopped and turned around. "I'm gonna miss you, my man. Have a good trip."

"God bless you, my friend," Jesse replied.

As Jimi rolled away, his fingers flashed across his guitar strings, and he sang, "'Scuse me, while I kiss the sky."

Six

THE PRODIGAL SON

Ό Ίησούς αγκάλιασε τόν παιδά, τό οποίο μερικοί είπαν ότι αμαρτωλός, αλλά είπε ότι όλοι καλοί έν μάτια τού Θεού.

Jesus embraced the child, which some said was a sinner, but He told them all were good in the eyes of God.

(The Gospel According to Trevor, chapter 8, verse 19)

Father Brian William Callum Robert O'Shea returned to the Starlight Gentlemen's Club on Thursday, and then again on Saturday, and then again the following Tuesday. Sometimes he stayed for half an hour, other times for much of the evening. His VIP status was now upgraded to Platinum, which afforded him two-for-one drinks every night of the week and one free table dance per month, perks indispensable to sustaining his resolute good stewardship of the parish discretionary fund. Other dancers complimented him, played with his hair, and grabbed his butt when he walked past, but they all knew he only had eyes for Simone.

Before long, the dancer and the priest became so close that one night she confided her real name was, in fact,

Simone.

Yet, ironically, during the past six weeks O'Shea seemed to perform his church duties better and with greater fervor than ever before. His homilies—a series on the Seven Deadly Sins and God's unremitting forgiveness—were incredibly compelling, almost as if spoken from the very depths of his own soul. His catechism exhibited warm, genuine human connection amidst its intellectual and theological scrutiny. His visits to sick parishioners were more heartfelt, and his work with children more joyful. One wedding he officiated was said to be so poignant that many in attendance were moved to tears, and one funeral so jubilant a celebration that the mourners ended up dancing.

The North Seattle Diocese even began drafting a letter to the Vatican, recommending Father O'Shea for bishop.

One Thursday afternoon, as he sat in his office at Saint Helen of Mercy Catholic Church, Sunday's homily nearly written and the meeting with the Youth Education Committee not until 6:30, he absently picked up a copy of *Catholic Digest* from the stack of daily mail. As a younger priest he used to read the monthly publication cover to cover, but through years of experience he learned to filter out the more useless articles. He especially recalled one in which a "noted vintner" assessed various communion wines using whatever criteria noted vintners use, concluding all were essentially crap. But since his parish had a long-standing wine supply contract with Devereaux Distributing of Seattle, and Ted Devereaux had been confirmed at Saint Helen and was now a member of the parish council, and Ted Devereaux, Jr. had been baptized and confirmed in the parish and would be taking over the distributorship in a few years, and Ted Devereaux III was about to be baptized in the parish next week, Saint Helen of Mercy's wine supply was pretty much locked in until roughly the Apocalypse.

Now O'Shea focused on the items most useful to him in his calling at Saint Helen of Mercy: financial policies, community outreach ideas, and of course those articles which discussed the mystery of faith and the good news of Christ.

Thumbing through the magazine, he stopped on page 28, at an article entitled "Professor Discovers New Gospel With Shocking Account of the Crucifixion." The first paragraphs seemed almost irrational, as if lifted from *The Onion*, but he became more intrigued as he continued reading. By the time he finished the article he was genuinely fascinated. He next visited Dr. Berkshire's website, where he read every word of her recent article, links to previous scholarship, and her biography and course syllabi. After pouring himself a cup of coffee, he researched various historical and theological accounts of the construction of the biblical canon and the Council at Nicaea.

It is possible, he thought. *I suppose.*

From that tentative conclusion, O'Shea began to search for assertions which might support or at least parallel Dr. Berkshire's work, but found none. He then Googled "Dr. Haley Berkshire reaction," and the payoff was immediate and overwhelming. Hundreds of negative reactions to the professor's preposterous ideas attacked her methodology, her qualifications, her previous scholarship, and her lack of any apparent filament of religious conviction. He was still reading when a parishioner knocked on his office door.

"Father, the Youth Education Committee is wondering where you are."

It was now 6:42, and he had been reading about Dr. Berkshire's research for more than four hours.

The Youth Education Committee meeting was interminable. Sure, replacing the chairs in the three-year-old room, listening to a presentation by the representative for the *Young Believers Bible*, and approving a new Sunday school teacher were all important, but none were remotely as interesting as the Gospel According to Trevor.

When the meeting finally adjourned at 8:30, he hurried back to his office and resumed his research. For the first Thursday night since early April, he did not visit the Starlight Gentlemen's Club.

Instead, O'Shea pored through dozens of anti-Berkshire op-eds. Some of the names she was called were, he admitted, quite creative. "The Wicked Witch of the Wasatch," ascribed to her by a bishop from Nova Scotia, was his favorite for its combination of cultural literacy, its exceptional use of alliteration, and the fact that it forced him to learn about the mountain ranges of Utah.

He could not find a single Google result in praise or support of her work, a fact which made her all the more compelling.

By eleven o'clock he was on his fifth cup of coffee, with the cost-benefit tilting toward the negative. He had already visited the bathroom four times, and while the physical activity helped him stay awake, it also sacrificed valuable research time. Sapped by growing fatigue and fading eyesight, he decided it was time for the *coup de grâce.*

He logged on to the website of the *National Catholic*

Reporter, typed in his password, and found the most recent issue. Browsing the Table of Contents, he located a commentary by James X. Shaver, lead editorial writer for the magazine—a man O'Shea found pedantic, closed-minded, condescending, intolerant, xenophobic, and (judging by his photograph) in need of a haircut from the current millennium. To Father O'Shea, James X. Shaver was a hateful, malevolent man, the ultimate opinion leader for the Inquisition but not so much for modern times.

Sure enough, Shaver had written about the Gospel According to Trevor:

> Dr. Berkshire's scholarship is bereft of logic, lucidity, and appropriate veneration for the inspired word of God. The Bible exists in its *praesens forma* for a reason, and her attempts to denigrate and trivialize its meaning are contemptible. Her work on the Gospel According to Trevor is no more than the musings of a lunatic theological hobbyist, and its abdication of Christianity is nothing short of apostasy. Anyone with designs to expand the Word beyond its current contents is a modern-day heretic, deserving of the same cleansing conflagration as Giordano Bruno and Joan d' Arc, the same sanctified necktie as the witches of Salem, and is ultimately welcome to join Dante Alighieri in his *Inferno*.

James X. Shaver had once written a lengthy essay condemning the film *The Night of the Hunter*, which happened to be one of O'Shea's favorites. If James X. Shaver hated Dr. Haley Berkshire so intensely, then she was certainly OK with Father O'Shea.

He stumbled into his home near midnight, exhausted, head spinning. That night's dream of Simone was interrupted when he woke with the dawn, muddled yet curiously inspired. He spent Friday pacing the grounds of Saint Helen, or back and forth across the church transept, always in prayerful contemplation. And with every step, the Gospel According to Trevor beguiled him further.

Saturday featured more walking and more contemplation, interrupted only when he stepped into his office to put the final touches on Sunday's homily, the last in his series about the Seven Deadly Sins. Many believe this message about the evils of Pride, about the destructive nature of vainglorious hubris, was the most inspiring sermon ever delivered at Saint Helen. Representatives from the North Seattle Diocese were especially impressed, and the entire Devereaux family tearfully thanked him after the service.

The next Tuesday, after his weekly visit with Mrs. Skinner, O'Shea headed straight for the Starlight Gentlemen's Club. Simone's shift started at nine.

She squealed when he swept through the door, then ran across the floor to embrace him. "I missed you," she said. "I was worried about you."

"Bless you," said the priest. "Bless your kind heart."

She led him to a table next to the stage. "Can you sit with me?" he asked. Apparently prepositions were not her strong suit, as she instead sat *on* him, straddling him so her breasts rubbed against his chest and their faces were only inches apart.

"Tell me what you were doing on Thursday night," she cooed, "and Saturday, too. You should have been here with me."

"Research," he said, and there was a long and uneasy pause.

"Do you want a beer?" Simone finally asked.

"Do you want to go on a journey with me?" he responded. The *non sequitur* threw her for a moment.

"Um, maybe," she replied. "Where?"

"New York, I think."

She clapped her hands and bounced on his lap. "I've always wanted to see New York."

Encouraged, and hoping to stop the bouncing, he touched her arm. "Let's leave tomorrow."

"I can't," she said, pouting. "I have my math final on Thursday. You know, weird quarter schedule at the University of Washington."

"How about the day after, then?"

Simone shook her head. "I'm going to a concert on Sunday with my friends. We're gonna see Stinkbomb."

"Stinkbomb?" O'Shea asked. "Never heard of them."

"Stinkbomb's not a 'them,' silly," she said, giggling. "It's a 'he.' A rapper. My friends and I just love him."

She took the Father's cell phone and, blessed with the dexterity of the social media generation, quickly located a Stinkbomb video.

"He's so young," O'Shea said as he watched the video, and Simone's laugh in response was telling.

"Wait. How old are you?" he asked her. She paused for a moment, shaken. "It's okay, Simone. How old?"

"Nineteen," she said, barely loud enough for him to hear.

If the same exchange would have taken place at a picnic, in a restaurant, or any place with more than five lumens of light, everyone would have seen his surprise.

Here, only Simone did.

"Under Washington state law, I'm old enough to serve alcohol," she offered in defense.

"But are you old enough to drink it? We shared a bottle of champagne, remember?"

"That stuff barely qualifies as alcohol," she rationalized.

"Fair point. Do they know you're only nineteen?"

"Thunderstruck" blasted from the speakers as a new dancer took the stage. Simone leaned in close and pleaded, "Father, please don't tell anyone."

"Of course not," he reassured. "Your confession is safe with me."

She threw her arms around him and kissed him. "Oh, thank you."

When she pulled back, he asked, "So you have a fake ID?"

Simone nodded.

"What about everything else?"

"Everything else is one hundred percent real," she assured.

As she gazed at him, seeming to study him, O'Shea waited with the patience of Job, mindful only of the glorious young woman who straddled him and the physiological effects arising thereby. After a moment, she smiled, threw back her head, and announced, "I could leave next Wednesday."

O'Shea broke into a grin. "I'll pick you up," he said.

The quest promised to be inspiring and the companionship stimulating, so naturally the week seemed everlasting. He saw her on Thursday night to inquire about her final exam and on Saturday to confirm trip details, but both times he left early, still a thousand loose ends to tie. He wanted to visit every sick parishioner and chat with every child, to thank every member of the parish council and bless each of his altar boys. Yet, because he had little idea of either the duration or the eventual outcome, he wanted to keep his journey a secret. Everything was now in God's hands, as it should be.

His Sunday homily was entitled "Sheep."

"Pope Francis," he said, "encourages priests and bishops to have 'the smell of the sheep.' He commands us to be as Christ, out amongst the people no matter how dangerous or uncertain it may be. Jesus taught in places where he was not welcome. He journeyed far and wide to spread his good news of love for fellow man and of the rectitude of the Heavenly Father."

Many in the pews nodded.

"Our 'Bringing the Collar to the Crowd' program allowed me to do just that, thanks to your generosity and the generosity of the Diocese. And as you look around the pews, you can see more new faces every week. You can see those hungry for the loving Word of God and the welcoming righteousness of the Catholic Church—new faces who have become new friends at Saint Helen of Mercy."

More nodding. The Father was certainly on his A game again today.

"Our job as clergy is not to remain safely ensconced in the parish office. We are called not just to experience the sweet smell of incense but also the musty smell of the lost and the forsaken, the sinners and the unbelievers. Our flock is found not just in our own hometown, but all throughout the world. And we must trust the Lord to lead us to wherever we are needed.

"I therefore ask for your prayers, your faith, and your continued support of this church as the rock of your spirituality. May I have your commitment?"

Had this been a Baptist church, the congregation would have jumped to its feet, shouted "Amen" and "Hallelujah," and burst into song. O'Shea believed the Baptists maintained wonderful traditions of joyful expression, traditions other denominations might be wise to emulate. But, here, nodding heads would have to suffice.

"I will be leaving on Wednesday, placing my fate in the hands of God on a most important spiritual journey. When and where it ends, I cannot say for sure. But the Lord beckons me to follow, and I must obey. *Me quaerere in Christo. Bonum est Deus.*"

Fifteen minutes later, as parishioners shook O'Shea's hand while filing out of church, many were still bewildered by what they heard.

Seventy-two hours later, Father Brian William Callum Robert O'Shea loaded Simone's luggage into the trunk of his Toyota Camry. After a stop at 7-Eleven for a blue raspberry Icee and a bag of nacho cheese Doritos, they turned onto Interstate 90, heading east.

Seven
SABBATICAL

Έκείνοι πού βρίσκονται κοντά σέ μπορεί πέσοιεν μακριά, καί έκείνοι μακρινές μπορεί πάλι πλησιάζοιεν. Τά σχέδιά αὐτῶν μπορεί αποβλήθοιεν, καί τό ίσιο μονοπάτι αὐτῶν μπορεί στραβόσοιντο.

Those near to you may fall away, and those distant may again grow near. Your plans may go astray; your straight path may become crooked.

(The Gospel According to Trevor, chapter 6, verses 17–18)

During the "Religious Discoveries and Antiquities" panel discussion which followed the four presentations, Berkshire scanned the room in search of Dr. Wexford. Since her boss was neither exceptionally tall nor exceptionally fat nor exceptionally bald nor even exceptionally bespectacled, she proceeded methodically lest she overlook his rather mediocre face. Halfway through her inspection, she heard her name.

"Dr. Berkshire, your thoughts?" the moderator asked.

"I'm sorry?" she said, turning her attention back to the discussion. "Could you please repeat the question?"

"Certainly," said the moderator. "The question was, how will these recent discoveries shared today affect religious scholarship going forward?"

"Well," began Berkshire, "I cannot speak for my colleagues here, but my research on the Gospel According to Trevor is far from complete. And I think this points out the realities of the field in general. There are always new discoveries, always more work to be done."

As the moderator directed a question at another of the panelists, Berkshire resumed her scan of the audience and thought maybe she saw Dr. Wexford sneaking out a side door of the banquet room. An hour later, when she tried his cell phone, her call went directly to voicemail. That evening, her email to him received an automatic reply:

I am attending a conference, then will be on vacation through Sunday, June 16. I will be back in my office on the morning of Monday, June 17. If you require immediate assistance, please contact our department secretary, Roxanne, at ext. 5231.

"Fuck," she said.

The snails in Berkshire's garden moved more swiftly than did the next two weeks. She passed the excruciating time tending her hydrangeas, eating lettuce-wrapped pork, cauliflower pizza, and other meals suggested by her cousin Jolene (who claimed she lost seven pounds on the keto diet), and most of all trying to decipher the biblical metaphors within the Gospel According to Trevor. Discovering the text was one thing, but what did it mean? If she needed to wait until midmonth, she wanted for damn sure to be ready. And, annoyingly, she picked up the beginnings of a summer cold.

Dr. Ronald S. Wexford, Chairman of the University of

Utah's Department of Religious Studies, was in his office the morning of June seventeenth, as promised. He typically arrived just after sunrise, allowing him to beat traffic on his commute from the suburbs, then called it a day not long after lunch, which left him time to play nine holes of golf and enjoy a couple of beers in the lounge before heading home to the oversensitive shrew to whom he was married. Madeline Wexford found crisis in everything. Once, upon discovering a moldy strawberry in the refrigerator, she called Dr. Wexford while he was administering a test in his Prophets of the Old Testament class. From that point forward, he left his ringer off to avoid calls while at school, but in their place he received frantic emails about spider webs, clogged drains, chipped dinnerware, and the time his adult son was fired from his job at Intermountain Healthcare for stealing prescription medications. Some days, when his wife seemed especially frantic, Wexford played a couple of holes and then enjoyed nine beers.

Dr. Berkshire also arrived on campus early Monday morning, although early for her was more like 7:15. Still, she thought that should provide sufficient time for an uninterrupted audience with Wexford and, if all went well, she could be gone before Roxanne arrived. Berkshire thought Roxanne was kind of a bitch.

Wexford's door was open and he was reading something when she arrived. With her knock, he lifted his head slowly, as if upholding the dignity of his lofty station.

"Dr. Berkshire. Hello. How are you?" She found his grin atypically peculiar this morning.

"Fine, thank you, Dr. Wexford. How was your vacation?"

"Jesus Christ," he said, pushing back from his desk. "I spent two fucking weeks in Cedar City with my wife's parents. At least I got to do a lot of fishing."

"Really? I didn't know you liked to fish."

"I don't," said Wexford. "In fact, I hate fishing. But I like it a helluva lot better than spending two weeks with my wife's parents."

She chuckled, somewhat knowingly.

"Enough about me, though." He interlaced his fingers and rested his chin on them. "I wanted to congratulate you on your presentation at the North American Society of Religious Scholars. Your research caused quite a ruckus."

"I suppose it did," she replied. "I guess it was provocative." She still liked that word.

"To say the least," Wexford affirmed, trying unsuccessfully to hide a smirk. "Research ... even the provocative kind ... is vital to our funding and to our academic reputation."

"That's what you tell me," she responded. A heavy pause now filled the office, Wexford allowing the drama to build.

"What brings you to school this early? What can I do for you today?"

"Well, sir, as you know, this will be my seventh year as a tenured professor at Utah." He nodded in agreement, so she continued. "And by our contract, I am entitled to a research sabbatical every seventh year."

"Do you know where the idea of a sabbatical comes from?" Wexford asked.

"It's biblical. Somewhere in the Old Testament, I assume."

"That's correct," he said, delighted. The Old Testament

was his area of expertise, meaning every time a Gay Pride parade took place in Salt Lake City, he received a call from a *Salt Lake City Tribune* reporter to ask his opinion on homosexuality. Wexford would cite Leviticus or sometimes, just to change things up, First Corinthians from the New Testament. The next day his name would appear in the newspaper and the University president would call him with congratulations. Some readers would express their anger at his intolerance in what should be a more enlightened twenty-first century, while others would respond with support for his reproach of such abomination. And, for a day, Madeline Wexford would know she was married to the most brilliant and conscientious man in Utah. Dr. Wexford loved Gay Pride parades. He loved Leviticus even more. His wife he tolerated.

"But in the seventh year there shall be a Sabbath of complete rest for the land—a Sabbath to the Lord," he continued. "Leviticus, chapter twenty-five, verse four."

"Of course," Berkshire responded. "Anyway, I hadn't planned on a research sabbatical this year. As you know."

"I do." Wexford leaned forward in his chair. "Go on."

"But, you see, in light of what happened at the conference ..."

"Yes?" beckoned her department chair.

"I was hoping I might be able to take one ... it's last minute, I understand ... but I was hoping I might be able to get some time to follow up on my research."

"To find the holy relic you described?"

Berkshire scuffed at the rug. "Well, yeah, maybe I was a little hasty. Maybe I shouldn't have ... But I'd like to try. So if—"

"'As God is my witness, I will find the Testicle of Christ!' God damn, I loved that part."

"I think I actually said 'discover,' but, um, thanks. I guess."

Wexford thrust a paper in front of her—a Department Approval form for her sabbatical, already filled out and signed by Dr. Wexford. "Just sign here. On the bottom, right there above my name. I'll handle the rest."

The moment she dotted the 'i' in Berkshire, Wexford said simply, "Good luck."

And all was well at the Department of Religious Studies until two months later, when the first day of fall classes revealed a new professor teaching Introduction to World Religions, and eleven members of Lambda Chi Alpha fraternity immediately dropped the class.

Berkshire drove home from campus as quickly as the law allowed, even skipping Jitterbug Coffee when she saw three cars in line. Her excitement was palpable, impossible to contain. She rushed through the door, tossed her keys on the table, and booted up the laptop which had taken permanent residency in her kitchen so she could research those stupid keto recipes. Moments later she opened Amtrak's website. She found she had only nineteen hours to get everything arranged if she were to make the next California Zephyr, which left Salt Lake City at 3:30 in the morning. With a change of trains in Chicago, the Lake Shore Limited would arrive in New York on Thursday, in time for dinner. And New York, she had concluded, was where she would discover the Testicle of Christ.

She had only one friend in her neighborhood on East Coatsville Avenue, the eccentric widow across the street whose husband purchased their house when he worked at the bank. The old lady now lived there alone, her husband having died of an *E. coli* infection in 2012 and her children scattered throughout the West. Berkshire thought the eccentric widow's name was Emily.

"I'm going to be gone for a while," Berkshire explained, speaking slowly and loudly because the old lady probably left her hearing aids in the house, or at the grocery store, or in Colorado the last time she visited her son. "I'm taking the train to New York. Leaving tonight."

Emily, whose name was actually Amelia, shook her head at the idea. She thought Dr. Berkshire was a dentist. They had lived across the street from one another for five years now, ever since Berkshire purchased her home in a foreclosure sale.

"Why don't you fly?" asked Amelia. Spittle flew from her mouth when she spoke. "It's not the goddamn 1930s, you know."

"I hate flying," Berkshire explained. "Scares the crap out of me. Besides, I'll still be there in two days."

"Have it your way," said the old lady with a dismissive wave. Young people had all the answers, but none of them made any actual goddamn sense.

"Can I leave you with a set of my house keys?" asked Berkshire, "In case anything happens?"

"Yeah, hell, sure," said the old lady, removing her upper dentures to examine them. "But I'm not gonna fix anything." Without her upper plate, she hissed as she spoke. "If your pipes break, I'm gonna call some ass-crack plumber."

"Oh, I don't expect you to–"

The old lady snatched the keys from Berkshire with speed so unexpected that it startled the professor. "What's so special about New York?" she asked as she replaced her plate, satisfied with its condition.

"It's research for my job," Berkshire replied. "The Gospel According to Trevor. I'm going to search—"

"I hope to hell this Trevor is cute," interrupted the old lady. "That's a long goddamn trip for an ugly man."

"Trevor is not ... I mean, Trevor is ... yeah, he's worth the trip."

"Good for you."

"Anyway, I need to get things in order. Thank you for watching my house."

"Sure thing," said the old lady as she picked at her teeth with Berkshire's front-door key.

The professor still needed to hold her mail, stop delivery of the newspaper, adjust the thermostat, wash and pack her clothes, and figure out how to get to the train station in the middle of the night. It occurred to her that maybe she could rent her house while she was gone, but she could not guess if this trip would last a week or a year. Maybe, once she got to New York, she could set it up as an Airbnb, with the old lady watching over the place. But, for now, only the train mattered.

She slept until one a.m., then showered, ate, and requested an Uber. A Buick Verano soon pulled into her driveway, horrible techno music playing much too loudly for the middle of the night. The driver blasted through the darkness, ignoring traffic signals, and dropped her a few minutes past three at Salt Lake Central Station. Less than half an hour later, while Berkshire tried to recall if she turned off all the burners on her stove, the train lurched forward and the lights of Salt Lake City began to fall away behind her.

A few hours of intermittent napping in her coach seat left her with a stiff neck when she awoke. Over the next hour, she saw other travelers stretching out similar kinks, contrasted with couples walking refreshed toward the dining car. *I bet they had a sleeper car*, she thought, longingly watching the invigorated couples. *I wish I booked a sleeper car. I've never even seen the inside of a sleeper car. I wonder if the bed really folds down like in the old movies.*

She spent the next few minutes daydreaming about sleeper cars, eventually deciding she absolutely must inquire about one for the second half of her trip, the leg from Chicago to New York. She passed the remainder of the day rereading the Gospel According to Trevor. In just over forty-eight hours, her train would pull into Penn Station and her quest would officially begin.

Around seven o'clock that evening, as she considered the bitter coffee in the dining car (the salmon salad was nothing special, either), Berkshire bumped into a middle-aged gentleman just boarding the train. They were in Denver. He was tall, with distinguished graying sideburns which matched his neatly tailored gray checked suit. "Oh, pardon me," he said.

"No problem," she answered, noticing the way his bright necktie made his blue eyes sparkle. "My fault. I was preoccupied."

He took the seat across from her. "My name's Edward," he said. "Haley," she responded.

They began talking, first innocuous stuff like the weather, then more serious topics like the news of the day. The conversation eventually turned to cocktails, so they relocated to the bar car for further research just as the train crossed into Nebraska. An hour later, she got her first-ever look at the inside of a sleeper car. Conveniently, the bed was already down, just like in the old movies.

But before things progressed any further, she heard a ping on her phone. It was a text message from Jolene.

"Sorry," she said as she watched him remove his tie. "It's my annoying cousin."

The message said: *Please call my mom ASAP.*

Jolene's mom. Aunt Sally. Berkshire had not spoken to Sally since 2011, an arrangement which offended neither of them.

"I need to make a call," Berkshire said, searching her contacts list for Sally's number.

"Hello?" said Sally, rather hoarsely. She had clearly been drinking, or smoking, or probably both.

"Aunt Sally, it's Haley Berkshire."

"Yes. Haley." Aunt Sally's voice dripped with obvious antipathy. "I'm afraid I have some bad news. My sister ... your mother ... had a stroke."

"Ohmygod, when? What happened? Is she okay?"

"No, Haley, she's not," Sally said with a cough. "She passed away this morning. The funeral is Friday at six p.m., at the Baptist church. The family would appreciate if you could attend."

And Dr. Haley Berkshire, the most reviled religious scholar in America, a woman with virtually no connection to her Texas family since she began teaching and a happily non-religious woman, began to cry.

"God help me," she said softly.

Eight
STAND AND WALK

Έιστέ πάντα ό φύλακας, έτοιμος κάνει καλά έργα.

Be always the watchman, prepared to do good works.

(The Gospel According to Trevor, chapter 9, verse 4)

Jesse was not entirely sure which day he left Venice, because he forgot to look at the morning newspaper, and not even sure what time of day. Sometime in the afternoon. But these details were inconsequential; when the Son of God is on a quest to make Himself whole again, time is both fleeting and eternal.

He spent his last few hours in Venice in resolute preparation for the journey ahead. He cleaned up in the newly repaired public showers—two of them already broken and a third scattering its sparse pressure into a fine mist appropriate for watering a fern but useless for scrubbing the body of a homeless man. Fortunately, though, his favorite nozzle still worked, the one right beside the Charles Bukowski quote engraved in the wall: "The madmen can find other holes to crawl into. I used to walk that pier when I was 8 years old." Jesse thought Bukowski would have been great fun to hang out with.

After his shower, he lazed on the concrete bleachers near the handball courts. Today, the handballs thwacked with an oddly soothing stridency, and the chatter of girls on their old-fashioned roller skates was positively serene. When the heat of the concrete finally forced him to move, Jesse sat up and watched the skater girls perform figure-eights as he put on his still-damp orange fake Izod polo shirt. Then he ambled fifty yards to visit his friends Tommy and Jeong at their stall along Ocean Front Walk.

"Jesse! You take shower and wash hair?" asked Jeong.

"Yes I did," Jesse said, proudly. His shirt clung to his body, outlining a man once strong and fit but now underfed and soft.

"You look good. Very handsome. Special occasion today? You have girlfriend?"

"Your English skills have gotten much better these last few months," Jesse said.

"Thank you. I watch *The Bachelorette* and *Survivor* to learn. But when excited I still speak Korean." She jerked her thumb over her shoulder and added conspiratorially, "Like when Tommy change TV at home to Dodgers."

Jesse laughed. "I wanted to tell you guys. I'm going away for a while."

"Going away?" she repeated, surprised. She turned toward the back of the stall. "Tommy, come see Jesse. He say he going away."

"He said what?" Tommy asked as he hurried to meet them. "What do you mean, going away?"

"I need to get to New York," Jesse said. "I must find the Testicle of Christ."

"The whaticle of who?" Tommy said. "What are you talking about?"

As Jesse explained the Gospel According to Trevor and its description of the crucifixion, and tied it to the mystery of his own painful scrotum, Tommy pursed his lips. His two years working as a bail bondsman in his twenties cultivated his suspicious nature, and this story was full of holes. But Jeong found it absolutely delightful.

"Oh, Jesse, I so happy for you to take trip. Go find left-side ball. Right, Tommy?"

Tommy smiled. "Sure," he said simply, chuckling.

"We give you gifts, for good safety and travel," Jeong continued. She became a whirlwind, gathering a purple camo-print Nike knockoff backpack they could not sell and filling it with a Venice Beach water bottle, a Venice Beach keychain, a Venice Beach hat, and a Venice Beach T-shirt.

"Much Venice Beach stuff," she explained. "So you not forget us."

"I don't think Jesse needs a keychain, dear," Tommy said. "He doesn't—"

If dirty looks had subtitles, Jeong's would have said, "*Dagchyeo, i babo ya.*" Even without the subtitles, its meaning was clear: *Shut up, you stupid man.* Jeong added a Venice Beach bandana and a Venice Beach postcard to the backpack while Tommy was smart enough to now watch silently.

Jesse's eyes grew moist as he accepted her gifts. "I'll never forget you, Jeong. Those who share their blessings with friends are rich in Christ."

"I am Buddhist," she said, laughing, and they embraced anyway.

He turned to Tommy and extended his hand. "And

thank you, too, my friend." Their handshake morphed into a hug.

"I will see you both again," Jesse said finally. "Either here or in Heaven." Then he walked away lest they see his tears.

"*Sarang-gwa chugbog-eul, joh-eun yeohaeng doeseyo*," called Jeong in a voice which sounded like honey.

Love and blessings to you as well, Jesse mouthed in response.

Jesse filled the water bottle from a nearby drinking fountain, then looked back at his friends one more time. Leaving them would make him melancholy, no doubt, but this was bigger than friends, bigger than home. This was the Second Coming, and it was his.

Jimi was right about one thing: It did not take Jesse long to pack. But, compared with ten minutes ago, he now owned actual luggage (such as it was). He was a man going someplace.

There remained a few minor issues Jesse had not considered, not the least of which was how to travel from West Coast to East Coast with only twelve dollars—the receipts from the last two days' panhandling—in his pocket. At an average walking speed of three miles per hour, it would take him one thousand hours to walk to New York, or forty days and forty nights. While that sounded like a reasonable amount of time to spend in the wilderness, as Jesus Christ had done prior to his ministry in Galilee, Jesse did not think he was up to the task. Besides, he hoped to get to New York more expeditiously, and doubted he could subsist on thirty cents a day. He could hitchhike, which theoretically would be much faster, but he had heard too many horror stories of hitchhikers getting murdered, organs harvested from their bodies before their carcasses were dumped in a ditch somewhere along a deserted highway. Jesse held infinite conviction in the goodness of mankind, so his occasional turn to the grotesque repulsed him. Nevertheless, as he balanced faith versus fear, Jesse knew deep down that he did not want to end up as a hollowed-out carcass on the side of the road.

All other options exhausted, he decided he would hop a train.

To the best of his recollection, Jesse had never hopped a train and did not know if it was even possible. But as long as nobody was shooting at him—something he seemed to recall once happening to him in a different place—he thought he might be able to do it.

He assumed the train yard was somewhere in downtown Los Angeles, and he knew there was a bus stop somewhere on Venice Boulevard. Armed with little knowledge but limitless hope, he boarded the 733 bus, a transfer ticket in hand, his purple backpack in his lap, and his mind already three thousand miles away.

Unfortunately for Jesse, there were pitfalls to his idea. First of all, traveling by bus across the dreadful traffic of one of the world's largest and most automobile-dependent metropolitan areas required no shortage of time and patience. Even Jesse, abundant in both, found himself growing aggravated at the length of the journey. Second, the end of the line for his bus route still left him several miles from the train yard, but nobody he asked seemed to know exactly where he should go. Sure, some people recalled crossing train tracks once, but was it in Monterey Park or Pico Rivera?

He eventually found a train track and followed it eastward, away from the setting sun, unsure whether it would lead him to the train yard or the middle of the Mojave Desert. At long last, exhausted, he stumbled upon the train yard. He estimated the time to be past midnight, perhaps even hours past. Other hobos were there as well, and some mocked his orange fake Izod polo shirt. Jesse eventually found a patch of dirt and, clutching his backpack tightly, promptly fell asleep.

He awoke two hours later to the sound of men running toward a moving train, but by the time he could gather himself it was half a football field up the track and gone.

That evening, Jesse finally hopped an eastbound freight train, destination unknown. An old man with sunken eyes stared at him from the corner of the freight car. The light was dim, but the old man appeared to be missing much of his left ear.

"Hello. My name is Jesse."

The old man answered with a stare.

"Do you ride trains much? I'm trying to get to New York."

Still nothing.

"Did something happen to your ear?"

The old man glared malevolently at Jesse.

Once again, Jesse clutched his backpack tightly and fell asleep. Sleep for him was often a paradox—an antidote for exhaustion and a chance to escape his hunger, but also a flood of violent, frightening images which seemed far too real. Too many nights he lusted for slumber; too many mornings his awakening offered a reprieve from its horrors. But this sleep was different. This night he dreamed of a canopy of stars, of a soft wind rustling the trees, of the loving cries of nature singing just for him. Jesse had not dreamed like this for a long time, longer than he could remember.

He slept for months, it seemed, and then he woke up and fell back asleep once again. This time he dreamed of the seashore—not like Venice Beach, but one untouched by the tackiness of mankind's greed. Waves crashed against the muted colors of the shore while birds soared freely in intricate formations across a dazzling blue sky.

This time when he woke, the old man was staring at him. "You smile when you sleep," the old man said, like an accusation of malfeasance. "Why?"

"Good dreams, I guess," Jesse said. He became aware of the protest in his empty stomach.

"I never have good dreams," said the old man.

"Me neither. But I've never had a sense of purpose like I do now," Jesse replied. Off the old man's curious look, he began to explain about the Gospel According to Trevor. He was just getting to the Testicle of Christ when the train slowed.

The old man held up his hand, signaling Jesse to stop speaking. "Albuquerque. Time to get off."

"But I don't want to get off at Albuquerque," Jesse dissented. "I need to go to New York."

"Don't matter. These bulls'll beat you up bad, then call the real cops." He scratched what remained of his left ear.

"What's a bull?"

"Railroad security," said the old man. "I gotta go." And he flung himself out the door, rolling as he hit the ground with a thud.

Jesse was momentarily paralyzed with fear. He finally moved to the door of the freight car and looked ahead. He could see the Albuquerque train yard drawing near in the fading light. The train was slowing.

"Father, please protect me," he said as he jumped out the door.

Jesse lay there for several minutes, performing a mental inventory of his current wherewithal. Purple backpack, check. Simple enough. Next he considered his health. Legs, unbroken. Arms, unbroken. Wrists, fine. Neck, no problem. Although the force of the impact surprised him, he was generally pleased with how skillfully he performed the escape. He wondered if he had once done something similar.

Thank you, Father, he said to himself.

In the distance, Jesse saw some lights, which he guessed were coming from a nearby park. Since it appeared he would be spending the night in Albuquerque, he decided he would rather sleep on the grass at a park than in the dirt near a train yard, and he began striding toward them.

He arrived during the fifth inning of a Little League game. The scoreboard indicated the Giants were leading the Cardinals six to one, and the Cardinals were at bat. Jesse loved baseball, so he took a seat in the bleachers, next to a man wearing a Giants hat.

"C'mon, Andy," the man called out. Strike one. "Attaboy, Andy. Nice pitch."

"Is that your son, the pitcher?" asked Jesse. The man looked at him and hastily ushered his family to the other side of the bleachers.

Andy was a big kid who threw very hard. He struck out the first two batters, both of whom seemed perfectly content to retreat to the safety of the bench. The next batter, number 6, appeared no more eager than his friends to face the hard-throwing Andy.

"Drew, dig in now," said the Cardinals' coach. "Don't let him scare you."

Following his coach's directions, Drew hacked up the dirt and set his feet for the challenge ahead. But it did not matter, as he swung awkwardly at strike one, then strike two, badly missing both pitches.

"You got him, Andy," called Andy's dad.

But Andy's next pitch sailed high and inside, striking Drew in the helmet with a sickening crack. The smaller boy was down instantly, and he did not move.

Coaches and players from both sides rushed to the fallen boy. The umpire pulled out his cell phone and, with shaking hands, called 911. The Cardinals' coach knelt and pried off Drew's helmet, split into two pieces from the violence of the impact. Drew's breath was shallow and he was unresponsive.

"Oh my God!" cried out his mother as she pushed players away to be at her boy's side. "Drew, honey, wake up!"

The director of the Little League ran onto the field but added nothing to the collective medical knowledge of those already gathered around the boy. The EMTs were still several minutes away. Barring a miracle, two dozen twelve-year-old boys were about to see their first dead body, and watch it happen in real time. Andy stood on the pitcher's mound, crying.

"Someone help, please!" wailed the mother.

Jesse stood and walked onto the field. Although several people tried to stop him, their attempts were half-hearted at best, as the gravity of the situation had already drained their strength and their resolve. Jesse managed to squeeze between some of the boys and he knelt beside Drew, who had stopped breathing. Drew's mother's eyes were pleading.

Jesse closed his eyes and touched the boy on his forehead. "Stand up, my son, and walk." Nothing.

"Get out of here, you bum," said the frantic Cardinals' coach. But Jesse believed.

"Stand up," he repeated. "I bid you, be well."

And then it became silent. The boy slowly opened his eyes, saw Jesse, and smiled. Jesse smiled back.

"Ohmygod ohmygod ohmygod," screamed the hysterical mother. Jesse trooped back to the bleachers while the boy sat up. His mother hugged him tightly. "I was so scared," she said through her tears as the EMTs finally arrived.

"Mom," Drew said in that *you're embarrassing me* voice seemingly preprogrammed into preteens. He turned to his coach. "Coach, I'm on first base, right?"

The EMTs examined Drew and pronounced him healthy. He took his base and, three pitches later, scored on a double to right-center field.

Twenty minutes later, the score now six to five in favor of the Giants, Drew hit a towering two-run home run to win the game for the Cardinals. Andy congratulated him before anyone, and Drew's mother's eyes filled with tears.

Jesse dined extravagantly on concession stand hot dogs, pizza, and Red Vines that night, happily provided by the Giants, the Cardinals, and the league. He slept under a picnic table until the next morning, when an off-leash Labrador retriever woke him by peeing on his foot.

He was still two thousand miles from New York City.

Nine
THE SMELL OF THE SHEEP

Ζήστε σύν τή σοφία καί τήν ταπεινοφροσύνη, διακηρύσσοντας χαρά περί τής ανυπολόγιστης ομορφιά αυτού τού κόσμου.

Live with wisdom and humility, proclaiming joy for the immeasurable beauty of this world.

(The Gospel According to Trevor, chapter 13, verse 26)

Central Washington rolled past that first morning, Father O'Shea driving and Simone buried in her earbuds as her fingers dashed across her various social media accounts. O'Shea tried to peek, but her screen was in a state of constant change. Instagram. WhatsApp. Twitter. Tumblr. YouTube. She occasionally paused to take selfies, some of just herself against the blurred backdrop of countryside rushing past at highway speed, others with O'Shea in the background concentrating on the road ahead. Then on to Snapchat. Her thumbs flew over the keys as she typed messages at warp speed. And all the while, she fiddled with iTunes and Spotify in search of her perfect playlist for the first day of such a momentous expedition.

"I can't believe how fast you go from one app to the

next," O'Shea said to her.

"It's what we do," she replied. She was dressed in a T-shirt and cutoff shorts, her remarkable legs on full display.

A trucker rolled past in the left-hand lane of I-90. "Hey, mister trucker," she said, waving at him. The driver answered with an extended honk before he eased back to the right lane in front of them.

"C'mon, catch up, Brian." O'Shea was glad to be just a first name with her, not a title. "Get in the other lane. I wanna flash him."

"No can do," said the priest. "I don't think my car will go over seventy-five."

She pouted in the flirty expression to which teenage girls and young women hold an uninfringeable patent, then wordlessly turned to rest her back against the passenger door, swung her bare legs onto O'Shea's lap, and returned to her phone for another cycle through social media.

They stopped for lunch in Spokane, where she enjoyed a hamburger and chocolate shake. He just enjoyed watching her, especially when the server brought her burger and she inhaled its charbroiled aroma, unconsciously accentuating her breasts as she did. O'Shea said a couple of "Our Fathers," but still had an inexplicable urge for a glass of milk to go with his chicken sandwich.

After filling the gas tank, they were back on the interstate by 1:30, with Coeur d'Alene just ahead across the Idaho border. She tormented him by lifting her shirt, offering just a peek at the busty pleasures inside. Even though he had seen those breasts many times at the Starlight Gentlemen's Club, he was now driving a five-year-old Japanese car in broad daylight with a family of four in an SUV in front of him, rather than sitting at a small table in a dark bar with a draft beer on a table in front of him. O'Shea did his best to keep his eyes on the road, but her mischievous temptation was relentless.

When they passed the sign which said "Welcome to Idaho," O'Shea honked his horn, and Simone, who had grown weary of teasing him and was currently engrossed in her Instagram account, actually jumped.

"What happened?" she asked.

"Nothing happened," he replied. "I just do that whenever I cross a state line. It's kind of a tradition."

"Tradition, huh? I like traditions." She pulled up her shirt, exposing her glorious breasts to the air and sun of Mountain Daylight Time. "This is *my* new tradition. You like it?"

"Simone, stop!" he said. "You're going to cause an accident."

"Fine," she said in that way which could mean almost anything (with the singular exception of *fine*), and she reluctantly lowered her shirt.

They rode in silence for a few miles as she took in the scenery. "Idaho is beautiful," she finally said.

"It sure is."

"I had no idea," she said.

"You've never been to Idaho?" O'Shea asked.

"I've never been out of Washington. I've barely been out of Seattle."

"Then you're in for a treat," he said. "For the next week, you'll witness the hand of God and all His glorious creation. It's a beautiful country."

"You wanna fuck?" she asked. Only the hand of God kept their Toyota Camry from crashing through the guardrail.

When he recovered, O'Shea began to speak several times, but each time it came out mostly as babbling and he was forced to retrench after just a few words. Finally gaining some degree of composure, he asked, "Do you know about the Seven Deadly Sins?"

"Sorta."

"For Catholics, you see, they represent the worst of all possible behaviors, the greatest failings of man." He let out a deep breath. For the first time in a while they were on his turf.

"As human beings," he continued, "we are blessed with free will. That's maybe God's greatest gift to us, but it's also the most dangerous. The Seven Deadly Sins are seen as abuses of free will. I just did a whole series of homilies at Saint Helen about it."

"Saint Helen is the name of your church?" she asked. "You never told me."

"Saint Helen of Mercy, to be completely accurate."

"Go on," she said. "About the Seven Deadly Sins." She leaned forward with genuine interest.

"A fourth-century monk named Evagrius Ponticus first wrote about them. Except his list had eight sins."

"Evagrius?" she asked. "That's a funny name. Where was he from, like Slovakia or something?"

"Turkey," replied O'Shea. "Except it wasn't Turkey back then."

"Oh, I know," she said, smiling. "It was part of the Roman Empire, and after that the Byzantine Empire, and then the Ottoman Empire. It didn't become Turkey until after World War One. I loved my World History class. Professor Tucker was just, like, sooooo interesting.

Anyway ..."

"Yes, anyway, Pope Gregory the First eventually modified the list to seven. He also created a list of seven virtues. The idea was that if you practiced the virtues, you would avoid the sins."

"I bet you five dollars I can name all seven sins," Simone challenged.

"Five dollars? I'll take that bet."

She sat up straight in her seat, ready to put the priest in his place. After clearing her throat, she began. "Dopey, Grumpy, Happy ..." O'Shea started to laugh. "Sleepy, Sneezy ..." She started to laugh, too. "Doc and, um, Bashful." They shared their laugh for a while longer before they caught their breath.

"You're very handsome when you laugh," she told him in a soft voice.

"You owe me five bucks," he replied.

"Are priests even allowed to gamble?"

"That was no gamble," he assured her. "That was a sure thing."

She went into her purse, peeled five ones from an impressive stack of currency, and tucked them one at a time into the waistband of his pants.

"So you're telling me the Seven Deadly Sins aren't even in the Bible?"

O'Shea pulled the bills from his waistband and slipped them into his pocket. "No, but they've become central to the Catholic tradition."

"What's the sex sin called?" she asked.

"Fornicating," he replied. *Fornicatio*. Or, more generally, *luxuria*. Lust."

"*Luxuria*," she repeated, drawing it out. "Like luxury.

That's a good thing."

"I suppose."

She crossed her legs on the seat. "And you've never had sex?"

"Never mind," he said, blushing.

"No, come on," she prodded. "We're travel buddies. Travel buddies share everything."

"Okay, fine. Once, in high school. With my sister's friend."

Now this was interesting stuff. "What was her name?"

"Dana. Deena. Something like that."

"You don't even remember her name?"

He shook his head. "But once I decided on the priesthood, I had to change my ways."

"And you haven't had sex since then? How long ago?"

"About thirty years."

"That's so unnatural," she pushed, genuinely perplexed as to how this was humanly possible. "People are sexual animals, right?"

"They are, I suppose, but as priests we are expected to be better than that. We are God's representatives in the human world, filled with the Holy Spirit, and we should be above mortal temptations and the pleasures of the flesh."

She put her leg on his shoulder, just the way she did at the Starlight Gentlemen's Club. "Oh, yeah? How's that working out for you?"

He allowed it to stay there, now unconcerned about the fact he was driving a five-year-old Japanese car in broad daylight with a family of four in an SUV in front of him, rather than sitting at a small table in a dark bar with a draft beer on a table in front of him.

She continued, "If it makes it any easier for you, I've

been with older men before."

No reply, but he gulped and loosened his collar.

"And I'm on birth control, obviously."

He wiped a trickle of nervous perspiration from his forehead, then drank from his water bottle and turned up the air conditioner a notch.

"Pull over up there, at the rest stop," she said. "We can do it in the back seat."

"No, Simone, I'm afraid I can't."

"You know you want to."

"Oh, I won't deny that. As a man. But as a priest, definitely not. Besides, I would probably throw out a hip or something. Backseat sex is for teenagers."

"Backseat sex is for everyone," she maintained. "It gets wonderfully sweaty, the windows get steamed up, you can be as loud as you want ..."

"You ruin your upholstery and your shocks," O'Shea countered.

"You know what they say," she replied. "If the Camry is a-rockin', don't come a-knockin'."

O'Shea shook his head. "This Camry will definitely *not* be a-rockin'."

"I guess," she sighed, but soon initiated a new gambit, puckishly running her bare left foot up and down O'Shea's leg. When he moved his leg, she simply adjusted her position, and before long he was jammed against the driver door. But no matter; the interior of a 2014 Toyota Camry is fifty-eight inches from door to door, so he could not escape without climbing onto the roof.

Ten minutes later, O'Shea turned on his right blinker and moved to the side of the road.

"Change your mind?" Simone asked, hopeful. "It

would be better if we got off the freeway, though."

"Definitely not," he said soberly, pulling to a stop.

"Then why are we stopping? What's wrong?"

"Cop."

A highway patrol officer approached his car and O'Shea rolled down his window.

"Afternoon, sir," the officer said, then noticing the priest's collar, added, "Father." He surveyed the car's interior, a bit surprised to see the scantily dressed girl. "Do you know why I pulled you over?"

"No, officer," the priest said. "Not a clue."

"You passed me going ninety-one miles per hour. Speed limit is seventy-five."

"I was going ninety-one?" he asked.

"Yes, sir."

"I didn't think this car could go over seventy-five," O'Shea explained. "But you see," pointing at Simone, "I need to deliver this young lady to a church camp." Simone waved at the officer. "She's a counselor, and the camp is just outside Missoula, and we're running a little late. I guess I wasn't paying attention to my speed."

The highway patrolman's eyebrows drew closer. "Church camp, huh?"

"That's right," O'Shea affirmed.

"Saint Helen of Troy Camp for Girls," Simone added with a smile. "I go there every year."

"Very well," said the officer. "You're free to go. But please watch your speed."

"Thank you, sir," O'Shea said. "I will, I promise."

The highway patrolman's shoes crunched the gravel as he returned to his vehicle. O'Shea watched through his side-view mirror, started the Camry, and accelerated back onto the freeway, now careful to keep his speed to the more comfortable seventy-five.

"You lied your ass off," Simone squealed.

"I did no such a thing. I merely offered a plausible explanation. He felt good about himself, giving a break to a man of God."

"Whatever," she said. "It was awesome."

"Saint Helen of Troy?" O'Shea countered, and they both broke into hysterical laughter.

Soon they crossed into Montana. O'Shea honked his horn and Simone lifted her shirt, but even that momentary pleasure could not appease his growing fatigue. Eleven miles past the border, they pulled into the Mangold General Store and Motel, where Simone bought a bag of Doritos while O'Shea stood at the check-in counter.

"One room, please, for one night," he said to the desk clerk, a stout woman whose arm jiggled as she typed on her computer. He handed her his driver's license and credit card, then quickly added, "With two beds."

A small boy approached. He carried a whisk broom in one hand and a toy truck in the other. "Hi, mister," the boy said. O'Shea guessed the boy was probably six or seven.

He squatted down to meet the boy at eye level. "Hello there, young man. What's your name?"

"Jack," he answered, staring at the priest's collar.

"That's my son," said the clerk. "You might see him around, but he's supposed to stay out of the way." This last part she directed at the boy.

"It's fine," O'Shea said. "I love kids."

"Why are you wearing that funny shirt?" the boy asked him, and O'Shea laughed. Mom was not so amused.

"Jack, stop bothering the guests," she said. "I'm sorry,

Father."

"You're a father?" continued the boy. "Is she your daughter?" he asked, pointing at Simone.

"Not that kind of father," O'Shea replied. "I'm a priest. I work in a Catholic church. This is called a collar, and it's what priests wear."

"What's a priest?"

"The man who officiates the church service," said O'Shea.

The boy mouthed the word *officiates*, trying to make sense of all those syllables. It was a big word. Finally, he asked, "You mean like a preacher?"

"Exactly," affirmed O'Shea.

"The preacher in our church just wears regular clothes," said Jack. "Right, Momma?"

"That's right, Jack," she answered before turning to O'Shea. "Father, here's your room keys. Room 138, on the backside of the building. It'll be nice and quiet back there. There's hot coffee in the lobby first thing in the morning."

"Perfect," he said as he took the key cards. "Thank you." Then he turned to the boy. "It was a pleasure to meet you, Jack. You are a fine young gentleman."

When they checked into their room, O'Shea wearily tossed his bags on a bed. "I need to take a shower," he said.

"Can I join you?" asked Simone.

"No. Absolutely, positively not."

"Ohhh kayyy," she purred as she bounced onto the other bed. She found the TV remote on the nightstand and turned on the television, watching a local newscast for a moment. "Actually, I have to be honest, I think you have amazing self-control."

"You're not making it easy, I promise you." he replied,

closing the bathroom door behind him. Simone, on the bed, twirled her brown curls.

Ten minutes later, O'Shea emerged from the shower, toweled off, and wrapped the towel around his waist. When he opened the bathroom door, steam rushed out, and in the middle of that steam cloud, reflected like Venus in a cheap hotel mirror, stood Simone. She was naked, and not by accident.

"Oh. My. God," O'Shea said. "Oh my God!"

When Jack stepped into the office of the Mangold General Store and Motel, he was smiling. "Momma, I think they must be having some kinda church service," he said to his mother, who was straightening out the various tourist flyers in the lobby. "Is that what they're doing?"

"Is that what who's doing?" she asked.

"Room 138. The priest and the girl. I walked past and I heard him say 'Oh my God' a whole bunch of times. Are they having a church service?"

"Something like that," the mother hissed, and went back to her work.

Ten
ON THE EAGLE

Ό Θεός ήμᾶς προσφέρει άφθονες δυνατότητες έν τόν ίδιο τρόπο ένας υπηρέτης φέρνει πιάτα φαγητού σέ γιορτή, επιτρέποντάς ήμᾶς ἵνα επιλέξουμε τινά φάμειν.

God offers us abundant possibilities in the same way a servant brings platters of food at a feast, allowing us to choose which to eat.

(The Gospel According to Trevor, chapter 12, verse 20)

Her original travel plans were simple enough, but now, once again, her mother had managed to disrupt Dr. Haley Berkshire's life. Being sent to Saint Mary Margaret of Grace when her friends got to attend Sinclair Elementary was the first of many humiliating disruptions she could recall. There was also the time nine-year-old Haley was forced to skip her ballet recital for a last-minute dental appointment, all because Mom read an article that very afternoon about the connection between lime Jell-O and gingivitis. Then there was the time Mom made fifteen-year-old Haley take a job at McDonald's when she would have preferred to work with her best friend at the Golden

Corral. On one occasion, Mom insisted on an emergency visit to Great Aunt Kristie in Nacogdoches, who was in the midst of an anxiety attack over the local Ace Hardware running out of vitamin-enriched potting soil. The six-hour round trip required seventeen-year-old Haley to cancel her prom date with Tony Scarpetta, a date she had cultivated since January when she found out he always kept a cooler of Zima in the back of his Mazda RX-7. Two weeks before eighteen-year-old Haley was supposed to leave for her freshman year at Tulane, Mom decided to get herself hospitalized with appendicitis, and Haley was stuck going to the University of Houston. And those were just some of the more vivid memories, the ones she could not keep suppressed.

Fortunately, Mom was now dead, so perhaps this would finally bring an end to her persecution. Or could she continue to torment from the grave?

Berkshire broke from her reflection to flag down the car attendant.

"Yes, ma'am?"

"Listen, I need to change my travel plans," she explained. "My mother passed away, and I need to get to Houston."

"I'm very sorry to hear that, ma'am," the attendant said.

"Thank you," she replied, somewhat bitterly. "Anyway, can you tell me what I need to do?"

"Not sure, ma'am," he said. "That's not my department, but I think you can just log in and change your reservation on the website."

"Okay, thank you."

The Wi-Fi on the train was pretty good, and Berkshire

could access the Amtrak site from her iPhone. She learned the train to Texas did not leave until the following afternoon, which meant that instead of her original six-hour layover, she now needed to kill twenty-three hours in Chicago, a city she abhorred.

She saw Edward again as he walked toward the dining car. "Edward," she said, waving him down. As he approached, she welcomed him with a flurry of sneezes, each louder than the one before.

"My goodness," he said when she finished. "That was epic. You know, according to superstition, sneezing is a way for your body to expel evil spirits."

"I must have a lot, then," she replied with a laugh. "Soooo," she continued, trying to navigate the uncertainty. "I'm sorry about last night."

"I understand," he sympathized. "I'm sorry about your mother."

"Don't be," Berkshire said. "She was a real bite in the ass."

He chuckled, almost uncomfortably, and she continued.

"Looks like I'm stuck in Chicago for a day, and I was wondering if you wanted to hang out. Take in some of the sights."

"Um, I really can't," he said, checking his watch. For the first time, she noticed the band of white skin around his left ring finger, behind the knuckle. "I have some business to take care of."

"I'm sure you do," Berkshire replied coldly.

"What is that supposed to mean?"

"Absolutely nothing," Berkshire said. "Just be sure to wash your hands before breakfast."

Edward looked at her, his confusion obvious, then stared at his hands as he labored to make sense of her remark. At last he clenched his left fist, and it was clear he now understood. “Oh, right,” he said, and slithered away.

She waved at the car attendant, who finished with another passenger and then hurried back to her seat.

“Is there something else I can help you with, ma’am?” he asked her.

“As a matter of fact, there is. Did you see the man I was just speaking to?”

“Yes ma’am.”

“Can you please put a cockroach in his breakfast?”

The attendant laughed. “I’m not personally in charge of the cockroaches, ma’am. I’ll have to check with the chef about that.”

Berkshire returned her attention to the Amtrak website and, a few minutes later, she was in possession of an electronic ticket for the Texas Eagle, departing Chicago the next afternoon at 1:45 p.m. Her new itinerary involved both train and bus, and would get her into Houston less than five hours before her mother’s funeral. But since she would not be caught dead on an airplane, glider, hot air balloon, the gondola ride at Universal Studios, or anything else not in direct contact with Mother Earth, there seemed to be no other choice.

Now, all that remained was figuring out what to do in Chicago.

When her train arrived at Union Station, Berkshire summoned a taxi. “Palmer House,” she said. Horrible techno music vibrated the car as the cabbie shifted into drive. He treated ten blocks of downtown Chicago traffic lanes as (at best) suggestions, until he jerked to a stop in front of the Palmer House. Berkshire exhaled audibly, uncertain as to whether she held her breath all the way from Union Station.

Rooms at the Palmer House were nearly three hundred dollars a night, but after the travails of the last thirty-six hours and the harrowing cab ride of the past five minutes, she believed she had earned it. She checked in, took the elevator to her room, and passed out before the bellman unloaded her luggage.

She napped for almost three hours, waking with a terrible hunger. After dinner and a glass of pinot noir at Vapiano, she returned to her room, read the Gospel According to Trevor once again, and fell asleep before ten.

The next morning she paid thirty dollars to enjoy the hotel's breakfast buffet, but in the end consumed only scrambled eggs, melon, and two cups of coffee. She briefly considered visiting the spa for a massage and facial before checkout, but balked at paying nearly two hundred bucks for something she would not consider at even half that price in Salt Lake City. The fitness center was out, as she refused to exercise anyplace someone might see her. She did not require the services of the hotel notary, florist, or shoeshine specialist. She reflected on the orderliness of her life, its simplicity the result of her ability to eliminate so many disagreeable choices. But she still had four hours before her train.

She packed her luggage and carried it down to the front desk, where she checked out. "Is it okay if I leave my bags here?" she asked the clerk. "I'm going to wander around the city for a couple of hours."

"Not a problem," the clerk said. "What time will you be picking them up?"

"About one o'clock, I guess. My train leaves at 1:45."

"Will you need a cab to the station?"

This one stopped her, as she doubted she could endure another harrowing ride like yesterday's. But unless she wanted to carry her luggage half a mile on a summer day in Chicago, what other option did she have? "Yes, I guess I will," she finally said.

Berkshire had no interest in visiting Buckingham Fountain or the Field Museum, nor in shopping at Marshall Field's. Fact is, she had grown to appreciate the slower pace of Salt Lake City, and felt Chicago was far too hurried for her. *I'm going to New York City, and that's even worse*, she thought. *But it's going to be worth it when I rub everyone's nose in my discovery.*

She turned left out of the hotel and began walking north on Wabash Avenue, her mind like a game of Pong as it bounced between her mother and the Gospel According to Trevor and the guy on the train and her aversion to Chicago. She absently stepped off the sidewalk at Randolph Street and was brought back to reality by a car horn. The driver, now stopped in traffic, glared at her from inside his Mercedes. She stared back, defiantly, and he leaned on his horn, its stridency echoing amongst the skyscrapers of downtown Chicago. The game of chicken played out as other drivers began honking as well, until the noise ultimately triumphed and she retreated to the sidewalk. The driver passed by and, from the sanctity of his expensive automobile, gave her the middle finger.

"Yeah, same to you," she muttered.

Now more alert, she continued northward, still without specific objective or direction. Just past Wacker Drive, on the right, she saw the Seventeenth Church of

Christ, Scientist and its attendant Christian Science Reading Room. Inexplicably, she was drawn in, as if the Reading Room contained a super-powerful electromagnet.

"Good morning," said the Reading Room attendant.

"Good morning," replied Berkshire. "Would it be okay if I just ..." And then, "Ah-choo!"

"Bless you," said the Reading Room attendant. "And, by all means, make yourself at home."

Berkshire wiped a sniffle and thanked the Reading Room attendant. There she stayed for nearly an hour, learning more about the life of Mary Baker Eddy and this strange denomination which rejected medicine in favor of prayer, believing illness to be a spiritual rather than a physical affliction. Although the Gospel According to Trevor and the Bible itself were filled with descriptions of Christ healing the sick, this seemed way too kooky. Bacteria and viruses, she was certain, were not agents of Satan but of science. With the time nearing eleven, she decided she should move on.

"Thank you," she said to the Reading Room attendant.

"Any time," the attendant replied. "Hey, looks like you stopped sneezing."

"Hmm," Berkshire said, realizing she had not, in fact, sneezed since she first entered the Reading Room. "How about that?"

She walked over to Dearborn Street and turned south, more or less back in the general direction of the hotel. Her mind once again a preoccupied pinball arcade of thoughts, she crossed Jackson Street and soon found herself in front of the Omkar Hindu Temple. The Hindus, she thought, were especially fucked up. Their polytheism offered so many gods and goddesses that it was difficult to keep them all straight, and besides, what kind of religious system allows its deities to evolve from one era to the next? At least Christians, despite many of them having a stick up their collective ass, believed in an unchanging God. What's more, the Hindus had all those levels of consciousness, all the way up to nirvana, which she thought was a great band name when capitalized but nothing special for a state of perfect enlightenment. Not to mention that their reverence for cows was unnatural. It seemed to her the entire religion had been co-opted into crystals and yoga pants, and she hated yoga pants because they made it abundantly clear to the rest of the world that her ass was fat.

Yet, for some reason, she drifted into the temple. For a few minutes she simply looked at the artwork, the pictures of Vishnu and Shiva and Brahma which lined the walls. Then she sat in silence for a few minutes longer. It was not a contemplative silence, not spiritual in any way. She just enjoyed the quiet.

When she looked at her watch, she was surprised to see it was already past noon. As she exited the temple, she spotted a Barnes and Noble a block away. She was hungry and knew there was a café at B-and-N, so she went inside.

She ordered a turkey and brie sandwich, which she ate briskly, and a chai tea latte, which she savored. After finishing, she located the Religion section of the store and searched the shelves for her self-published book about the Shroud of Turin. She knew it would not be there, but every time she went to a bookstore she felt somehow compelled to indulge in this exercise in self-flagellation. On her way out, as she wandered past the cashiers and the point-of-sale displays of calendars, bookmarks, and greeting cards, an eighteen-month 2019-2020 calendar entitled Cats of the Rocky Mountains caught her eye. Stopping to take a closer look, she thought the February 2020 photo of a cat on snow skis was especially cute, so she paid eight-fifty for this new treasure which would probably end up stuffed in her filing cabinet at work.

It was now after one. She hurried back to the Palmer House, where she picked up her luggage and went outside.

"Dr. Berkshire?" asked a bellman.

I suppose they ought to know me, she decided, *for three hundred dollars a night*. "Yes, I'm Dr. Berkshire."

"Cab to Union Station?"

"Yes, please," she replied.

The bellman hailed a taxi and it zigged through traffic to a stop in front of the hotel. Horrible techno music blasted when the cabbie opened the door. Berkshire rolled her eyes and sighed, and before she even fastened her seatbelt the driver raced off like it was the start of the Daytona 500.

Five minutes later he screeched to a stop in front of Union Station, both himself and Berkshire jolting forward as real-life examples of Euler's First Law of Motion. Yet, as she paid the driver and collected her luggage, Berkshire was completely calm, perfectly tranquil, absolutely unruffled, and realized she had been quietly chanting "Om" for the duration of the drive.

The Texas Eagle left Union Station at exactly 1:45 p.m., Berkshire already settled into her sleeper car. She left only for dinner, and when she awoke it was morning and the train already into Texas. Gathering her luggage, she waited for the stop in Longview, where she would have just twelve minutes to switch to a crowded Lone Star

Coach for the four-and-one-half-hour trip to Houston.

The portly man seated on the aisle already claimed both armrests, so she leaned against the window, hoping to avoid conversation, as the bus accelerated to highway speed.

"Whatcha goin' to Houston for?" asked the portly man, oblivious to her body language.

"Funeral," she said simply.

"Guess you didn't get the life insurance money," the portly man chuckled. "Else you'd be flying first class."

"I guess not," she said, pulling out her notes on the Gospel According to Trevor. By now she pretty much had it memorized, but she hoped this would dissuade the portly man from talking.

The ploy worked for less than five minutes. "Whatcha reading there?" he finally asked.

"Work stuff," she said, not looking up for fear it would be interpreted as an invitation.

He plowed ahead anyway. "Whatcha do for a living?"

"College professor."

"Very interesting. Me, I'm not that educated, but I've made a good living anyway. Mel's Sand and Gravel is my company. I'm Mel," he said, extending his hand.

Fuck my life, she thought as she shook his hand with absolute disinterest.

"Don't sound like much, I know, but I've got a house in Longview, a cabin on Lake Martin, and a condo in Houston. I go there twice a month for meetings. You ever been to Houston?"

"I grew up in Houston."

"I grew up here in Longview. Got my start in the business right out of high school."

By now the bus was going seventy miles per hour, fast enough to ensure certain death if she could somehow just squeeze out the window. But the risk management department of Lone Star Coach was one step ahead, its internal memos convincing Lone Star Coach to purchase a fleet of buses whose windows were too small for a full-sized adult to fit through. For the next two hundred miles, Dr. Haley Berkshire was forced to listen to a stream-of-consciousness lecture which included the intricacies of sand and gravel as well as boar hunting in east Texas, mid-level bourbon, tractor pulls, conspiracy theories, the relative merits of catfish versus largemouth bass, and a position-by-position analysis of the Dallas Cowboys.

The bus pulled into the Houston Amtrak Station at 1:15, and Berkshire was met by her cousin Jolene, the only member of the family she could tolerate. As usual, Jolene wore clothes at least a size too small, and better suited for a high school cheerleader than for the mother of one.

"Haley darlin'," screeched Jolene as she hugged her cousin. "How was the trip?"

"Let's see," said Berkshire, thinking it through. "My back hurts, I got hit on by a married man, I spent a fortune for one night's hotel in Chicago, and a fat guy talked my ear off for the entire bus ride from Longview. But I'm here."

"Yes you are, bless your heart." Jolene struck her best modeling pose. "So what do you think?" she asked.

"Um, I don't know," Berkshire replied. "New top?" It was tight, sequined, and somewhat revealing.

"New everything! I lost twelve pounds and I had to get a whole new wardrobe. I'm a size six now."

You're actually a size eight, and your old clothes would

probably fit correctly now, Berkshire thought to herself. But she said, "That's great, Jo. Keto?"

"I'm on the paleo diet now. Ninety-Day Super Macro Ultra Paleo. I read the book."

That's a first, Berkshire thought. But she said, "How's your love life? You still doing Match.com?"

The portly man walked past, dragging a heavy wheeled bag behind him. "It was a pleasure chattin' with you," he said to Berkshire. "Sure made the time go by faster."

"If you say so," Berkshire said under her breath as she watched him lumber away.

"Bumble now," Jolene replied. "And Ashley Madison, for when I'm feeling especially naughty. Y'all find yourself a man yet?"

"You just saw my best prospect," Berkshire answered.

She wheeled her luggage to Jolene's car, and Jolene popped the trunk. "Can you manage that yourself, Haley? I'd help, but I just got my nails done," said Jolene, displaying her sparkly new manicure. Berkshire sighed and wrestled her luggage into the trunk while Jolene sat in her car and tapped her nails on the dashboard. They exited the parking lot, and when Jolene merged onto the I-10 without looking, she forced an Amazon delivery truck to slam on its brakes in order to avoid a collision.

Jolene glanced in her rear-view mirror. "Can you believe that crazy Amazon driver? Bad drivers are so annoying."

Berkshire, her feet jammed into the floorboard and her back stiff against the seat, sat in silence, slowly calming her breath. Once her death grip on the armrest loosened, she finally asked, "How's your daughter?"

"Chloe's fine and dandy, thank you for asking. Head

cheerleader, dating the star player. She won queen of the 4-H, too."

Destined to be pregnant by nineteen, just like her mother, Berkshire thought. But she said, "Fantastic. How about her academics?"

"She's probably gonna graduate on time," Jolene beamed, as if Chloe had just been selected for a fellowship at NASA.

Even on a good day, Houston traffic moves like gravy through a bar straw, but after thirty minutes of small talk they arrived at Aunt Sally's house near Jaycee Park. "Mom made up the guest room for you," Jolene told her, then grabbed a beer from the fridge, plopped down on the sofa, and found *The Ellen DeGeneres Show* on TV. Berkshire showered and changed into the most funeral-appropriate clothing she brought: black pants, a white blouse, and a red jacket. Jolene, meanwhile, remained dressed in the same outfit, which seemed more appropriate for a Las Vegas burlesque show audition. A few minutes before six, they pulled into the parking lot at Lazybrook Baptist Church and took their seats in the second row of pews. Other members of the extended family hugged Jolene but offered little such warmth to Berkshire.

The pastor began speaking exactly at six. "We are gathered here to celebrate ... yes, I said celebrate ... the remarkable life of Sarah Landsdowne Berkshire. A kind, gentle, loving woman, full of grace, adored by her family and her church community."

Over the next hour, in between Bible readings and favorite hymns, family members offered loving tributes to a woman who bore no resemblance to Berkshire's mother. No fan of church music, she occupied herself by reading and rereading the printed program, unconsciously reassuring herself she had not accidentally stumbled into the wrong funeral.

At the end of the service, family members arranged themselves in a receiving line in the church lobby, greeting mourners who had come to pay tribute.

"I'm Agnes Mumple," an older woman said to Berkshire. "I taught Sunday school with Sarah."

"I'm Haley, her daughter." She noticed Aunt Sally giving her the side-eye from the opposite end of the line.

"The college professor?"

"Yes, ma'am."

"Ohhh," the older woman recognized, and then hurried along.

So it went for the next fifteen minutes–friends and acquaintances offering tight-lipped platitudes to Berkshire before turning their attention to the more favored sisters and cousins. Once the last mourner passed, it was mercifully time to adjourn to the community room for stories, slide shows, BBQ beef sandwiches, potato salad, and Lone Star beer. As it turned out, though, even that environment proved no more hospitable.

Worst of all, the Sunset Limited did not leave until Sunday afternoon, meaning she would be expected to join the family for Saturday dinner, the same tradition she once hoped to flee with high school graduation and finally escaped when she moved to Kansas to begin her master's degree program. In retrospect, her twenty-three hours in Chicago did not look so bad anymore. She bolstered herself with the knowledge that once Jolene dropped her at the station on Sunday, she would likely never see any of these people ever again.

Guessing nobody would be troubled by her absence, and not really concerned if they were, she excused herself and went outside, passing Jolene and a tall man wearing Tony Lamas and a Stetson. Jolene and the cowboy talked in low voices, his face only inches from hers. Their body language did not suggest they were reminiscing about the deceased.

Berkshire found a bench, closed her eyes, and tried to summon even one good memory of her mother. When that proved futile, she recalled the pastor's words about her mother's soul being "lifted home to the glory of Heaven," and began to contemplate various theories and beliefs about what happens to the human soul. She eventually concluded that if Sarah Landsdowne Berkshire had been a Hindu rather than a Baptist, she would probably be reincarnated as a snail.

Eleven

THEY FLATTER THEMSELVES

Μή δουσούσιν όλοι σαφήνεια, αλλά ὁ Θεός τούς πάρει ἵνα επιτελέσει έν αυτήν τρόπον.

Not all will see clearly, but God will take them to task in His own way.

(The Gospel According to Trevor, chapter 10, verse 14)

Jesse was growing concerned.

For two days, his attempts to get back on a train were stymied. Security at the train yard was too thick, and he was down to his last package of Red Vines. Something had to give. He needed a ride and, for that, he needed to summon faith.

There has to be a truck stop somewhere along the interstate, Jesse guessed, so he headed north through downtown. From their enclaves in an alley or beneath a tree, languishing on cardboard and wrapped in blankets, desperately in need of a bath and holding tightly to their meager belongings, the wretched refuse of Albuquerque watched Jesse as he slowly worked his way past them. Other than the fact that he was moving, they saw little difference between Jesse and themselves. Jesse, however, saw a multitude of difference; he was a man with a plan, vague as it may be. Although he despaired for his brothers and sisters in distress, mankind would now best be served by him completing his calling. So onward he marched.

He eventually arrived at Love's Travel Stop along I-40, tired and hungry yet resolute. *If I am to fail*, he thought, *let it not be for want of effort. And if I end up a hollowed-out carcass on the side of the freeway, then it must be God's will.*

Besides, having enjoyed the largesse of appreciative parents from his intervention two days earlier, he now had greater faith in the goodness of others, even though he ate most of his remaining Red Vines for breakfast during his walk.

His problem, though, was how to proceed. Did people still stick out their thumbs if they wanted a ride? Would a handmade sign work better? If so, what should it say? Would people be more willing to pick up the Son of God, or intimidated by His glory?

He finally decided upon the direct approach.

"Excuse me," he said to a man walking from the building toward the fuel pumps. The man wore an Albuquerque Isotopes T-shirt and carried an armful of snacks. "I need to go east, to New York. Any chance you could give me a ride, however far you're going. I'd appreciate it."

"Dude," said the man. "Are you serious?"

"Yes, sir," Jesse replied. "I am the Second Coming of the Lord, and I am on a holy journey—"

"Not with me, you're not," the man said as he dropped a package of mini-donuts. "Now fuck off."

Jesse met with similar rejections for the better part of an hour. A few people, seeing him approach, preemptively handed Jesse their spare change with hopes of warding off any significant contact. Transportation, not funding, remained his primary objective, but at least he would be able to afford some food on his journey, should it ever continue. *But what price my dignity?* he thought.

Recognizing he needed to change tactics, Jesse moved to the shadows of the eighteen-wheelers to contemplate a new approach. For some reason he felt more comfortable among the enormous vehicles, as if their huge engines were a welcoming blanket he could not explain. Although he felt no inspiration, and in fact was becoming resigned to another night in Albuquerque, he felt especially drawn to a red Peterbilt truck. He ran his hands along its graceful fender, examined its front grill, and marveled at the intricate pinstriping which, while once beautiful, was fading and chipping away with age. Just like himself.

"What are you doing up there?" he heard. The harshness of the voice jerked Jesse's head instinctively.

"Is this your rig?" Jesse asked.

A man advanced toward him, waddling from too many years spent on the road. "Damn right it is." He was a large man, wearing a faded black and green flannel shirt and a beard in need of trimming. And he was not happy. "Now what do you want?"

"Nothing. I'm just admiring the truck. Two-thousand-eight?"

"Oh-seven," the driver said, softening. "You a trucker?"

"No," answered Jesse. "I'm the Son of ..." He thought better of it, and changed course. "I'm the son of a trucker."

It was a lie, or at least a convenient fabrication, as Jesse had never actually known his father. But in the interest of his health and safety, it seemed the most expedient story at the moment. "What kind of engine?"

"Caterpillar C-15," said the trucker.

"Great engine," Jesse said.

"She's taken care of me for twelve years," said the trucker, caressing the hood of his vehicle. "Almost nine-hundred thousand miles."

"I used to work on the Cat-15 ..." Jesse trailed off, without the slightest notion when or where he worked on them, or if he really did at all.

"'Zat so?" said the trucker, his tone shifting. "You know, I got a little ping in the engine. I don't think it's anything ... It ain't bad, but I gotta get my load to Oklahoma City by tomorrow morning. You mind taking a look?"

Jesse shrugged, so the trucker opened the hood and Jesse buried his head in the immense engine. It did not take long before he announced, "I need to adjust your injection timing."

The task swiftly completed, Jesse came out for some air. "Has your engine been smoking?" he asked the trucker.

"A little, yeah. I figured I dripped some oil last time I topped it off."

"That's not it," Jesse said. "Your intake is a little off, so your EGT is probably high." He disappeared back into the engine compartment to make the necessary adjustments.

Jesse reappeared and tried to wipe the grease from his hands. "Start it up and let's give it a listen." The trucker climbed into the cab and soon the engine roared. "Sounds better," he announced.

"You should be ready to roll now," Jesse said. "But when you finish your run, you might want to check turbo number two."

"Thanks, friend," the trucker said. "What can I do to repay you?"

"You said you're going to Oklahoma City?" Jesse asked.

"I did."

"Can I get a ride?"

The trucker extended his hand, but Jesse pulled back from the handshake, displaying his palms blackened with engine grease. The big man chuckled. "My name's Carl. This here's Jezebel," he added, pointing at his truck.

"I'm Jesse."

"Go get cleaned up, Jesse, and let's hit the road."

Jesse returned a few minutes later, his hands scrubbed clean. Carl pulled Jezebel onto the I-40, accelerated to highway speed, and slotted himself between two other big rigs, the sun painting the sky orange as it set behind them.

"What are you hauling?" Jesse asked. He smelled of industrial hand soap.

"Canned food of some kind. Not exactly sure what. Beanie weenies, I think maybe."

"What kind of range does Jezebel have?"

"Got a hundred-and-fifty-gallon tank, so about eight or nine hundred miles give or take. Depends on the hills, of course, and if I can catch a draft. OKC's about five-hundred-and-fifty miles, so unless I gotta drive all over Texas looking for a place to piss, we're good to go. Coffee?"

"No, thank you," said Jesse. "I don't drink coffee."

"I couldn't survive without it," Carl said, filling his travel mug from the sixty-four-ounce Thermos he kept in the center console.

Carl slid a Garth Brooks CD into the player in his dashboard and began humming along to the music. Jesse, meanwhile, listened to Jezebel, who hummed along the asphalt, her engine performing flawlessly.

"You been on the road awhile?" Carl asked, finally. Jesse pulled back, unsure if there was any pretext or judgment in the question, and Carl seemed to notice. "I don't mean anything by it. Just making conversation. I usually drive by myself, and sometimes it gets awful lonesome. No offense."

Jesse relaxed. "None taken. I hopped a train from L.A. to Albuquerque."

"Why'd you get off there?"

Jesse paused, conspicuously.

"I'm not trying to pry, friend," Carl said. "Tell me if it's none of my business."

"It's fine," Jesse reassured. "It's just a little, I don't know, strange." Off Carl's curious look, he continued. "I jumped off the train, and then I went to the park to watch some kids play baseball, and one kid got hit in the head with a pitch, and he was dead."

Carl's travel mug stopped halfway to his mouth, and he lowered it slowly. "What do you mean, dead?"

"He wasn't moving or breathing or anything. The parents were screaming and the other kids were crying, and the ambulance didn't get there fast enough. So I saved him."

"Holy shit, that's unbelievable," Carl said, excitedly. "You did CPR to save a kid's life?"

"Not CPR," Jesse said. "Faith. I don't know how, exactly, but faith is a remarkable thing."

"God bless you, friend," said Carl, who smiled and turned up the stereo. "I'm in the company of a God-blessed miracle worker." And he began to sing along to Garth Brooks.

For the next two-hundred-and-fifty miles, they sang, they talked of Carl's family and Jesse's friends, and they spent long stretches simply enjoying the lights of a big Western sky. Carl seemed to know them all, and spent considerable time describing Jupiter and Venus, Orion and Ursa Minor, Cassiopeia and Perseus. "I guess you could say astronomy's kind of a hobby of mine. I spend so much time alone with these guys, it's like they're family, too."

Jesse looked at him and saw a man truly at peace.

"I'm excited about the Perseids meteor shower," Carl continued. "I already booked a run for August twelfth, just to make sure I'm out here to watch. It'll be glorious, like God throwing handfuls of diamonds from Heaven."

"I like that," Jesse said, and then he felt brakes and looked at Carl.

"I gotta piss," Carl explained. "There's the downside of all that coffee. Plays hell with my bladder."

"Where are we?" Jesse asked.

"Just outside Amarillo. The TA truck stop's got an all-night restaurant, so I'll get us a couple of burgers." Carl's hand wiggled as he pointed at the restaurant lights ahead. "I hope you like hamburgers."

"Very kind of you," Jesse said.

Carl parked his truck and headed for the building. Jesse sat for a few moments to contemplate God and His diamonds before he decided it might be a good idea to stretch his legs. He climbed down from the cab and walked a couple lengths of the truck before a woman approached him. Her tight jeans barely contained an ample bottom, and her breasts spilled from her half-buttoned blouse.

"How's your trip?" she asked Jesse. Her voice sounded like an alley cat dancing on sandpaper.

"Fine. I just got on back in Albuquerque."

"I love your long hair," she said, reaching tenderly to touch it. "You've got a nice face. Do you like my face?"

"Yeah, sure," Jesse said, and with that he found himself pinned to the truck.

"You wanna have some fun before you take off?" she offered, pressing against him.

Jesse was speechless, but the sound of footsteps made them both turn their heads. It was Carl, carrying his Thermos and a bag with the sandwiches.

"Hey, Lizzie," Carl said.

"Hi, Carl."

"C'mon, Jesse, we gotta go."

Jesse scrambled back into the cab while Carl fired up the engine. As he pulled out of the truck stop, he asked, "How'd you like Lizzie?"

"You know her?"

"Oh, yeah," Carl said. "She's one of the regular lot lizards here."

"What's a lot lizard?" Jesse asked.

"A hooker. A truck stop whore. She's a nice one, though. It coulda been a lot worse." He handed Jesse a hamburger, then added, "You coulda met Yolanda. If you don't sleep with her, she flattens your tires." Apparently, a tryst between Jesse and Yolanda was the funniest thing he could imagine, and he laughed so robustly that his seat bounced for the next couple of miles.

Jesse and Carl talked for a while, but the hamburger

was comforting and the humming of Jezebel's engine was soothing, and Jesse felt his eyelids grow heavy. "I got my coffee, and we'll be in OKC in a few hours," Carl said. "Go ahead and sleep." Jesse obliged, and before they even left the Texas panhandle, he was dreaming of a similar big rig and a similar magnificent night sky, except the vehicle in his dream was tan, the road was bumpy and dusty, and the load something more consequential than beanie weenies.

They pulled into Oklahoma City under a still-dark sky. Jesse woke to the bump of brakes. "Made it before sunrise, praise the Lord," Carl said. "I hate driving into the morning sun."

"You're welcome," Jesse said.

"Excuse me?"

"Nothing."

Carl dropped his load and signed off. Jesse was full of gratitude for the ride and the hospitality, but he also had no idea what lay on the horizon. Nevertheless, he felt reassured to be halfway across the country, still in possession of his purple backpack and all his internal organs. And, truth be told, it was a long time since he had eaten as well as these past few days.

"What's next for you?" Carl asked above Jezebel's rumble.

"Keep going east," Jesse said. "Don't quite know how, though."

"Sorry I can't help you out, but I gotta go see the wife if you know what I mean. Head north, though, and you'll get back to the interstate soon enough."

"Thank you, Carl," Jesse said, and Carl waved as he maneuvered Jezebel out of the parking lot.

North it is, Jesse said to himself, and he started walking.

Before long, he cut through the parking lot of a Motel 6. Parked in front of the motel was a white Chevy van, its rear end adorned with a hodgepodge of bumper stickers. They featured different colors and different fonts, but all carried the same message: God Hates Fags.

I do? Jesse asked himself.

He moved to the side of the van, which displayed the logo of the Westboro Baptist Church on its door. This confused Jesse; churches were not supposed to hate.

He pressed his face against the van's side window and cupped his hands to shield his eyes from the early sun. The interior was strewn with a dozen or more signs, and the ones he could see contained a variety of odious messages, all similar to that of the bumper stickers.

As he continued to survey the van's interior, Jesse did not notice a man shut the door to his hotel room and begin striding across the parking lot. Still fifty feet away, the man said, "Son, I recommend you step away from the van." Jesse jumped in surprise and complied with the suggestion.

"Can I ask what you think you're doing?" the man snapped. He was a large man, although not as large as Carl, with brown hair, a beard, and eyes with an incendiary flicker.

"I'm just curious about your bumper stickers and your signs," Jesse said as he extended his hand. "My name's Jesse, by the way."

"Steve Drain," responded the man. He did not shake Jesse's hand. "Do I know you?"

"If you are a church, you should," Jesse replied.

"What the hell is that supposed to mean?" Drain stiffened. "Of course we're a damn church."

"Then why the hatred? God loves all living things."

"God hates anyone who blasphemes against the Holy Bible," Drain seethed. "He hates all immorality, depravity, and evil. God hates all sin and all sinners."

"No," Jesse said calmly. "He doesn't. He hates sin, but He loves all, since all were created in His image."

Drain cackled. "Suddenly every vagrant is an expert on religion." He inserted his key to unlock the van and turned back to face Jesse. "I bet you've never even read the Word of God."

"I am the Word of God," Jesse corrected, softly.

"You are the ..." Drain shook his head. "You're full of shit is what you are."

Jesse remained unruffled. "Let he who is without sin cast the first stone."

"Listen, pal, we're doing God's work in a world where nobody else will step up." He waved his finger at Jesse. "Last night we picketed a concert by that country music singer Blake Shelton."

"I don't understand why a church would picket—"

"Because his music is vile, that's why," said Drain, his face puckered as if he bit into a lemon. "His lifestyle is even worse, with that wife of his. Let me tell you, mister, we will not sit quietly while the world parades its corruption down Main Street USA. No way. Not on our watch."

Drain opened the driver's door and heaved himself into the van. "Right now I don't have time to debate a crazy man. I gotta make a Starbucks run. This afternoon we'll be in Tulsa protesting a fag funeral, so get your ass out of the way."

"But God is love, not hate," Jesse argued. "It's far better for two men to hold hands than to make fists."

"Disgusting," said Drain, absolutely certain of the rectitude of his position. He slammed the door and defiantly held up another God Hates Fags bumper sticker for Jesse to see.

Love your enemies and pray for those who mistreat you, Jesse thought as he walked away, shaking his head. *Bless those who curse you.* In the background, he heard the van's engine struggling to turn over. He kept walking, eventually turning around to see Drain pounding on the hood, the universal affirmation of an angry, frustrated, mechanically inept human being. And even though he knew he could help, and should, Jesse kept walking.

Still grappling with this latest failure of conscience, his unwillingness to come to the aid of a fellow man in need, he arrived at the Flying J an hour later and eventually secured a ride with a trucker hauling chickens from Oklahoma City to Montgomery, Alabama. As they pulled onto the freeway, a laden tow truck drove past, with the Westboro Baptist Church van secured atop its flatbed.

In Montgomery, Jesse hitched another ride in the bed of a cucumber farmer's pickup. Sharing space with approximately eight thousand cucumbers (by Jesse's math) provided little opportunity for conversation, so Jesse studied the night sky, searching for Jupiter and Venus, Orion and Ursa Minor, Cassiopeia and Perseus. His groin tingled in anticipation of becoming whole again, but when the cucumber farmer dropped him somewhere in Georgia, Jesse's eyelids were heavy. Up ahead he saw a farm, and it did not take long before he was asleep in a haystack.

Twelve

TRIBUTES GREAT AND SMALL

Άκομά όπως εσείς αγαπάτε αυτούς πού έζησαν πρίν, δώστε τήν καρδιά εσάς όσους πλησιάζουν. Οί μεγαλύτεροι θησαυροί εσάς είναι.

Even as you revere those who lived before, give your heart to those nearest you. They are your greatest treasures.

(The Gospel According to Trevor, chapter 11, verse 3)

Father O'Shea woke first, looked at the alluring angel still asleep in the other bed, and knew he needed a walk. Walking was therapeutic for him, providing exercise, a clear head, and a peaceful soul—a combination he found nowhere else. The gym was too chaotic, swimming too monotonous, riding a bike too fraught with the hazards of broken glass, potholes, and inattentive drivers. Walking took him back to the more innocent days of childhood, a time when he often took long strolls along the Boise River at sunset before dinner.

During his monastic stay in the Pyrenees, he dived into the writings of Henry David Thoreau, who insisted the words 'walking' or 'hiking' were too mundane for such a transcendent act. Instead, Thoreau wrote, it should be called *sauntering*, essentially walking toward holiness. O'Shea sauntered a thousand miles during his year in southern France, and viewed more than three hundred sunsets. And he felt obliged to admit they were even better than those in Boise, each a brilliant canvas newly painted by God to celebrate the close of day.

Since walking around this small town would take only minutes, O'Shea turned south instead. Crossing the interstate led him to the Olympian Trail, where he paralleled the Saint Regis River and sauntered east into the morning sun. As he inhaled the fresh scent of pine, he said his morning "Our Fathers," congratulating himself on his ability to avoid temptation yesterday and last night. Where a lesser man might have faltered, he held steadfast. *But what of today, and the next two thousand miles?*

Returning to the Mangold General Store and Motel, he entered his room just as Simone emerged from the bathroom after her morning shower. Her lithe body, still damp, was magnificent, and somehow she managed to accomplish something as mundane as toweling off with an ephemeral grace.

Looking in the mirror, she noticed O'Shea standing in the doorway. "What are you staring at, silly?" she asked, smiling.

"Was I staring?" asked O'Shea, who knew for damn sure he was.

She wrapped the towel around herself and turned on the hairdryer, while O'Shea packed his bags before using his phone to research the local possibilities for breakfast.

When she was nearly ready, Simone noticed that O'Shea was dressed in jeans and a button-down shirt, the clothes of a civilian.

"Not Father O'Shea today?" Simone asked.

"Nah, just Brian today," he responded as he watched her pull a camisole over her bare breasts. "Do you realize the only people who call me Brian are you and my mother? Sometimes it's nice to be a person rather than just a title."

On their way out, they saw young Jack hand-in-hand with his mother, headed toward town. "Oh, hi, mister," Jack said. "Hi lady." They waved at him, and he continued, "I hope you had a good church service."

"Excuse me?" O'Shea said.

The mother turned back and shot them a withering glare. "He heard you last night."

"Heard me doing what, exactly?" O'Shea responded.

"I know what you were doing ... Father." This last word she spat out like poison, and then she glowered at Simone. "You and her."

"But we didn't do anything," O'Shea protested. He turned to Simone. "Tell her."

"We didn't do anything," Simone affirmed.

"Of course you didn't," the mother said. It was not compliance.

O'Shea stopped fast, allowing the mother and son to gain some distance while he considered the implications of her comment. "The last thing I want is to scar some cute little kid," he said to Simone.

"But we didn't do anything," Simone repeated. "If the mom wants to make assumptions, that's on her. Besides, in five years when the little guy figures out what mom *thinks* happened, he'll think it was funny as hell."

They found a breakfast joint in the next small town, and every male stopped chewing as Simone breezed past.

She was Peisinoe, Aglaope, and Thelxiepeia, all three Sirens poured into one pair of size four cutoff shorts, and in western Montana of all places. It would be reasonable to speculate that more than one man suffered a bruised shin from an under-the-table kick by his wife, or a bruised ego from her furious stare. But none betrayed any pain, their focus resolute. They returned to their meals once Simone was seated, but like missile lock on an F-16 fighter jet, their eyes found her again whenever their wives went to the restroom or were distracted by their fussy three-year-old. Simone said nothing about the gawking, but O'Shea could tell she enjoyed the attention.

Once they ordered, Simone began scrolling through her phone, so O'Shea picked up a newspaper left behind by previous diners. Their food arrived within minutes, and Simone dived in.

O'Shea was done with his meal first, half his hash browns uneaten.

"Not hungry?" Simone asked, her mouth full of pancake.

"I don't usually eat a big breakfast," O'Shea replied. He patted his stomach. "I'm trying to lose a few pounds."

"You know, something to think about, sex is a great way to lose weight," she said, shoving another forkful of pancake into her mouth.

"Not for me it isn't, which is why I need to watch my calories," O'Shea replied.

She picked up her phone and said, "Siri, how many calories do you burn having sex?" But when several nearby heads swiveled to investigate, she realized she may have said it a bit too loudly, shrugging an apology as the waitress stopped by to refill O'Shea's coffee.

Simone offered her phone and O'Shea leaned in closer to look. "That's not a lot of calories. Seems like I'd need to have sex ten times a day to lose any weight," he said.

"It's worth a try," she twinkled. She scrolled through the article and again shared her phone with O'Shea. "For future reference, this is my favorite sex position."

A family shuffled past with the husband trailing. He stopped and put his hand on O'Shea's shoulder as he passed. "Have a nice trip," he said with a wink. Simone laughed, covering her mouth just in time to stop half-chewed pancakes from spewing onto the table.

As they left the diner, they were the subject of stares from almost every patron, although the subtext of those stares varied greatly between men and women. The women mostly glared at O'Shea with utter disgust. The men reached a much different conclusion. Indeed, had they known the details of these two travelers, many would have considered joining the clergy themselves.

Back on I-90, Simone posted to her social media accounts and found a playlist on Spotify. Once her virtual world was in order, she turned to O'Shea.

"What made you become a priest?"

"You want the long version or the short version?" he replied.

"We're driving to New York. I think I have time for the long version." She slipped on her sunglasses to fight the morning glare.

"I suppose we do," he said. "I was in high school ... Actually, let's start with grade school. In grade school, I used to love science fiction, and I wanted to be an astronaut. That's when they were doing all the space shuttle missions, which I thought were so cool. You take off on the back of a rocket and shoot out into space." He mimicked the flight trajectory with his right hand. "Then you drive this awesome airplane-slash-spaceship around for a while, maybe see some Martians, look at a couple of planets, and when you come back to earth everyone treats you like a hero."

"Plus you get to wear that awesome helmet that makes your head look like a bubble," Simone added, holding her hands around her head to illustrate.

"Exactly. But then came 1986. The Challenger disaster." After adjusting his sun visor, he continued, "When the Challenger blew up, my career choice didn't seem quite so attractive."

"And that's when you decided to become a priest?" Simone asked.

"Not yet," he answered. "Remember, this is the long version. Now I'm eleven years old and it's January and my friends are all outside throwing snowballs, but I just wanted to sit in my room and cry because my whole future is gone. Eleven-year-old Brian O'Shea was very dramatic, I'm afraid."

Simone giggled in response.

"Eventually I figure out I'm a science kind of guy, and I actually liked Biology more than Physics. So I decide I'm gonna be a doctor."

"Dr. Brian O'Shea," Simone said. "I like it. You want to examine me later?"

"Only your soul." He paused for a sip of water. "Anyway, now I'm in high school, just doing what high school kids do, drinking a little, chasing girls ..."

"Having sex with Dana or Deena," she added.

"I finally remembered, her name was Diana," he

countered. "And it was just once. At any rate, my grades are pretty good, I'm kicking butt in my honors science classes, I'm gonna go to college, then med school, and then I'm gonna be a radiation oncologist."

"What's a radiation oncologist?" Simone asked.

"An oncologist treats cancer," he said. "A radiation oncologist treats it specifically using radiation therapy. Kinda like shooting a ray gun at the bad guys, except in this case the bad guys are cancer cells. I'd still get to do the science fiction stuff, and help people at the same time."

Simone, spellbound, crisscrossed her legs in the passenger seat. "That's very noble," she said.

"That's what I thought, too. Anyway, one day we're at the dinner table and my mom tells us about Dolores Anderson, our neighbor down the street. She has cancer, my mom says, and my ears perk up because I know they can use radiation on her and she'll be cured, right? Because cancer is just that easy."

"My friend's mom died of cancer," Simone pouted.

"Nasty stuff," O'Shea affirmed. "So I say, 'But she's gonna be okay, isn't she?' And my mom says, 'No, they're putting her in hospice care. She only has a few weeks to live.'"

"How sad." Simone's voice broke slightly.

"I know. It turns out she'd had cancer for years, and her doctors had done everything they could for her. Radiation, chemo, everything."

"So what happened?"

"Mrs. Anderson went into hospice, and she spent her whole time there praying and reading the Bible. Morning, noon, and night, that's all she did."

Simone leaned forward. "And?"

"And a month later, she walked out of hospice care and went home. Dolores Anderson was saved by faith when medical science could not help her. And *that's* when I decided to become a priest."

"Wow, what a story."

The next ten miles passed in silence, until Simone asked, "What happened to her?"

"Who?"

"The lady with the cancer."

O'Shea shook his head. "She died six months later when she choked on a chicken bone."

"Brian!" she yelped, and playfully hit him.

"Hey, hey, I'm driving here," he said, and she stopped. He worried over his next question for a few moments, then eventually offered, "We're travel buddies, right?"

"Of course."

"And travel buddies share everything?"

"We haven't quite shared *everything* ... yet. But yes."

"Okay." He took a deep breath. "What made you become a ..."

"Stripper?" she completed what he could not. "You can say it. I'm not ashamed. Although I prefer dancer."

"Good," he said. "I was worried."

She sat up taller and pushed her wavy hair back from her face. "Don't be. Three years ago my dad finally left, good riddance, and then a few weeks later my mom lost her job. We really struggled for about six months."

"My goodness," O'Shea said, "That's rough."

"You're right, it was. And not like 'I can't buy the expensive makeup' rough. I mean, like, I care about school and I want to do something with my life, and I don't want to have to depend on anyone ever again."

"So you've been a stripper, I mean a dancer, for three years?"

She shook her head. "Three years ago I was still an A cup. I got a part-time job at a bagel shop for about six months, and after that I worked as a hostess at a restaurant. I was there for a long time, and all that time I was, you know, blossoming." She held her breasts to ensure there was no confusion as to her meaning.

"And quite spectacularly," added O'Shea, and she touched him in appreciation.

"I was making decent money for a teenager, but not enough so I didn't have to worry. Especially since I have to pay my own tuition at U-Dub now. Anyway, one day last year I was shopping at the mall, and I notice this old guy peeping on me."

"Old guy?"

"Yeah, like forty."

O'Shea winced. "Ouch."

"Don't worry, Brian," she reassured. "My perspective has changed a lot since then. Anyway, this guy is totally checking me out, like following me around to different stores, pretending to be interested in the same stuff I'm buying. It was soooo obvious. Do you know who Morgan Fairchild is?"

"She was a little before my time, but what red-blooded male of the nineteen-eighties doesn't know Morgan Fairchild?"

"I read that Morgan Fairchild didn't realize she was hot until she went to a Halloween party and all the dads were staring at her. Kinda like what happened to me, except mine happened at Northgate Mall. Anyway, I realized maybe I could take advantage, you know. The next week I invested a hundred dollars on a fake ID, another hundred on costumes, and I started dancing at the Starlight. I'd been there about two months when you first asked for me."

"And I was mesmerized," O'Shea added.

"Besides, think of it this way. If I still worked at the bagel shop, I never would have met you."

"Good point," he said. "Thank God for upward mobility."

She laughed, then added, "Thank God for great tits."

They drove through breathtaking mountains and seemingly endless prairie that day. Midafternoon, Simone informed him she wanted to visit Mount Rushmore.

"Why?" O'Shea asked. "Don't you want to get to New York?"

"You know I do, but you forget a couple of things," she explained. "First, remember, I've never been out of Washington state before. Second, I love history, and it's pretty much on our way. We can take a few hours, can't we?"

"Sure, of course. We can take as much time as you want."

A trip to Mount Rushmore required a slight detour, so they got off the interstate an hour past Billings and traveled one hundred miles on U.S. Highway 212, arriving in Broadus, Montana around seven. O'Shea had driven more than six hundred miles since the morning, from a hamlet at one end of Montana to a dusty speck on the other. After experiencing the local dinner cuisine, they were directed to the Sagebrush Inn for their lodging needs. O'Shea negotiated the dirt roads of Broadus and located the motel, but since this particular establishment was located directly across from the Powder River County Sheriff and two blocks away from Faith Bible Church, he requested a room in the back.

A sheriff cruised past as they unloaded their luggage. O'Shea disappeared into the room with their bags, so the sheriff stopped to ogle Simone, who was bent over the front seat, the bottom of her shorts cut so high it made her legs go on forever. When she stood up, the sheriff asked, "Everything okay, miss?" His voice cracked when he said it.

"Everything's great," Simone assured him. She sashayed to his patrol car and leaned over, resting her palms in the open window. "Why do you ask?"

The sheriff shifted in his seat, trying to remain inconspicuous in his obvious efforts to examine her cleavage. "Just making sure," he said, and then drove away.

That night, the Siren tried once again to tempt Odysseus. While O'Shea brushed his teeth, she selected music, removed her camisole, and swiveled her hips in that way which typically shoots electrical current directly to a man's netherworld. As she shimmied seductively toward him, he did not even realize he had stopped brushing his teeth and now stood motionless, openmouthed, toothpaste dribbling from his lower lip. But her dance was interrupted when headlights shone through the flimsy curtains, followed by a knock at the door which roused him from his stupefaction. "Thank God," O'Shea said. He spat his toothpaste into the sink and moved across to the door while Simone pulled on a sweatshirt and zipped it just past her navel.

"Who is it?" O'Shea asked.

"Sheriff."

When O'Shea opened the door, the sheriff looked right past him. "Everything okay, miss?" he said.

"Everything's fine, officer. Just like I told you before."

"What's with the music?"

"Oh, sorry," Simone said, turning it off. "Am I disturbing other guests?"

"No. Just wanted to make sure you were all right."

"Everything's good. In fact, I'm getting ready to go to sleep now, if you don't mind. Thank you for checking on me."

The sheriff surveyed the room, stared at O'Shea for a moment, then offered one final glance at Simone, who zipped her sweatshirt to her neck and back to her navel and lingered there. "Sure," he said, his voice cracking again. "Goodnight, miss."

For the rest of the night, a spotlight from the sheriff's patrol car swept across their curtains every few minutes. Simone's soft breathing confirmed she was asleep, but O'Shea lay in bed for what seemed like weeks with his eyes wide open and the faded wool blanket pulled up to his chin, an insubstantial fortification against a raid by local law enforcement. In another context, the alternating darkness and bright light might have carried some sort of religious symbolism, perhaps a metaphorical sign from God about temptation and redemption. But in a motel room in Broadus, Montana, thanks to the stalwart efforts of the County Sheriff, O'Shea thought it was like trying to sleep in a bad seventies disco. All he could do was lie there, watch the lights, and wait out the interminable night, finally drifting off near dawn.

After sorting through shriveled oranges and generic

breakfast cereals at the Sagebrush Inn's free continental breakfast, they started for Mount Rushmore. They negotiated summer tourist traffic to arrive early afternoon, ate lunch in the cafeteria, and spent several hours exploring the grounds of the formidable monument. By the time they were ready to leave, Simone was halfway through an ice cream cone and O'Shea was spent. "Let's just stay in Rapid City tonight," he suggested with a yawn. Later, at a cowboy cookout, they debated the significance of the four Mount Rushmore presidents until the band started to play. As soon as they returned to their room, O'Shea fell asleep in his clothes, exhausted from the day's activities and the previous sleepless night. Simone sighed, removed his shoes, and watched television on mute until she grew tired.

When O'Shea awoke the next morning, he turned to look at Simone's bed. It was empty.

"Simone?" he said, but there was no answer. "Simone?" he said, a little louder this time, and again nothing. Alarmed, he jumped out of bed and went to the window. Parting the curtains, he was relieved to see his Toyota Camry still parked in front of their room. Then he detected sounds coming from the bathroom. As he cracked the door, there was Simone, sitting on the toilet, earbuds in place, singing along to the music of Stinkbomb as she meticulously shaved her pubic hair.

"Oh hi, Brian," she said. "Look, I made a heart!" And indeed she had.

Thirteen

AN EARLIER HELL

Ενώ ή δόξα τού ανερχόμενου ήλιου μπορεί προσφερθοίτε ΐνα βιαστείτειν, καί προσελκυσέτω σού παρά τήν Κύριον.

While the glory of the rising sun may bid you hurry, let it also draw you to the Lord.

(The Gospel According to Trevor, chapter 9, verse 23)

Dinner at Aunt Sally's promised to be a contentious affair, intermingling mashed potatoes and green beans with long-held grudges and grievances. For every "please" and "thank you," there would just as likely be some thirty-year-old story whose resultant angst remained, to this day, unresolved. So while family members and their guests were expected to follow the rules of civil dining—dress nicely, keep their elbows off the table, eat with the proper fork—it was a good idea to wear big-girl panties, as a fond memory could, at any given time, abruptly transform into a hurtful affront and develop into an unforgivable offense. Berkshire knew she was badly outnumbered, to the approximate dimensions of the Texans at the Alamo, so she sharpened her tongue in preparation.

Aunt Sally sat at the head of the table, the matriarch lording over her vassals, not all of whom fully understood the rules of this game.

"Let's say grace," she said, a mandate badly disguised as suggestion. And she began, "Heavenly Father, thank you for preparing this table for us. Keep dear Sarah in our hearts as you lift her to Heaven. We thank you for her presence in our lives, and for reminding us that ..." Now she paused for the scripted part, which everyone in the family joined in: "A happy family is an earlier Heaven."

This family, though, is an earlier—, thought Berkshire, unconsciously chewing her lower lip. But she could not finish the thought before everyone said "Amen" and attacked the food.

Jolene brought her new beau with her, wearing the same Tony Lamas. "The happy family part," she confided to him, "George Birmingham Shaw said that."

"The guy from Oklahoma?" he asked. "The football coach?"

"No, sweetie. I think he's from California."

Berkshire turned toward them. "It's George Bernard Shaw, and he's from Ireland. He was a writer."

"Never heard of him," said Tony Lama. "He must not be a very good writer."

Berkshire decided to bail on this conversation before the boat completely sank, so she focused instead on scooping mashed potatoes and green beans onto her plate. They ate in an edgy silence for a few moments, the only sounds coming from forks hitting plates and the chatter from the kids' table in the living room.

"Haley, dear, what time do I need to get you to the station tomorrow?" Jolene finally asked.

"My train leaves at 12:10, so I'd like to leave here by eleven if possible. If not, I can take an Uber."

"Don't be silly," Jolene replied. "We can go to early church service."

"Are you sure it's no bother?" Berkshire asked.

"It's no bother at all," Jolene affirmed, even as Tony Lama frowned almost imperceptibly.

"Do you go straight to New York?" asked Aunt Sally. Her tone was not particularly inquisitive, but rather suggested that the sooner Berkshire was located in a different time zone, the better it would be for everyone.

"No, this train only goes to New Orleans. I stay there overnight, then catch the Crescent on Monday morning."

"Explain to me again why y'all are goin' to New York," Jolene said. "And can you pass the biscuits, please?"

Berkshire complied, and then answered, "It's a research project for work."

Next to Berkshire, a prematurely gray man sliced up his dinner. "The meatloaf's especially good today, Mom," he said to Aunt Sally, who replied, "Thank you, Jimmy."

Jimmy shoved a load of meatloaf and potatoes into his mouth. As he chewed, he turned to Berkshire and said, "Tell us about it."

"You wouldn't be interested."

"Of course I would," he said, waving his fork for emphasis. "Else I wouldn't have asked."

"Jimmy's an engineer," Jolene explained to Tony Lama. "He's always askin' questions about things. My curious brother."

Berkshire sighed. "I suppose. My research team and I discovered a new book of the Bible." She noticed their disapproving looks and continued, "What I mean is, we discovered a book that did not go in the Bible and then was lost. Until recently."

"And you, of all people, found it?" asked Aunt Sally, her head tipped to the side, dubious about the prospect.

"My research team and I did, yes," Berkshire affirmed.

"What's it say?" Jimmy asked.

"It pretty much goes along with the other Gospels, but it adds some additional details. That's what I'm researching."

"What details?" Jimmy pushed.

"Mostly about the crucifixion. According to the book, one of the Roman soldiers wounded Jesus."

"We know that already," Jolene said. "A Roman soldier stabbed Jesus in the side." She beamed at her biblical expertise.

"And then another cut off his testicle," Berkshire added. Tony Lama suppressed a laugh. Jimmy's wife, wearing a plain floral dress, stopped chewing and looked at her husband. Berkshire's older brother Todd set down his iced tea, and his wife shifted uneasily in her seat, while Berkshire's brother Trent, youngest of the three, took the opportunity to snag another biscuit.

"His testicle?" asked Jimmy. "Did I hear you right?"

"That's correct."

"And is that what you're researching? Christ's holy nut?"

"I am," she said. Tony Lama looked away, lest he betray his amusement.

Jimmy cut his meatloaf and then paused with a piece on his fork. "You actually get paid to do this?"

"I do. Research is vital to our funding and to our academic reputation."

"And where, exactly, do you think y'all are gonna find this Jesus nut?"

"New York City. At least, that's how I interpret the text."

"May I ask," Jimmy continued, putting the meatloaf in his mouth, "what's this book called?"

"The Gospel According to Trevor."

Tony Lama snorted. Jolene looked at him, glanced around the table, and began to titter with the restraint appropriate for a Southern belle, no matter how fictional her self-characterization. Soon, the combination of Jolene's comical giggling and the academic's absurd theory made everyone bellow with laughter. Everyone except Berkshire, of course, who ate in silent anger as even the children, from the kids' table in the other room, joined in the uproar.

Calm was not restored for several minutes, and even then it bore a palpable tension, capable of snapping at any moment.

"You know, Haley, maybe you should join us at early church tomorrow," Aunt Sally suggested. "Might do you some good."

"What the hell is that supposed to mean, 'might do you some good'?" Berkshire asked, hackles up.

"Please watch your language around the children," Sally scolded.

Berkshire held up her hands apologetically. "I'm sorry. But what is that supposed to mean?"

"It's supposed to mean ..." Aunt Sally waited until everyone concentrated their attention on her. "It's supposed to mean that you have certainly drifted away from the Lord, and from this family. You pushed us all away when you were a child, and you never looked back. Jimmy teaches Sunday school and Jolene works as a greeter. Your brothers helped retile the sanctuary when we remodeled a few years ago. But all you've got is this cock-and-bull story about a new Bible book. I know you think you're too good for Lazybrook Baptist Church, but now you're too good for the Bible, too?"

"I didn't push you away," disputed Berkshire. "My own mother pushed *me* away!"

"She did no such thing, God rest her soul," Sally argued.

Berkshire's fork clanked onto her plate. "Oh no? Then why the fuck was I sent to Catholic school?"

"Haley!" Sally said.

Jimmy leaned back in his chair. "Kids, why don't you all go outside and play?"

"Aw, Dad, we want cherry pie."

"You can have cherry pie later," Jimmy said. "Right now I need you to go outside and play." Obediently, they did.

Jimmy turned to Haley. "You've got a lot of nerve—"

"Haley," brother Trent interrupted, "we all went to religious school. Not just you."

"Bullshit," she fired back. "You went to preschool at the Baptist Church is all, and then to Sinclair Elementary. I had to endure six years of hell with the nuns at Saint Mary Margaret of Grace. And let me tell you, there was no actual grace at that school."

"Then I guess you shouldn't have gotten thrown out of Baptist preschool," Aunt Sally said. "Your mother knew she needed to straighten you out. Didn't work, though."

"Obviously," added Jolene.

Berkshire dropped her biscuit on her plate. "Maybe that was a stupid way to do it. It's like 'Haley doesn't like turnips, so for the next six years we're going to make her eat turnips at every goddamn meal.' That's a ridiculous fucking plan."

"My gracious, your language is atrocious," Jolene said.

"Yeah, well, at least I'm not sleeping with the guy I just met at my aunt's funeral."

"Oh, we know that," Jolene responded coldly. "You're not sleeping with anybody."

"Haley, let's face it," Trent said. "You've always thought you're better than everyone else in the family just because you have a Ph.D."

As Berkshire started to protest, Aunt Sally added, "He's absolutely right, and guess what? You may have a Ph.D., but your soul is empty."

"You know," Jimmy said, "I was reading about some religious assembly they're gonna have up in Philadelphia on Tuesday. Lots of big names are gonna be speaking. Falwell, Franklin Graham, maybe Joel Osteen."

"Have you seen pictures of Joel Osteen's house?" gushed Jolene. "My goodness, it's incredible." Others chimed in with their own admiration for the televangelist's megamansion.

"Anyway," Jimmy continued, "it just seems to me, if y'all are a religious scholar who hates religion, maybe it would be interesting to you."

"Maybe it would," Berkshire said, mostly to mollify her attackers.

"I bet your mother would like if you went," Aunt Sally said.

"I have no doubt," Berkshire answered crisply. She

stood up and placed her napkin on the table. "I'll take care of my own transportation tomorrow. Thank you for dinner, Aunt Sally. It was nice to see everyone."

That night, covered in both metaphorical bruises and one on her left thigh from running into the dining room table as she hurried out of Aunt Sally's house, Dr. Haley Berkshire cried herself to sleep in room 1105 of the Magnolia Hotel in downtown Houston.

She left Houston a few minutes past noon the next day, and nine-and-one-half hours later her train pulled into New Orleans. The temperature outside was only in the eighties but the humidity stood at about eight-hundred percent, and by the time she hailed a cab she was already wet with perspiration.

"Hotel Saint Marie," she said.

She checked into her room, changed into a tank top, and decided to explore the French Quarter. *Just one drink*, she thought, *and maybe a little music.*

But the Quarter at night is intoxicating, filled with street performers and ornate hotel balconies and the smell of crawfish and the sounds of live music and the ghosts of its colorful history. She enjoyed a Hurricane at a bar on Bourbon Street with dueling pianos and a Sazerac in a lively jazz bar on the next block, and was drawn into the karaoke bar where she quaffed two Abita ambers and ended up onstage with several other women singing "Love Shack." When the song ended, the women all flashed the appreciative crowd, and Dr. Haley Berkshire realized she might be a little bit drunk.

I'll be tired tomorrow, she thought, *but I'll just take a nap on the train.*

The group of women convinced her to join them as

they continued to explore, and about half an hour later they walked into a gay bar at the far end of the Quarter. Berkshire joined her new friends in a tequila shot, soon thereafter she was on the dance floor, and eventually she found herself in a dark corner booth, sipping yet another Sazerac and kissing a woman named Beth whom she had just met. Her train was scheduled to depart in less than five hours.

Just before the bar closed at three a.m., Berkshire went to the ladies' room. A glance at the mirror revealed her tank top partly askew, her hair a mess, and her eyelids heavy with fatigue. The mirror also showed the face of a woman who, surprisingly, did not mind any of these. Except maybe that last Sazerac. *What the hell,* she thought. *I'll just sleep all day on the train.*

As apparently required by Louisiana tourism statute, it was suggested that her night would be incomplete without beignets from the Café Du Monde. She walked there hand-in-hand with Beth, sober reflection still a couple of hours in the future. After feasting on the sugary treats, they sat on a bench overlooking the Mississippi River, where they kissed the sugar off each other's lips and talked until the effects of the alcohol dissipated, the conversation waned, and the sun peeked over the bayou.

"Oh, crap, I gotta go," Berkshire said. "My train leaves in an hour."

"Stay an extra day," urged Beth.

"No. I must be on that train. My work depends on it." Her tone was resolute and her goodbye awkward.

She hurried back to Hotel Saint Marie, took a five-minute shower, changed clothes, and tossed the offending tank top into the trash. A two-mile cab ride got her to the

Union Passenger Terminal in time to make her train by six minutes.

"Happy Monday, miss," said the cheerful conductor as Berkshire boarded. "Where you headed?"

"New York," she said, groggily. The pace of the last hour made her feel as if poisonous frogs were breeding inside her stomach.

"Have a nice trip," he said.

She slept through breakfast and woke feeling parched. She bought a bottle of water from the bar car, drank it in what seemed to be a single gulp, then bought two more. She spent much of the afternoon inert, except for five minutes somewhere in eastern Alabama when she visited the bathroom to vomit a revolting combination of bourbon, rum, beer, tequila, various fruit juices, and chunks of fried dough—her souvenirs of New Orleans. The toxic blend smelled so bad that the frogs in her stomach started kicking, and she vomited a second time.

Her head hurt until the next day, when she awoke to see the University of Virginia out the window. As the train pulled out of Charlottesville, she realized she was absolutely famished, and dragged herself to the dining car.

By ten a.m. they had left Washington, D.C. and she finally felt better. New York, the Big Apple, the fruition of her research, the chance to prove all the haters wrong and establish herself as a bright light among religious scholars, lay just three hours ahead.

But then she thought of her night in New Orleans. So much in just nine hours. She thought of karaoke, and cocktails, and beignets, and Beth. And the more she thought of New Orleans, the more conflicted she became. *What was Beth thinking? Hell, what was I thinking?* And the kicker: *What would Mom think?*

"Next stop, Philadelphia," the conductor announced. "Arriving in five minutes." Berkshire's stomach knotted. New York beckoned. Her brothers and cousins rebuked. Trevor summoned. Aunt Sally ostracized. Her thoughts swirled like the ocean at high tide, although they were so disjointed they could scarcely be called thoughts. She reached for her luggage, then stopped. She began to stand up, but felt the train's brakes and sat back down. *Only ninety more minutes to New York,* she told herself. *Just relax.*

"Philadelphia," the conductor announced.

Instinctively, Berkshire grabbed her luggage and rushed for the exit, and next thing she knew she was standing on the platform. The doors closed, the train pulled away, and the passengers dispersed.

What the fuck am I doing?

Only then did she fully comprehend that Sarah Landsdowne Berkshire, dead a week, still somehow managed to disrupt her life. Again.

Fourteen
A CARPENTER'S WORK

Πολλά πράγματα γίνονται έν ἀγαθῇ καί καλῇ πνεύμῷ. Όλά είναι αντανάκλαση τής χάριτος τού Θεού.

Many things are done in a kind and good spirit; all are a reflection of the grace of God.

(The Gospel According to Trevor, chapter 4, verse 16)

Jesse woke to a shotgun being racked, and by the time he forced his eyes open, both barrels were ready for business—Jesse's forehead being the customer. *Surely this cannot be my demise,* he thought. Raising his hand to request a moment's consideration, he gained a temporary reprieve.

"Who are you?" asked the black man on the other side of the shotgun. His overalls hung from his thin frame like a shower curtain and his straw hat looked like an umbrella atop his small head.

"Jesse Morales. I just—"

"You jus' what?" asked the farmer. "Are you spyin' on me? You from the bank?"

"Am I from the ...?" It took Jesse a moment to process

the question. "Do I look like I'm from a bank?"

"Then where *are* you from?"

"California. Los Angeles, to be exact."

The farmer scrutinized him. "You're a long way from home, son."

"I'm on my way to New York."

"Musta took a bad wrong turn to end up in Taylor County, Georgia."

"I'm hitchhiking. I take whatever I can get. My last ride dropped me down the road there," Jesse explained, pointing into the distance, "and I walked as far as I could before I got tired."

"And you just happened to get tired right heah, right in front of my farm?"

"I didn't know it was your farm," said Jesse. "I just saw a comfortable place to sleep."

The farmer tugged his straw hat in deliberation.

Jesse continued, "And why do you even think someone from the bank would sleep in one of your haystacks?"

"Because they're sneaky." The farmer jabbed with his shotgun as he explained, "They've been tryin' to run me off my land. I owe foah thousand dollars else they gonna take my farm."

"Four thous–?"

"That's right," affirmed the farmer, finally pointing the shotgun away from Jesse. "I had a bad yeuh last yeuh, so I took a loan so I could keep this place, which means the world to me. Y' see, six generations ago my family were slaves, right heah on this farm. The next foah generations we were sharecroppers, right heah on this farm. Then my daddy had a payin' job, as field foreman, right heah on this farm. I'm the first person in my family to evah own anything other than the clothes on our back, that bein' this heah farm. And now the bank wants to take it away."

"I'm sorry," said Jesse. "I wish I could help. I'll just be moving on. I apologize for the inconvenience."

"Not so fast. You sleep on my farm, you owe me either rent or labor."

"It'll have to be labor," said Jesse, hauling himself to his feet. "I don't have any money."

"Labor it is, then. I'm Silas Felder. The house is right up the road. We'll get you some breakfast b'fore you get to work."

They walked side by side up a dirt road to a small farmhouse.

"Bernard, we got company," Silas said when he entered the house. "This heah's Jesse. Can you fix him up a couple eggs and some grits? He's gonna help me out on the farm today."

Bernard, who might have been even thinner than Silas, nodded a hello as he pulled a skillet from the dish rack.

Silas went outside while Bernard got busy in the kitchen. Jesse waited patiently, examining the sparse interior of the truly humble home. Five minutes later, Bernard set a plate before Jesse. "Thank you," Jesse said meekly, and presently was overcome with emotion.

"What's the matter? Eggs not prepared to your liking?"

It took Jesse a few moments to regain his composure. "No, sir," he said. "This is beautiful."

"It's just eggs, honey. Why you cryin'?"

"I can't remember the last time I ate a meal on regular plates with a real fork. It's been years." He remembered eating with other men, long ago, but it was much noisier than here.

"You a funny man. Eat your breakfast. Silas is waitin'."

Jesse quickly finished breakfast, thanked Bernard, and went outside to find Silas.

"What are you growing," he asked, "besides hay?"

"Peanuts. This heah's west Georgia. In west Georgia, everybody grows either peanuts or pecans." They walked a dirt path, leafy peanut vines on either side, and Silas pointed. "I got peanuts on this north half, alfalfa on the south. Next yeuh I switch."

"Where's the hay?" asked Jesse.

Silas chuckled at this. "Alfalfa is what makes hay. I leave some behind to help the soil, what we call 'green manure.' But most of it I bale up and sell for livestock feed."

"How do you know when it's time to harvest?" asked Jesse.

"Alfalfa's most a yeuh-round thing, 'bout once a month, just b'fore it blooms. The peanuts gonna be a while yet. I planted in April and we won't harvest until August."

"What do you do until then?"

"Mostly I walk the fields, makin' sure they're okay and wonderin' how I'm gonna raise foah thousand dollars. Otherwise I do projects, keepin' things fixed and workin' properly. Like right now I gotta bale the hay and patch my back fence. Don't have the money to afford a new fence, so I gotta use chewin' gum and balin' wire, as they say."

Jesse squinted against the morning sun.

"Which one you wanna tackle first?" Silas asked. "Hay or fence?"

"Fence," Jesse said.

They walked to the rear of the farm, nearly a quarter of a mile, and began working. Jesse pushed or pulled while Silas' bony fingers threaded or bent or secured wire like a skilled weaver. Bernard brought lunch and lemonade when the sun was overhead, and they enjoyed a brief respite from their labor.

When Silas removed his straw hat to pour cold water on his head, Jesse reached over and picked it up. The hat was frayed and filthy, with a hole in the front and a chunk of the brim missing. "Looks like you could use a new hat," Jesse said.

"I could use a lot o' new things, but right now we're barely gettin' by. Let's get back to work."

By late afternoon, Jesse had the hang of it and they were working with machine-like efficiency. The faster they moved, the more Silas smiled, a genuine expression of a man who appreciated the simple pleasures of an honest day's work and the assistance of a friend.

"Tell me about Bernard," Jesse said. "Does Bernard help on the farm?"

"Not much," said Silas. "He's sick, so he mostly takes care of the house."

"Is he your brother?"

Silas chuckled. "He's my husband."

They worked silently for a while as Jesse tried to make sense of it. "Your husband?" he finally repeated.

"You think it's strange, a gay farmer?" Silas asked. He was not angry or even defensive. Facts were facts, no more and no less.

"I don't see why it should be," replied Jesse. He squeezed two pieces of fencing together for Silas to patch.

"Mm-hmm," said Silas. "That's what we think, too. Not

everyone around heah agrees, though, so we mostly keep to ourselves."

"Are you a good farmer?" Jesse asked.

Silas nodded. "I think so."

"Are you honest?"

"As the day is long."

"Then what else matters?" asked Jesse.

Silas removed his hat and scratched the top of his head. "We're all done heah, Jesse." He pointed at the sky. "We fixed the whole fence b'fore the sun went down. Much obliged."

They walked back to the farmhouse, where Jesse kept a respectful distance while Silas hugged Bernard. They spoke quietly between themselves and, at one point, Silas gestured over his shoulder at their guest.

"Don't just stand there like a statue," Bernard said to Jesse. "Get washed up. Dinner's almost ready." And as Jesse slipped past him and entered the farmhouse, he thought he heard Bernard whisper, "Thank you."

When the three took their seats around a small table, Bernard looked at their guest and asked, "Jesse, you mind sayin' a blessing?" Jesse turned uncertainly toward Silas, who put up his hands and said, "Don't look at me. Inside, Bernard's in charge."

Jesse shrugged, closed his eyes, and bowed his head. "Lord, thank you for each day," he said, "for leading me toward my destiny, and for all the kind people I have met along the way. Bless Silas and Bernard for their hospitality and, if it be Your will, deliver them from the shackles of debt. Amen."

"Amen," echoed Silas and Bernard, and they all picked up their forks.

"How's the chicken?" asked Bernard after a moment.

"Delicious," Jesse said.

"Special recipe I got from my momma," said Bernard. "Though mine's not nearly as good as hers."

Jesse hoisted a green leafy substance with his fork. "What's this vegetable? I like it."

"Them's collard greens," said Bernard. "We eat lots o' collard greens around heah."

"Can I ask you somethin'?" Silas said, and Jesse nodded, his mouth now full of collard greens. "How'd you learn to mend fences so good if you're from Los Angeles? Cain't be any farms where you live."

"I'm not exactly sure," Jesse said, and they could tell he was completely serious.

"Tell me this then," Silas continued. "When you prayed, you said somethin' about your destiny. What did you mean by that?"

"I'm on my way to New York to become whole," Jesse explained between bites. "To fulfill my holy purpose as the Redeemer, the one true Son of God come again." That one perplexed them, and for a while they all ate in silence.

Finishing his meal, Silas stood and said, "Excuse me just a moment." He slid his chair underneath the table and went out to the front porch. Jesse could hear him talking indistinctly from outside.

Bernard finished next but remained seated, seeming to take quiet pleasure in watching the stranger eat. When Jesse ate the last of his collard greens, he gently set down his knife and fork and turned to Bernard. "That may have been the best meal I ever had," he said. "Thank y—"

Silas interrupted when he reentered the house. "Good news," he said. "A friend o' mine named Luther Thompson is drivin' up to Philadelphia, leavin' tomorrow night. He said he'd welcome the company, if you want. It's not New York, but it's gettin' closer."

Jesse clapped his hands like a child on Christmas morning. "That would be wonderful!"

Silas smiled. "And you'll stay heah tonight. We got a guest room. Right, Bernard?"

"That's right," Bernard agreed.

"Now, lemme show you somethin'," Silas said, with more than a hint of intrigue. He led Jesse ten feet into the living room, parked him in a chair, and took a small box from a shelf. Bernard chuckled from the kitchen sink, where he scrubbed the frying pan.

"Peanuts are my life," Silas explained, still holding the box. "I been around peanuts and peanut farmers since I was born. Yet I haven't never seen anything like this."

With such a sublime introduction, he opened the box and showed its contents to Jesse.

"A peanut?" asked Jesse, frowning, underwhelmed.

The farmer leaned in closer. "Not just any peanut. This one is special. Look heah." Silas gently removed the peanut from the box and held it in the palm of his hand for closer inspection. "Look closely. Look at it from different angles. You see it?"

"Umm, maybe ..."

"This heah's the best view," Silas said, tipping the peanut slightly. "This is not just any peanut. No sir. This peanut looks just like—"

"Like Jesus," Jesse said. "I'll be ..."

"Ain't that somethin'?" said Silas, grinning. "And I grew it myself."

"It's late," said Bernard as he moved toward a room at

the back of the house.

"Sure enough it is," Silas said, returning the peanut to its box and the box to its shelf. "Let me show you to the guest room. Bernard, honey, I'll be there in a minute."

Silas walked Jesse to the small guest room on the opposite side of the house, a room so small it barely contained a twin-sized mattress and a small table. "It's not much," Silas said, "but the bed's comfortable and the sheets are clean."

A few minutes later, Silas joined his husband in their bedroom.

"Strangest thing happened," Silas said. "Soon as he saw the bed, he started cryin'. Over a simple twin-size bed."

"He sure is a funny man," Bernard said.

Jesse was up before the roosters and, after breakfast, he and Silas set out for the barn. Silas carried a one-gallon water jug and now sported Jesse's Venice Beach hat, a gift which brightened his whole face.

"Silas, I've been thinking about something," Jesse said.

"Go on," said Silas. "I'm listenin'."

"I had a brainstorm," continued Jesse. "Isn't there some website where you can sell things?"

Silas pushed open the barn door. "There's lots o' websites where you can sell things. In fact, I sell most o' my crop on the internet now'days."

"Is that so?" Jesse crossed his arms. "Here's what I'm thinking. The peanut you showed me last night. What if you sold it?"

"Sold it?" asked Silas. He checked the hitch to confirm the baler was securely attached to the tractor and, once satisfied, hopped into the driver's seat.

Jesse explained, "I don't know, maybe it's a crazy idea, but I understand people buy just about anything. Maybe you could get a little money for it, help you out a bit. You know, since it is such an unusual peanut."

Silas turned the key to start the tractor, which rumbled in response. "C'mon, man," he shouted over the noise. "Don't nobody want to buy a single peanut, even if it does look just like Jesus."

"Maybe not," said Jesse. "It was just a thought."

"Hop aboard, unless you'd prefer to walk."

Once they covered a quarter of the alfalfa field, Silas turned off the tractor and opened his water jug. Jesse examined the hay baler, intrigued. "Did you always want to be a farmer?"

"My whole life," replied Silas, using his sleeve to wipe the sweat from his forehead. "I even went away to college to learn more about it." Silas passed the water jug to Jesse and continued, "Abraham Baldwin Agricultural College, in Tilton. Took me six yeuhs because I was also workin' a full-time job. Since we never had a college student in our family b'fore me, I promised my daddy I would graduate. And I did."

"How was it?" asked Jesse, his eyes wide. "What was it like?"

"Funny thing," said Silas, "my daddy knew as much about farmin' as any of 'em."

"And then you came back here?"

"Wasn't plannin' to, but when my daddy passed, the owner asked me if I wanted the field foreman job. I said, 'No, thank you, but I'd like to buy the place from you.'"

They worked until midafternoon, then walked the peanut fields until dusk before they went inside for dinner.

"I gotta apologize, Jesse," said Bernard. "We ain't got much, and I wasn't expectin' to be servin' three."

"Prob'bly not even enough for two," added Silas. "I think maybe that's why we're both so skinny."

Jesse looked at the small helping of fried catfish and the loaf of cornbread. "This will be plenty." And half an hour later, even though all three of them were stuffed, Bernard still had leftovers to put in the refrigerator.

"My belly feels funny," Jesse said, pushing back his chair.

"Two days o' home cookin'll do that," said Silas.

Luther Thompson arrived about nine p.m., and soon they were off in Luther's truck. Silas and Bernard stood in front of their house and waved goodbye at the disappearing cloud of dust.

"Funny man," Bernard said.

"He sure is," Silas agreed, resting his thumbs in his dirty overalls. "And I didn't even tell you 'bout the crazy idea he had today ..."

Luther bumped along the Taylor County farm roads. "I hear you're headin' for New York." He was an older man, stocky, weathered by a lifetime of work in the hot Georgia sun. "I got me a job in Philly, helpin' move some furniture for my cousins. They're movin' up to Norristown. Sorry I can't get you any farther."

"Oh, no, that'll be great," Jesse said.

"You know, every time I visit my cousins, I can't wait to get back home to the wide-open spaces," Luther said. "They're from Taylor County, too. Never thought they'd make it in the big city, but they love it. Silas says you're from LA."

Jesse ran his fingers through his stringy hair. "That's

right. Venice Beach, to be exact."

"Ocean livin', huh? Must be nice there."

"It is," Jesse said, deciding this was not the time to disclose his typical accommodations back home.

"Pretty girls?"

"Sure," said Jesse. "Lots of 'em."

"Then why you goin' to New York?" Luther asked as he turned onto the state highway.

Jesse spent the next fifteen minutes explaining about the Gospel According to Trevor, his missing testicle, and his divine purpose. Luther listened quietly, intently, occasionally offering an "uh-huh," which emboldened Jesse to spare no details. When he finished, Luther paused, took a sip from a Coke can, and proclaimed, "Son, that's the most ridiculous damn story I ever heard."

Jesse wanted to protest, but two days of labor had exhausted him, so he sat in silence for what seemed like hours. *Could Luther be right*? he wondered. Before they reached Atlanta, Jesse was asleep.

Around nine a.m. the next morning, Luther detoured onto Interstate 495. "Washington, D.C. traffic is the worst," Luther offered.

Jesse shifted in his seat, craning his neck to get a better view of things. "You happen to know what day it is?"

"Tuesday," said Luther. "You on a time schedule to get to New York and find your testicle?" He laughed like thunder.

"You think I should skip it, don't you?"

"Son, don't be a fool," Luther said, shaking his head slowly, insistently. "In the end it don't matter what I think, or nobody else for that matter. It only matters what you think. You done traveled all the way across the country.

You must believe in this."

"I do," said Jesse.

The big man placed his hand on Jesse's shoulder. "Then you'd best see it through."

They arrived in North Philadelphia just after noon. Luther dropped him at a Sunoco gas station on Broad Street. "Good luck to you, Jesse," Luther said. "I hope you find what you're looking for."

"Thank you for the ride," Jesse said, "and the advice." He slung his purple backpack over his shoulder and started to walk.

Ten minutes later, he encountered a building adorned with the Greek letters ΚΨΒ. Young men carried lumber through the open door, through which the unmistakable sound of hammering could be heard. Jesse stopped and listened, and decided to go inside.

"What do you want?" asked a young man who eyed Jesse contemptuously. The young man's T-shirt bore the same Greek letters.

"Hey Brad, I need that two-by-four over here," came a voice from inside.

"Be right there," Brad shouted over his shoulder. "I'm talking to some dude."

"What's he want?"

"I'd like to help," Jesse said.

"He says he'd like to help."

"Then let him help, for Christ sakes. We need all the help we can get."

"Tony says you can help, so let's go," said Brad, and Jesse followed him into the next room.

Jesse surveyed the project. A few large pieces of wood were joined together, but scraps and sawdust littered the room and a handful of clueless frat guys spent more time arguing than working. "What are you building?" asked Jesse.

"A bar, dickbrain," said Brad. "What's it look like?"

"Right now it looks like a large box. You should cut some trim pieces. You have a miter saw?" One of the guys found one, and Jesse took charge of the aesthetics. Within an hour, it looked more like a bar and less like André the Giant's coffin.

Jesse stood back to survey their progress. "How are you going to decorate it?" he asked.

"Dude, we need it to hold booze on one side and people on the other side," Brad said. "We're not trying to win a fucking art contest."

"But you could carve something into the face here," Jesse said. And soon, while the other men of Kappa Psi Beta were cleaning and sanding, Jesse took mallet and chisel in hand and began working on the front of the bar.

Brad glanced at his watch. "You gotta work faster, dude."

"Why? What's the hurry?" asked Jesse, tapping his chisel.

"We need to be ready for these Zeta Pi Thetas coming up from Widener for the God thing tonight."

Jesse stopped carving. "What's 'the God thing'?"

Brad pursed his lips and huffed, "Some stupid fucking rally at the Liacouras Center. Bunch of jerkoff preachers talking about who-knows-what-the-fuck."

"But if we're gonna score with those Widener chicks, they said we gotta go with them first," added Tony.

"Very well," said Jesse. "Pursue the earthly pleasures if you must."

"Oh, hell yes we must," affirmed Brad.

Jesse finished carving the bar and set down his tools. Brad, Tony, and the others gathered around.

"Sorry it's not that great," Jesse said, using his finger to flick off a small fragment of wood. "It was a rush job, after all. Plus I had to keep looking at Brad's shirt."

"It's awesome," said Tony, admiring the ΚΨΒ carved into the front of the bar. "Thank you."

Brad backhanded Tony on the arm. "I told you he could help us." Then, turning to Jesse, he asked, "How long have you been a carpenter?"

"Two thousand years, give or take."

They looked at him curiously. "Um, right," said Tony as he reached into his pocket. "Look, I know we didn't talk about pay or anything, but how about twenty bucks?"

Jesse lit up at this unexpected bounty. "Twenty dollars would be most welcome." He took the money and folded it into his pocket. "Thank you."

With another look at his watch, Brad ushered Jesse to the door and urged him outside, and he resumed venturing northward as before. He stopped at the Wendy's across from the Liacouras Center, filled his Venice Beach water bottle, and spent eight dollars plus tax on two "4 for $4" deals. As he left, he gave one of the meals to a homeless man outside.

"What's your name?" Jesse asked.

"Robert," said the homeless man.

Jesse noticed the homeless man's hat. "Marine Corps, huh?"

"Yessir," said Robert.

"I'm Jesse. I hope you like chicken."

They chatted for a moment, but the allure of the meal

was too great and Robert became an unwilling conversationalist. Jesse understood, having felt the same way hundreds of times himself, and crossed Cecil B. Moore Avenue.

The electronic marquee in front of the huge building scrolled: Tuesday, June 25 ... 7:00 p.m. (doors open at 6:00) ... God's Power Makes People Flower ... Featuring Jerry Falwell, Kenneth Copeland, and Franklin Graham.

I guess this is 'the God thing', Jesse thought. *I may as well see what they have to say about me.* He found the end of the line which hugged the building, took a seat on the concrete sidewalk, and with maybe three hundred people ahead of him, waited two hours for the doors to open.

Fifteen
THE LONG WAY HOME

Οἱ ἄνθρωποι μετατοπίζονται όπως ὁ άνεμος επί πεδία ή βροχοπτώσεις έν ουρανόν. Μόνος ὁ Θεός είναι ακλόνητος.

People shift like wind across the fields or rainclouds in the sky. Only God is unwavering.

(The Gospel According to Trevor, chapter 12, verse 7)

O'Shea drove east through the farmlands of South Dakota, flat as toast. Simone read a *Cosmopolitan* magazine she picked up before they left Rapid City. Today she wore a tank top (braless, of course) and another pair of cutoffs from what seemed to be an endless collection, these so short they would make Daisy Duke blush. O'Shea wore shorts as well, but his extended to his knees.

"It's hotter than it was before," Simone observed, the midmorning sun beating through the windshield. "It's too hot for all these clothes." She peeled off her shirt, and the car next to them swerved.

"Did you see that?" she giggled, bouncing on her seat.

"You can't keep doing that," chuckled O'Shea. "Somebody's going to crash, and I can't have that on my conscience."

"But I don't wanna get tan lines," she protested, reaching for her sunglasses. "One dancer told me tan lines are like a twenty-five percent reduction in tips, at least."

"I really don't have any choice in this, do I?" O'Shea asked.

"Nope. None whatsoever."

As temperatures climbed and trickles of sweat rolled between her breasts, Simone said, "Too bad you don't have a dash camera. I bet we could make some money." She tossed the *Cosmo* on the floor and dabbed at a droplet of perspiration, adding, "And here you get the show for free."

Every glorious, agonizing mile, thought O'Shea.

He endeavored to keep his eyes on the road but the challenge was monumental, so he searched for any sort of diversion. Unfortunately, central South Dakota does not offer an abundance of roadside attractions, although he tried to entice her with every billboard's promise of the remarkable. "Hey look," he said, pointing out the window. "It's the South Dakota Tractor Museum. Wanna check it out?"

She answered with an indifferent laugh, dabbed another droplet of perspiration from her chest, and slowly sucked it off her finger. Try as he might, O'Shea could not avoid sideways glances, which grew more frequent as she repeated the exhibition. That same finger then rolled the salty moisture around her nipples, conjuring demons in his head. Smiling, she swirled her tongue around her finger. "Ahhh," she hummed, like it was the most satisfying refreshment she could imagine. Another droplet, and this one she held to O'Shea's lips. He tried to focus on the road, but she had the endurance of youth and hundreds of highway miles ahead, so he eventually succumbed and licked it from the end of her finger. She grinned mischievously, then began to flick sweat at him. Although he did his best to ignore her, his efforts were an excruciating dance in which resolve and resignation took turns leading and the song went on forever.

When she grabbed his right hand, dabbed at her breast with his index finger, and sucked on it, he could bear no more.

"Simone! I need both hands on the steering wheel. Ten and two!" He yanked his hand back and returned it to the wheel.

"Who taught you how to drive? Henry Ford?" Simone laughed. "It's nine and three now."

"Whatever," he said, sliding both hands down the wheel to the correct position.

The femme fatale knew she had him on the ropes. She unbuckled her seatbelt and turned around, her shoulders against the dashboard and her feet over the top of her seat. She arched her back and pointed her breasts heavenward, glorious living shrines to human desire. Many of the world's greatest artistic talents—from Roman sculptors and Renaissance painters to mixed-media artists of today—have tried to capture the beauty of a reclining nude, but none of their efforts could rival the aesthetic masterpiece of Simone's current pose. And, unlike those other works of art, she was still half-dressed.

She sipped from her water bottle, allowing some of its contents to dribble down her chin. O'Shea watched the rivulet slink down her body, creeping between her breasts, pooling for a moment in her navel until it continued its path, finally turning the waistband of her cutoff shorts dark with moisture.

"Oh my God," O'Shea whimpered.

"I know, right?" she replied with an impish grin.

He reached for the *Cosmo* and tented it on his lap. "Please stop."

"I can't help it. It's hard to drink in this position. I have no control over gravity."

"Oh my God," he repeated.

Over the course of a few miles, this process made her shorts grow ever more damp, and O'Shea had little doubt they would be coming off soon. But then, salvation. He turned on his right blinker and took the exit.

"What are we stopping for?" Simone asked.

O'Shea exhaled. "Mitchell, South Dakota. Home of the world-famous Mitchell Corn Palace."

"Why is it world-famous?"

"Because it's a building made out of corn. Pretty cool, right?" He knew it sounded ridiculous, but at least it was true, and it was all he could come up with.

"Not particularly," she replied.

O'Shea held zero interest in construction practices utilizing agricultural by-product, but he stopped anyway. He needed to get out of the car, away from Simone. Right now.

He shoved the car into park and, holding the magazine discreetly in front of himself, sprinted toward the Corn Palace. Once inside, he spent ten minutes walking the halls, his purposeful stride bearing no resemblance to sauntering. *Just don't look*, he said to himself as he paced, as if it were just that simple. *Just keep your eyes on the road*. He found the restroom and splashed cold water on his face. *Don't think about it ... them ... her*. When he left the building, he clenched his fists to summon the courage of Jesus. He was Custer against the charging Sioux, and almost out of bullets.

As he negotiated the parking lot, Simone waved at him. She stood outside the car, her top back on, eating from a bag of Doritos. *How can she make eating chips look so damn sexy?* he asked himself. *Hail Mary, full of grace ...*

"You want me to drive some?" Simone offered, her nonchalance suggesting the past one hundred miles never happened.

"Great idea," O'Shea said. "I could use a break." What he meant, really, was a break from the lascivious tease, theorizing she might have to keep her shorts dry, her hands on the steering wheel, and her feet on the pedals.

Her tank top stayed on as they returned to the freeway. They stopped briefly for lunch in Sioux Falls before they crossed the state line, where Simone honked and still managed to flash the Welcome to Minnesota monument.

"Why are we going to New York, anyway?" Simone asked. "Weird that I never asked before. I just trusted you, but now that I'm driving, I'm curious, you know?"

"I'm looking for something," he said, staring at the road ahead.

She waited for elaboration, but when it became apparent none was forthcoming, she asked, "That's all? We're travel buddies, remember?" Poking him in the arm, she added, "What's the big secret?"

"I just don't want you to think it's strange," O'Shea explained.

"Sometimes you think too little of me."

"Fair enough," he said. "Okay, here goes. Even though I'm a priest, I've spent much of my career struggling with my faith. There are so many things that don't make sense to me. Too many questions and not enough answers. My desire to experience God is too often sabotaged by mankind's interpretation of Him. One writer put it something like this: 'Man is supposed to be made in God's image, but instead we've remade God in man's image.' Obviously, this falls way short of the all-powerful, perfect God to whom I have pledged my life."

"I can totally see what you mean," she said, "but what's it have to do with New York?"

"Remember when we were talking about the Seven Deadly Sins, and you pointed out how they weren't in the Bible?"

"Yeah."

"That's just one example ... one of many ... where humans had too much contribution to how we are told to perceive God. Another example is the Bible itself, how it was assembled. Did you know that over the course of something like six hundred years, Jewish and Christian religious leaders essentially decided what went in the Bible and what didn't?"

"Really? Why did *they* get to decide?"

"Money and power, basically," O'Shea continued. "But it certainly begs the question: Is the Bible really the inspired Word of the Lord—"

Simone completed his thought. "Or does it just say what a bunch of guys want it to say?"

"Exactly."

"I see your point," Simone said, "but you still haven't told me what it has to do with New York."

"I guess I haven't. Recently, there was a discovery of a rejected text, a text they decided not to include in the Bible.

Or, at least, that's what the person who discovered it claims. And now here I am, torn between faith and doubt, wanting—no, needing—to find out if her claims are true. And, based upon my reading of the text, I think the answer is in New York."

"Wow," she said. "All this time I thought you were just going to visit your mother."

"My mom lives in Idaho, actually."

"Awesome! We can stop by on the way home."

They crossed into Wisconsin late in the day. Simone engaged in the usual ceremony while O'Shea looked absently out the window.

"What are you staring at?" asked Simone.

"The Mississippi River," O'Shea said. "It's the third-longest river in the world. We're now officially in the eastern half of the United States."

"How do you know so much about geography? You're like Google."

"I've done a lot of driving," he said. "The Catholic diocese can assign you wherever there's a need, so until you get settled at a church, priests have to move around a lot."

Simone frowned. "I don't want that lifestyle. I just want to open an office and stay there."

"What kind of office?"

"Family therapy," she said. "My childhood was so shitty, I'd like to help others before it's too late for them. Make sure they don't become fucked-up adults. I'm studying Psychology at Washington."

"Do you have a favorite psychologist?"

"That's like me asking if you have a favorite pope," she replied, "but I do like Maslow's hierarchy, his idea how we need to feel safe before we feel loved."

"And do you?"

"Feel safe?" she said. "Not yet, but I'm getting there. The more distance I have from my father and the more money I have in the bank, the better I'll be."

"Money does not buy safety, you know."

"True, but neither does poverty."

It had been a long day on the road, and they decided to stop half an hour later in Tomah, Wisconsin. They cruised through town and settled on the Pleasant Acres Motel.

"What is there to do in this town?" Simone asked the man at the desk as they checked in.

"Let's see. We've got a movie theater, a skate park, the Cranberry Discovery Center, a couple of museums." None of the choices elicited any reaction from Simone. "And there's a casino a few miles out Highway 21."

"A casino?" Simone said, and the desk clerk nodded. "Can we go there, Brian? Please?"

With her fake Washington driver's license, Simone instantly became the featured attraction at the craps table, old men transfixed every time she bent over to pick up the dice. The atmosphere was supernatural. O'Shea magically turned into Frank Sinatra, the weathered pit boss became Humphrey Bogart, and grizzled farmers and Social Security widowers at the far end of the table were now George Clooney and Brad Pitt. Simone, though, needed no such wondrous transformation. Her flip-flops sufficed as glass slippers and her tank top and cutoffs as a formal ball gown. She had no idea what she was doing, no concept of the rules of the game, but every time the croupier said "Winner!" she squealed with delight and her breasts jiggled in a celebration which made the other players deliriously happy. In the history of the Ho-Chunk Casino, it was the first time the casino workers ever tipped a patron. Before long, between her winnings and gratuities, the pockets of her minuscule cutoffs were stuffed with money.

She turned to O'Shea. "What do I do if I don't want to play anymore?"

"Just set down the dice, I think." She did, and the croupier said, "New shooter." He looked at O'Shea, who shook his head.

They stopped at the casino cage to cash her chips. Simone beamed at her prosperity, $427 in profit making her front pocket swell.

O'Shea trailed her toward the exit, pausing for a final look over his shoulder. Every eye seemed upon them. Once Simone glided out the door, all the energy whisked out with her, the glamour vanished, and the players transformed back into the same tired, ordinary, desperate men they were before her arrival.

It was nearly eleven o'clock when they got back to the Pleasant Acres Motel. "What a rush," Simone said as she went into the bathroom. "In five minutes, I'm going to give you the best private dance you've ever seen." But when she came out of the bathroom, O'Shea was already asleep or, more accurately, pretending to be.

"Damn it, Brian O'Shea! So help me, one of these nights I'm just going to crawl into bed with you."

He faked it well enough, apparently, that she fell asleep soon thereafter. He was relieved but also starving, a beer at the casino being an insufficient dinner. Recalling a sign for Denny's on the way back, he slipped out of bed, dressed quietly, and stole his way out the door.

There were two waitresses working: an attractive younger woman and a grandmotherly sort. "No offense, but I'd prefer to sit in her section," O'Shea told the younger waitress, who huffed but led him to an empty table.

O'Shea found late nights at Denny's to be comforting. He appreciated the solitude and the bottomless coffee, both staples from his days in seminary when he used to sit in a booth and spread out his notes while studying for exams. His current experience with Simone was not an exam, but it was damn sure a test, and even after four days he was still not confident in his ability to pass.

After his meal, he returned to the hotel and to his bed, which thankfully was unoccupied by Simone. A few hours later, she shook him awake.

"Something's wrong with the car," Simone said.

"Huh?" He blinked his eyes into focus.

"I wanted to get supplies while you were asleep, but it drives funny."

O'Shea tugged on some pants and went outside to check. "Flat tire," he announced, and she wrinkled her nose. He crouched and ran his hand along the tire's surface. "It feels like there's a nail in it. Not a problem, though. I have a spare."

He opened the trunk and rearranged its contents so he could access the spare tire well. "Bad news," he said.

"What?" asked Simone, scurrying to the trunk for a look.

"Spare's flat, too."

Simone moved around the car and explored the tire tread with her hand. "How did this happen?"

"I don't know. Maybe I ran over something on my way back from Denny's last night."

"You went to Denny's without me? You shit!" She paused to study her dirty hand, and her tone shifted. "What are we going to do?"

"Find a garage that's open on a Sunday." However, multiple phone calls produced no satisfaction, and they became resigned to their fate.

"We'll have to wait until tomorrow morning," O'Shea said. "You want to go to the movie theater, the skate park, the Cranberry Discovery Center, or a couple of museums?"

"I want to go to New York," she pouted.

Her frost obvious, Simone spent most of the day on her bed, immersed in her phone, earbuds blocking out the world. O'Shea took a long walk to Lake Tomah and back, but upon his return the room felt no less chilly. He checked the spare tire again, even though he knew his efforts were futile, that it had not miraculously reinflated itself. After watching television for an hour, he walked to Fred's Corner Market to purchase a copy of the *Milwaukee Journal Sentinel*, which he read cover to cover. When he asked Simone about dinner, she grunted a response and returned to her phone. He went out by himself and brought her back a hamburger and fries, which she picked at until he fell asleep with pencil in hand, the Sunday crossword puzzle half-finished.

Monday morning they called a local garage as soon as it opened, and were on the road with a fresh tire and functional spare by nine.

"I'm sorry about yesterday, Simone," O'Shea said.

"It's fine. I'm over it now."

He glanced at her as she fiddled with her phone. "What were you watching on your phone all day yesterday?"

"Different stuff," she said. "TED Talks. Tony Robbins.

Stand-up comedy. Extreme sports videos."

"TED Talks?" he asked, opening a package of cheese and crackers.

"Yeah, nine of them. I watch at least one every day. It's part of my daily routine."

He took a bite from the cracker. "Really? That's amazing."

"Why is it amazing? I like to learn new things," she said. "So where are we going today?"

"Your choice. We can spend the day and night in Chicago, or we can keep going and get to Cleveland."

"Cleveland?" Her tone conveyed her uncertainty about the city's merits.

"Home to the Rock and Roll Hall of Fame," O'Shea announced with aplomb. "Total bucket-list destination for me."

"Why?"

"Why? Are you kidding me? I grew up with rock and roll. So did my parents. Every bit of angst you've ever felt, we felt it too. Rock and roll was the soundtrack of our rebellion."

"Rebellion reshmellion. You're a priest, for fuck's sake."

"I thought you liked to learn," said O'Shea. "Come on, it'll be cool."

"Like the Corn Palace?" she joked.

"Maybe even better."

"When will we be in New York?" she asked. "I want to see a Broadway show. Is *King Kong* still playing?"

"We should get there on Wednesday, I think," he said. "And sure, we can go see a Broadway show."

That seemed to satisfy her for a while, and as they

rolled along I-90, she researched New York City, Broadway shows, and tickets to the Empire State Building's observation deck.

"New York's expensive," she finally declared. "Did you know anything less than two hundred dollars a night is considered a budget hotel?"

This was a detail O'Shea had not considered.

"Maybe we can stay in a hostel," she continued. "But I kinda wanted to have a drink at one of those rooftop bars."

"A drink? A Coke, maybe. Simone, you're nineteen years old."

"*Au contraire*, Father Brian." She pulled out her fake ID. "I'm twenty-two, according to the great state of Washington. And therefore eligible for all the rights and privileges of any other adult. I want to drink a Manhattan *in* Manhattan."

O'Shea chuckled. "We'll see."

"Besides, you took me to a casino, so don't be a hypocrite." She had him cold with that. "I tell you what. You promise me a drink, I'll go to the Rock and Roll Hall of Fame with you."

"It's a deal," he announced.

They skirted the edges of Chicago, crossed through Indiana, and arrived in Cleveland after dark, taking a room at the Renaissance Cleveland Hotel.

"This is nice," Simone said. "Much better than those other dumps we stayed in." She bounced on one of the beds and pulled down the bedspread. "A girl could get used to this, expensive sheets against my bare skin." Her bewitching look, O'Shea well knew, would be prelude to trouble if he did not promptly change direction.

"Wanna go to a movie?" His storehouse of resolve

nearly empty, he hoped watching a movie in a crowded theater meant her clothes stayed on and her libido stayed off. Simone's enthusiasm was tepid but she went anyway, and they shared an order of nachos while watching *Aladdin*. O'Shea found the film kind of amusing, but since it was Simone's second time, she ended up half asleep on his shoulder before crashing at their hotel.

As Simone's velvet breaths filled their hotel room, O'Shea contemplated his circumstances: a stunning young woman six feet away, her very presence daring him to break his vow of celibacy. If he broke that vow, which many outside the church thought was idiotic anyway, who would know? *Other than myself and God, that is, and God is supposed to be merciful. But could I forgive myself?* Maybe doing it just one time would help him better appreciate the desires of the flesh to which his parishioners were so often prone. It wasn't like he planned to start fornicating on a daily basis. Besides, it wouldn't be nearly as bad as what some priests have done. She's female, legal, and clearly willing, not to mention smart, interesting, and ravishingly beautiful.

When he slept that night, he dreamed of a tennis match between devil and angel, but he was roused before he found out the winner.

"Brian!" Simone shook him awake early the next morning. She was already dressed, and for the first time the entire trip she wore pants. And, underneath her T-shirt, a bra.

"What's going on?" he asked. It was not yet seven a.m.

"We need to hit the road, pronto."

He stretched, with no sense of alacrity. "What's your hurry? The Rock and Roll Hall of Fame doesn't open until ten."

"Not the Rock and Roll Hall of Fame," she said. "Pittsburgh. Take me to the airport, please. I'm going home."

His jaw dropped, but no words followed.

"My flight leaves at ten-thirty, American Airlines. I'll be in Seattle this afternoon."

"Is it because I wouldn't ... you know? Because I thought about it last night. I think you can break me today. In fact, I'm sure of it."

"Too late, Brian. Don't you know you shouldn't keep a girl waiting? He who hesitates–"

"Is lost?" asked O'Shea.

"Is celibate," corrected Simone. He cringed, and she continued, "I had a great adventure. It was wonderful, really." He stared at her, the hurt obvious. "You were a fantastic travel buddy. But I miss Seattle. I miss my friends."

"Your friends?" he stumbled. "W-what are you going to tell them?"

"That I was at the Saint Helen of Troy Camp for Girls, of course," she said, winking.

O'Shea sighed with relief.

She added, "I'll see you at the Starlight when you get back. You can buy me my Manhattan. But right now, you need to get moving." She threw a pair of pants at him, packed both their bags while he dressed, and waited in the passenger's seat until he emerged from their room.

"When did you decide this?" O'Shea asked as they left Cleveland behind. The dark clouds and impending rain seemed wholly symbolic.

"I've been thinking about it for a while," she said.

"When you pretended to be asleep after the casino in Wisconsin, I'm not gonna lie, that hurt. Then last night when you took me to a movie just so you didn't have to be alone in the room with me—"

"I didn't ..." But he did, and he knew it. "Why didn't you say something before? Yesterday you still seemed excited about New York. Even last night, on the way back from the theater."

"I offered a plausible explanation," Simone said, and he could tender no rebuttal. She continued, "It's just not as much fun as I hoped. We did some cool stuff, and the country is beautiful like you said, but to be honest I'm kinda bored now. I can make it back for summer school. Even though classes started yesterday, I contacted the professor and he said I could start Abnormal Psychology tomorrow. Who knows, maybe I'll use you as a case study."

"What do you mean, a case study? I'm not—"

"Just kidding."

O'Shea forced a smile.

"One thing I still wonder, though," probed Simone. "Why did you ask me to come?" Five billboards passed while he struggled for an answer, until she rescued him with a gentle touch. "It's okay. Tell me whenever you figure it out."

It took them less than two hours to get to Pittsburgh International Airport. When O'Shea pulled to the curb in front of her terminal, Simone gathered her belongings and kissed him tenderly before she stepped out. "Peace be with you," she said, turning to wave as she hurried into the airport. He watched her grow smaller in the distance, fought back a tear, and then put the car in drive and headed east, alone.

O'Shea covered half of Pennsylvania by early afternoon, every mile a simmering stew of thoughts and emotions peppered with increasingly unbearable munchies. A pit stop at a mini-mart alongside I-76 assuaged the latter, but the deeper stuff would take longer to sort. Near Harrisburg he encountered a light sprinkle. He fiddled with the radio, settling on a talk show airing out of Philadelphia.

"... It's expected to be one of the most important religious events the Eastern Seaboard has ever witnessed," said the radio voice. "Falwell, Copeland, and Graham, all in one place. The greatest luminaries of American religion ... and it's free. Seven o'clock tonight."

The Pennsylvania Turnpike was not the most direct route to New York, but this event in Philadelphia intrigued him. Maybe it was exactly what he needed given the turmoil of this particular day. He arrived in Philly a couple of hours later and paid twenty dollars to park his car at the Liacouras Garage. After changing into his clerical clothing, he joined the gathering throng which now numbered in the thousands. Immediately behind him, four young men excitedly told a group of women about the sweet new bar at their fraternity house.

A crack of thunder startled him, and he looked at the dark clouds and their imminent threat. Mercifully, the doors opened moments later, precisely at six, and O'Shea was swept inside with the crowd just as the sky unleashed its torrent.

Sixteen
UPSETTING THE TEMPLE

Οἱ χρηματιστές καί οἱ τσαρλατάνοι αμφισβητήθηκαν από τού Ιησού. Ἀνεβάλε τά τραπέζιά αυτούς καί κάλεσε τήν αντιπολίτευση αυτήν ἵνα πάντες μαρτυρίασωσιν.

The moneychangers and the charlatans were challenged by Jesus. He flipped their tables and called out their vice for all to witness.

(The Gospel According to Trevor, chapter 5, verse 48)

By seven o'clock, the Liacouras Center was packed with more than ten thousand people. Both Berkshire and Jesse, by virtue of having arrived several hours early, were seated on the floor level, perhaps fifty feet from the stage and within a few seats of each other. O'Shea, who arrived much later, sat in the upper tier on one side of the arena, directly left of the stage and one seat left of a brunette Zeta Pi Theta who traveled from Widener University with her friends.

The multitudes chattered excitedly while Christian rock music was piped through the public address system. When the lights dimmed a few minutes past seven, the crowd began to cheer.

"Ladies and gentlemen, welcome to God's Power Makes People Flower," announced a low-pitched disembodied voice with gravitas befitting the Almighty. "And please welcome the president of Liberty University, and our host for the evening, Mister Jerry Falwell, Jr."

Colored lights spun wildly and the crowd cheered passionately as Falwell paraded onto the stage. This was big, like the WrestleMania events O'Shea remembered as a kid in Boise. He smiled, unsurprised at the crowd's reaction.

"Good evening, Philadelphia," Falwell, bathed in spotlight, said from behind a stage-right podium festooned in purple and gold. "We are delighted to be here at Temple University in the City of Brotherly Love. You know, 'brotherly love,' or *philia*, is the foundation for both this great city and for the life of Jesus Christ. Now, I know there's nothing the people of Philadelphia love more than sports, so it's appropriate for us to be meeting tonight in the basketball arena for the Temple Owls. We could fill the football stadium if we wanted to, but we like this more intimate space. Plus we can stay dry." More cheers.

Falwell continued, "It's also appropriate for us to be meeting tonight at Temple University, which was founded in 1884 by the Baptist minister Russell Conwell, so there's a great history here." More applause from the crowd, and he added, dramatically, "The love of Christ courses through the veins of this Temple."

Hearty, enthusiastic cheers, which Falwell generously absorbed.

"We're going to do things a little different tonight," he continued. "First we'll have a brief panel discussion, then each of us will share our individual messages with you. We'll have some audience participation, some music, and of course some prayer. And we'll take a faith offering toward the end of the program, so when you leave here tonight you will surely be filled with the Holy Spirit."

Jesse sneaked a look at the contents of his pocket, at the money left over from his carpentry work and subsequent trip to Wendy's. *I hope eleven dollars will be enough*, he fretted.

"I know you're anxious to meet the rest of our esteemed panel, but first we'd like to set the mood with some music." A curtain rose behind him to reveal a full band, which immediately broke into "Amazing Grace." Many in the crowd, including both Jesse and O'Shea, sang along.

"Amen," said Falwell when the song ended. "You know," he continued, "the United States of America is a nation first touched by the amazing grace of God in its struggle for independence more than two hundred years ago, right here in this very city. Our great nation has long been the champion of freedom, fighting oppression around the world. And today, we are still a nation lighted by God's holy lamp, with leadership that we can say, with the utmost confidence, finally represents the Christian values necessary to make us great again."

Berkshire looked around the crowd and, for the first time, noticed more than a handful of red MAGA hats.

"And now, it brings me great pleasure to introduce two of the most important and respected preachers in America." The house lights dimmed once again. "The first is head of the Eagle Mountain International Church in Tarrant County, Texas, and one of the most successful evangelists in American history. At eighty-two years old, he still travels far and wide to spread the Good News. Please welcome my friend, the Reverend Kenneth Copeland."

More twirling spotlights greeted Copeland's entrance, and the crowd responded enthusiastically.

"Our other panelist is the son of the late, great Reverend Billy Graham. He is now an evangelical superstar in his own right, president of both the Billy Graham Evangelical Association and the organization Samaritan's Purse, allowing him to use the Lord to provide much-needed relief to millions of people each year. Welcome to the stage, Reverend Franklin Graham."

More spotlights, more cheering.

"Brother Graham," Falwell said solemnly, "would you open with a word of prayer?"

Graham nodded and moved to the podium, bowed his head and began, "Beloved Father who grants us all such abundance, I pray that as we touch these good people with Your message, it inspires them to open their hearts. Forgive their sins and encourage them to follow our path of righteousness as we work to restore traditional Christian values to America. Amen."

The three men took their places in comfortable leather chairs arranged in a semicircle, attaching lavaliere microphones to the lapels of their thousand-dollar tailored suits. Stage lighting came up to reveal a set which reeked of pomposity. Combined with the garish drapery on the podium to their right, the impression of moral superiority was unmistakable. Yet the working-class Philadelphians in the building seemed not to mind.

"I want to first thank you for putting this together,"

Graham said to Falwell, "and for your leadership at Liberty University. Your school does great things in the name of God."

With a façade of sincere modesty, Falwell replied, "My father did most of the heavy lifting. I'm just trying to keep his legacy intact."

"As am I with my father," said Graham. "And God's hand is certainly a part of both of our efforts."

"You know, there's a great place to start," Falwell said, and the stage lights dimmed dramatically. "God's hand is all around us. We see Him in the kindness of others, in the beauty of a sunset, and in the actions of our leaders. Sometimes we take it for granted, but God is always in control. God's message, His power, is everywhere. Lightning might indicate God is angry with us. Birds are His message of freedom. Sunsets show us His majesty."

"And the wind and rain can reveal evil and wash away the transgressors," added Graham. "The story of Noah and the ark shows how God used the rain in Genesis to cleanse the sins of the world and start over. That's why there are ten thousand good Christians inside this building while it's raining on the evil out there." The audience cheered lustily at that one.

"The world is a cesspool of iniquity, in constant need of sanitizing," Copeland added. "Only by coming to God can we purify ourselves. My ministry is dedicated to that purification, to facilitating the transition from sinner to saved."

Falwell shifted in his seat. "Are people open to your message, Brother Copeland?"

"Yes and no," Copeland replied. "There are good people who seek salvation, but too many people want the easy way. Sexual gratification without the selfless commitment of marriage. Wealth without the dignity of labor. Microwave ovens, so we lose the joy of preparing meals for those we love. Cell phones, so we can text instead of loving our neighbors. Those devices are evil, yet the world glorifies them as false idols." The dark arena seemed to contain a thousand fireflies, as men and women recorded Copeland's remarks on their cell phones. He continued, "That's not the way of the Lord. I fly to all fifty states every year to explain that, preach that, and welcome new believers to the flock."

"God bless your diligence," Falwell said. "Now, in doing what you do, you've managed to become a wealthy man. What do you say to those who take issue with your wealth?"

"True, the Lord has blessed me. I've made a comfortable living from spreading the Good News. I admit it, but I do not apologize for it." Copeland paused to take a drink of water. "Yes, I have a private airplane. But understand we couldn't get our work done otherwise. Have you ever been on a commercial flight?"

"Not recently," Falwell admitted. Copeland turned to Graham, who added, "Me neither."

"My airplane keeps me away from distractions," Copeland continued. "It allows me to talk to God in my own space. It protects my spirit from being agitated by people who want me to pray for them. It keeps me from the sinfulness of the dope fiends and unbelievers."

"I totally agree," Graham added. "Licentiousness is all around us, and it's our job to identify it, expose it, and remove it from the world."

Falwell said, "Tell us some of the ways you're doing

that, Brother Graham."

O'Shea glanced at the Zeta Pi Theta sitting next to him. Although engrossed in the discussion, she still made eye contact and smiled.

"Marriage is between a man and a woman," Graham said. "We all know that. The Holy Bible tells us so. Anything else is unnatural. Evil. Sinful." He leaned forward for emphasis. "I'm working to make sure local school boards are filled with evangelical Christians who understand the sanctity of marriage, and who work to bring God back into the classroom and restore the proper order of things."

"Jesus Christ," said Copeland, with enough emphasis that Jesse popped up, "wants us to be pure of heart, wants us to return to the values that made this country the greatest nation on Earth."

"USA! USA! USA!" began the chant from the audience. Falwell encouraged it for a long time, motioning for calm only when he sensed the chant running out of momentum.

"Would anyone in the audience like to share their testimony?" Falwell asked.

Berkshire jumped to her feet and hurried to the stage. "I would."

"She's very enthusiastic," Falwell joked, and the other two evangelists laughed while the crowd cheered.

A stagehand gave her a microphone and stepped away. "Tell us your story," urged Falwell.

"For my entire life," she began, "I have rejected religion and all it stands for. Not just Christianity, but every religion. I'm what you might call a nullifidian. And this event, in just fifteen minutes, has brought me great clarity."

"How wonderful," said Falwell. "What's your name, sister?"

"Dr. Haley Berkshire. I'm a professor of Religious Studies at the University of Utah."

Jesse recoiled, astonished. The agent for his wholeness, seated in the same row as him. If only he had known, for he had so many questions to ask her.

O'Shea could not believe it, either. The woman whose research inspired his cross-country journey was now in the very same building. He sat up in his seat, his arm accidentally brushing the leg of the Zeta Pi Theta. "Sorry," he offered.

Meanwhile, a flicker of recognition caused the three evangelists to whisper amongst themselves on the dais. Graham fired the first salvo. "You're the professor who wants to rewrite the Bible," he accused.

"Don't be obtuse," she responded. "I simply want to find out why some books made it into the Bible and others ended up in the trash. It's an intellectual inquiry, not a religious one."

Jesse moved to the edge of his seat. He knew there was much more of his story yet untold.

Berkshire continued, "Besides, it's not like you think the Bible is perfect as is. You all support Miriam Adelson's recent call for a Book of Trump, which seems more than ironic."

"That's different," said Copeland.

"Bullshit it's different," she said. "Your view of Christianity is narrow, closed-minded, and hateful." Falwell gestured to security, and two guards moved toward her.

"Let her speak!" Jesse shouted from the audience.

Others from his row joined the call, then other rows nearby, and it grew into a chant: "Let her speak! Let her speak!" Jesse pumped his arms to encourage the entire arena, which responded enthusiastically. "LET HER SPEAK! LET HER SPEAK!"

Falwell stood and motioned for calm. Once the noise subsided, he said, "If that's really what you want. But I need to tell everyone, this woman is well known for some of the most preposterous religious conclusions you've ever heard. We'll allow her to speak so you can understand just how ridiculous she is, and how much she hates the Lord." Many in the crowd responded with jeers.

O'Shea turned to Zeta Pi Theta. "This could get interesting."

"Now," Falwell said to Berkshire as he returned to his seat. "Say what you must. I'm sure it will be just as misguided and stupid as usual."

"Thank you," said Berkshire. "Mister Graham, you talk about wanting to get more evangelicals on school boards. What would that accomplish?"

"I'm glad you asked, Professor," Graham responded. "We need to teach God, not science. We need to teach children they are in the image of God, not a monkey."

"But what about the separation of church and state?" asked Berkshire.

"Nothing but a liberal distortion," Graham said.

"Which has been in the Constitution since the beginning," she replied. "You claim to love the Constitution, but in reality you only do when it fits your agenda. What a bunch of frauds!"

Graham stiffened. "You're the one teaching your liberal agenda. We serve the people of God."

"Oh, really?" she replied. "Jesus was poor and commanded us to be giving, yet each of you is a multi-millionaire. There are ten thousand people in this building, and I bet our total net worth does not equal the three of yours. Yet you get a 'parsonage exemption' on your homes ... your mansions, to be more accurate ... while we still pay property taxes."

"We welcome a generous spirit," Copeland offered, "as a personal choice that demonstrates one's commitment to God. "We—"

"That's just a fancy way of saying you're happy to get rich off the guilt of the suckers who follow you," replied Berkshire, who was in no mood for empty rationalizations. Falwell looked nervously at his two guests as she continued.

"Not to mention the fact that, in your world, women are second-class citizens. That's not Christlike. In fact, more and more scholarly evidence suggests Mary Magdalene played a major role in Jesus' life—a possibility totally dismissed when the Bible was constructed. By men, I might add. As a result, throughout history, our job was to be the 'helpmate' of the man, either servants or sexual objects. It's no surprise so many famous evangelists have been caught in sex scandals."

The crowd began to boo, although it was unclear whether their target was Berkshire or the three evangelists, or perhaps a fifty-fifty split.

"I don't think this is going the way they hoped," O'Shea said to Zeta Pi Theta. Brad eyed the priest suspiciously.

Berkshire continued, "You claim to care about human life, but you act as shills for the NRA—"

"If more good people carried guns," Falwell

interrupted, "we could stop those Muslims before they committed their atrocities."

"Guns don't kill people," added Copeland. "People kill people. Guns are just tools, and they're our God-given right."

"Whoa there," said Berkshire, waving her arms. "Moments ago, you blamed cell phones and microwave ovens for our problems. But those are just tools, too. So which is it, Mister Copeland? Is the problem the person, or is it the tool?"

"It depends ...," Copeland stumbled. "It's a matter of, you know, the circumstances ..."

Graham jumped in, "Listen, young lady—"

Copeland held up his hand. "I've got this," he said to Graham.

"It doesn't appear that way," answered Graham snidely.

"As I started to say," continued Berkshire, pounding the stage with the palm of her hand, "You act as shills for the NRA while marginalizing entire groups of people for their nationalities, religious choices, or sexual orientations."

"We've heard enough now," Falwell said testily. "Like I said, good people of Philadelphia, we can all see how preposterous this woman is." But the crowd's reaction suggested not everyone agreed with him.

Berkshire spotted security approaching from both directions. "Christians believe in grace. You're not Christians, you're Pharisees! You're Leviticans!"

"This is what happens when we let women out of the kitchen," Copeland said to Falwell, loud enough for his microphone to catch the remark. Many in the crowd murmured in response.

Zeta Pi Theta rolled her eyes and turned to look at O'Shea, who shook his head in disbelief.

Graham jumped to his feet and pointed sternly at Berkshire. "You need to fear the Lord."

"Why should I be fearful of what's supposed to be a loving God?" she asked.

Now surrounded by security, Berkshire continued, "You have completely disregarded the love of Christ in favor of your own power and wealth!" She barely got this last part out before security ripped the microphone from her hand. One security guard grabbed her underneath the armpits and another by her legs, but she kept kicking while they dragged her away.

Zeta Pi Theta turned to speak to O'Shea, but the now-boisterous crowd made it difficult for him to hear. He leaned closer, innocently placing his hand on Zeta Pi Theta's shoulder.

Falwell raised his hands in a call for quiet. Once the commotion subsided, he said, "Sadly, friends, too many people have been led astray. You've just seen an example of Satan's debasing influence at work, right here in our midst. I hope you'll all pray for—"

Brad's voice pierced the arena. "You fucking pervert!"

"Excuse me?" said Falwell. He turned to the other evangelists. "What did he say?" Shrugs all around. Then, to the audience: "What did you call me?"

"Not you, shitbag. This guy." Brad pointed at O'Shea. "He's trying to feel up my date."

"I'm not your date, you jackass," Zeta Pi Theta said. But it was too late; security had already converged on the area and was motioning for O'Shea to follow, and the crowd again turned raucous.

In the bedlam, Jesse crept to the edge of the stage.

"It is written," he shouted, "My house will be called a house of prayer, but you are making it a den of thieves."

Copeland turned to Falwell and said, "What kind of shit show are you running here?"

Jesse hopped onto the stage and pushed over the podium. "As I did two thousand years ago, I will upset the temple when it is being used for profit. You three are the most deceitful, the worst of the charlatans!"

Security ran to the stage, but Jesse swung his purple backpack in defense, spinning to repel attacks from all sides. The weight of the full Venice Beach water bottle gave the backpack just enough heft to make it a useful defensive tool. Thinking he had an angle, one guard charged Jesse, but was clocked in the head by the backpack and sent sprawling at Falwell's feet. Others tried to maneuver for position, but Jesse's quick movements stopped their advances. Finally, the head security guard tackled Jesse from behind and immobilized him with a knee in his back, but it still required the efforts of three men to carry Jesse away.

Pandemonium swept through the building like a middle-school rumor. With the event clearly ruined, many in the audience moved toward the exits. Nobody would flower on this day. Recognizing this, Falwell ripped off his lapel microphone and rushed from the stage in pursuit of the security guards, who shoved Jesse through the doors and onto Broad Street alongside Berkshire and O'Shea.

Falwell pushed past the brawny guards and stood face-to-face with the three degenerates who ruined his event. He stared at them, scarcely able to contain his rage, his eyes aflame with wrath as raindrops bounced off the sidewalk. "May the Lord have mercy on your souls, you reprobates," he snarled. "Because you can be goddamn sure I never will."

A breeze ruffled Berkshire's hair, followed by another gust, even stronger. Falwell began waving frantically, as if a lizard just landed on his head, and then his toupee skittered down the sidewalk, carried by the brisk Philadelphia wind. O'Shea burst into laughter as Falwell shuffled after his rug, dodging others who were exiting the arena, while a student at the Temple Law School, across the street, recorded everything on his cell phone. By midnight, the YouTube video of Jerry Falwell, Jr. chasing his hairpiece down Broad Street in the rain would have almost 200,000 views.

In the distance, police sirens drew ever closer, a fact which the head security guard indicated by tilting his head in the direction of the sound. "You three should disperse," he deadpanned.

"Come on," O'Shea said to the others. "I have a car."

As the trio hurried past, Jesse quietly said to the security guard, "Nice tackle." The big man's faint smile was barely noticeable.

They splashed their way around the Liacouras Center to the garage and dashed up two flights of stairs to locate the Toyota Camry. Pulling onto Fifteenth Street, O'Shea turned on his windshield wipers and asked, "Anyone else hungry?"

Seventeen
BREAKING BREAD

Συνδεθείτε ώς αγαπημένοι προσκυνητές τού Θεού. Οί διαφορές αὐτῶν δέν έχουν σημασία.

Bind together as God's beloved pilgrims. Your differences are of no matter.

(The Gospel According to Trevor, chapter 3, verse 40)

As O'Shea drove through the northeast Philadelphia rainstorm, they recounted the transgressions each committed to get themselves expelled from the event.

"I guess I might have been a little too aggressive," Berkshire admitted. She pulled down the passenger-seat visor and examined her wet hair in the small mirror.

"You just posed questions," said Jesse from the back.

"Forcefully," Berkshire noted.

"But valid questions," Jesse continued. "Me, I lost my temper and turned over the tables and chairs on the stage. I wonder if that's a crime."

"It could be criminal mischief," O'Shea said as he glanced in the rearview mirror at his passenger. "Did you break anything?"

Jesse leaned forward, sticking his head between the front seats. "I'm not sure. The big security guard tackled me before I could perform a BDA."

"A what?" asked Berkshire.

"Battle Damage Assessment," he said, without the faintest idea where the term came from.

"And what did you do?" Berkshire asked O'Shea.

O'Shea sighed, signaled for a lane change, and said, "I had a difference of opinion with one of the audience members."

"You got in a fight?" Jesse's voice pitched with disbelief.

"Goodness no. Some guy thought I was being overly friendly with another audience member, but we were only having a conversation. It was a total misperception."

He parked on Erie Avenue, across the street from Pat's Pub. The place seemed far enough from Temple to avoid the Liacouras crowd and the embarrassment of being recognized or, perhaps, questions from law enforcement.

They made an odd trio, with little in common save their interest in a rejected text buried for the last seventeen hundred years. They were like the start of a bad joke: A scholar, a preacher, and the Messiah walk into a restaurant ... With the punch line still to be determined, they found a table in the back corner, ordered, and waited for their meals.

"You are the infamous Dr. Haley Berkshire," said O'Shea, his tone almost reverential. The Phillies game played on televisions scattered throughout the establishment.

"I am. How do you know me?"

"The Gospel According to Trevor, of course," he

responded. "An article in *Catholic Digest* piqued my interest. To be honest, I found myself absolutely riveted. I looked up your other scholarship, your reputation, whatever I could find out about you. I have never seen anyone so universally reviled."

"It seems my research is a bit too provocative," she said. She still liked that word.

"To say the least," O'Shea said. "A beach towel?"

"I stand by my conclusions, even if they do make people uncomfortable."

"Oh, they certainly do," O'Shea affirmed.

Their food server approached the table. "You ordered a beer?" she asked Jesse. He pointed at O'Shea, and the server placed the mug in front of the priest.

O'Shea took a sip and continued, "James X. Shaver—who, I might add, is an unenlightened and repugnant Neanderthal of a human being—said your work on the Gospel According to Trevor was—"

"Apostasy. I read that, too," she said. "But he's wrong, ironically enough. It cannot be apostasy."

O'Shea leaned closer, and she explained, "I did not abandon any religious beliefs because I don't *have* any religious beliefs. I don't believe in God, or Allah, or Buddha, or the Good and Evil Manitos, or any omnipotent being for that matter."

"Fair point," said O'Shea.

Their sandwiches arrived and each thanked the waitress. O'Shea added extra mayo to his Italian sub, while Berkshire gently applied the sauce (ordered on the side) to her turkey club. Jesse put half his cheesesteak in the to-go box he requested and secured it in his purple backpack, then took a bite from the remaining half.

"What's your story, Father?" she asked between bites. "In fact, what's your name?"

O'Shea held up his hand to request a moment. He finished chewing, swigged his beer, and offered, "Father Brian William Callum Robert O'Shea."

Berkshire shook her head to allow the volley of letters to settle, while Jesse used fingers to count out the names—all five of them.

"Brian is fine," O'Shea chuckled. "Truth is, I kind of liked just being 'Brian' for the past week."

Berkshire extended her hand. "Pleasure to meet you, Brian. Call me Haley."

"Haley," O'Shea repeated as he shook her hand. "That's a nice name." She smiled in response, and he continued, "I'm curious about something, Haley. Why would you, of all people, be at an evangelical love-in?"

"I guess that's a reasonable question," she replied, shifting in her chair. "It's a long story, and to be perfectly honest, I'm not sure of the answer. My family. Professional curiosity. Guilt, maybe. I don't know." After a pause, she pointed her sandwich at O'Shea and continued, "Same question. Why would you?"

"I've been a Catholic priest for sixteen years," O'Shea began, "currently serving at Saint Helen of Mercy Catholic Church of the North Seattle diocese. At least I was a week ago Sunday. As I said, I was fascinated by the Gospel According to Trevor, and I needed to know more. So I drove across the country."

"Why Philadelphia?" she asked.

"This is not my ultimate destination. I just ended up here today. I was traveling with a passenger who decided she wanted to go home."

"She?" asked Berkshire, but O'Shea waved it away.

"I'm headed to New York," he continued. "I agree with your conclusion from reading the text."

"So do I!" said Jesse, midbite.

For the first time, Berkshire looked at him in detail. She scowled, unimpressed. "How long have you been wearing that shirt?"

"On and off since Los Angeles," he replied. "I alternate it with my Venice Beach T-shirt."

"You're from Los Angeles?" asked Berkshire.

"I don't know exactly where I'm *from*. Things are a little hazy, you know. But I've been living in Venice Beach for a long time."

"Do you like it there?" asked O'Shea.

"One alley is really the same as any other," Jesse said, and they did not immediately understand.

"Wait," said Berkshire, finally. "You're homeless?"

His downward gaze suggested it was not a fact of which he was particularly proud, especially considering her somewhat accusatory tone.

"And you made it all the way from California to Philadelphia?" asked O'Shea. Jesse nodded meekly. "That's amazing!"

Encouraged by the validation, Jesse sat up taller. "This is important to me. It's important to the world. My name is Jesse Morales and I am the Second Coming of Christ, but my ministry is mostly rejected because ... you know ..." He indicated his unkempt appearance. "This."

"You're the Second Coming," Berkshire echoed. Her head was cocked and her arms were folded impudently, as if cross-examining a three-year-old who blamed the family dog for stealing the bonbons.

Jesse wiped the corner of his mouth with his napkin. "It's true. And the Gospel According to Trevor proves it."

"How?" asked Dr. Berkshire, unfolding her arms. "Please enlighten me." O'Shea thought he noticed the hostess eying them from the front of the restaurant as she spoke on the phone.

"The Testicle of Christ," Jesse explained. "That's *my* testicle. I have hurt ... down there ... for as long as I can remember. I don't remember much ... Something happened years ago, I don't know what ... but the pain has been a daily part of my life. I am unwhole. And Trevor proves I'm right. A Roman centurion took my nut."

O'Shea grimaced at the thought.

"That's a rather, shall we say, *unusual* story," Berkshire concluded, her voice dripping with doubt and her volume increasing with each word. "In fact, it sounds downright ..." When several diners glanced her way, she realized she was too loud and continued in a softer voice, "In fact, it sounds downright delusional."

"But I know it to be true," said Jesse. "And if it is, wouldn't it prove your research is also true?"

Berkshire shook her head, unconvinced, and boomed, "There's no way—"

Before she could finish, the door opened with a whoosh, the rain still hammering Philadelphia. Two police officers entered, water dripping from their uniforms, and scanned the restaurant. O'Shea softly cleared his throat, just loud enough to make his companions aware of the intrusion.

The hostess hustled to greet the officers, who spoke to her indistinctly. She pointed toward the rear of the restaurant and the officers moved in that direction, scrutinizing the tables of diners as they passed.

"They're coming this way," O'Shea whispered, his voice shaky. "And they're not just checking to see who brought umbrellas."

"What do we do?" squeaked Berkshire.

"Act natural," Jesse whispered. "Keep eating. Don't stare."

But neither Berkshire nor O'Shea could avert their eyes as the policemen approached—ten steps away, now only five, until one officer stopped and leaned against the wall a foot from their table.

"Be right back," said his partner, who disappeared into the restroom.

Jesse chuckled to himself and O'Shea, who had been holding his breath for most of their approach, let it escape all at once.

The policeman noticed and turned to them. "How's the food?"

"Oh, it's great," said Berkshire, and the others voiced their agreement.

"What's the score of the game?" asked the officer, pointing at one of the TVs which now showed a Jack-in-the-Box commercial, the one with Jack and his giant head in a business suit.

"We haven't been watching," O'Shea said.

"Mets, five to two," Jesse interjected. "Bottom of the fifth."

"Phillies are gonna take ten years off my freaking life," the officer said.

Berkshire pulled lip gloss from her purse and, with unsteady hands, tried to apply it. O'Shea, equally desperate for distraction, nervously picked up his phone.

He was surprised to find a text message from Simone:

Made it home, took a nap, back at the
Starlight tonight. Starting class tomorrow.
Just wanted to send this to you. Hope
you like it.
xxx♥

O'Shea scrolled below to find a picture—Simone reflected in her bathroom mirror, spectacularly naked as God made her—and gasped. He quickly set his phone face down on the table, but his reaction attracted the policeman's attention.

"Everything okay, Father?"

O'Shea took the final slug from his beer and nodded in the affirmative, just as the other policeman emerged from the restroom.

"Have a good evening, folks," said the first policeman, and they walked away. O'Shea watched the two officers thank the hostess before returning to the rainy night outside, and Berkshire followed them through the window until their patrol car left the parking lot.

Once her hands stopped shaking, Berkshire returned her attention to the others. "Where were we?"

"My testicle," Jesse said as he turned away from the baseball game. "Our quest."

"Right," said Berkshire, staring at Jesse. "Let's be honest here—"

O'Shea interrupted, "I don't think it's a coincidence we were thrown together." He tossed his napkin onto his plate, covering a pile of uneaten fries. Jesse eyed them enviously but decided to let it pass.

"You're saying this is fate?" Berkshire scoffed.

"Kismet?"

"Maybe," said O'Shea, signaling to their server for the check. "Or maybe divine intervention."

"You know I don't believe in such things," said Berkshire. "But fine, go ahead. I'm listening."

O'Shea looked to Jesse, urging him to make his case. Berkshire tapped the table impatiently.

"In the great metropolis of the modern world," recited Jesse from memory, "a place both west and east, in a gathering place used by many."

"New York City," said O'Shea.

"Central Park," added Berkshire.

"Look to the strategizers, who tarry at games but know much more," Jesse continued.

"Chess and Checkers House?" proposed O'Shea.

"I agree," replied Berkshire.

"Me, too," added Jesse, smiling.

Berkshire turned to Jesse. "Chapter thirteen, verses five and six, word for word," she said. "I'm impressed."

"We share the same goal," O'Shea said, "even though we have different reasons. I'm on a spiritual pilgrimage. "You," he added, nodding at Berkshire, "are on an academic one. And Jesse's quest is—"

"Anatomical?" Berkshire interjected.

O'Shea chuckled. "I was going to say epistemological, but yes, that too."

Jesse tapped him on the arm. "What does epistological—"

"Epistemological?" O'Shea corrected.

"Yeah," said Jesse. "What does that mean?"

"It's the study of knowledge," O'Shea explained. "How do we know something is true?"

Jesse's nod affirmed the relevance of the megaword to his present undertaking.

O'Shea continued, "We've reached the same conclusion about how and where to fulfill our shared goal, although maybe not the exact details yet."

"What are you thinking?" asked Berkshire.

"I propose we work together," O'Shea said. "It's not like we're at cross-purposes, and maybe we can help each other." After Berkshire shrugged her acquiescence, he added, "Great. We can sleep here tonight and go into the city in the morning."

Jesse shifted uncomfortably. "Sometimes I tend to be overly cautious, but I wonder if maybe we should get out of Philadelphia, just in case."

"I agree with him," said Berkshire. "Although I need to get my luggage first. It's in a locker at the train station."

"How about Trenton, then?" O'Shea asked. "I think it's about half an hour."

They agreed on Trenton, fetched Berkshire's wheelie suitcase, and soon were northbound on the I-95. As they paralleled the Delaware River, O'Shea observed, "Rain's stopping, finally. You'd think a guy who lives in Seattle would get comfortable driving in weather like this, but I never did."

Berkshire asked, "You know how they said the rain is a sign from God? Which guy said that?"

"Graham," said Jesse, and being purposely bombastic, reenacted, "'Rain can reveal evil and wash away the transgressors.'" Again, it was word for word.

"Which it did," Berkshire said, mimicking Falwell's gesticulations from when he tried unsuccessfully to keep his toupee from being blown off his head. They all enjoyed a laugh at the expense of Falwell's flying hairpiece. After some measure of contemplation, Berkshire added, "You know, I think maybe I believe in God after all."

O'Shea flicked on the radio. "Let's see if there's any news about the rally. Any stories about the trio of reprobates."

"The Trio of Reprobates," repeated Berkshire. "I like it."

"Maybe we can get team T-shirts. I sure could use a change of clothes," joked Jesse.

The radio announcer said: "Our final story tonight, and it's a good one, comes from Taylor County Georgia ..." Jesse sat up to listen more closely, motioning to stop the laughter. "... where a local peanut farmer, Silas Felder, just sold a nut on eBay." Jesse broke into a broad, satisfied grin, but the others, focused on the announcement, did not immediately notice. The announcer continued: "That's right, one nut, posted on eBay for less than twenty-four hours. What made this particular nut special, you ask? This is a unique peanut, maybe even a sacred peanut, which apparently looks exactly like Jesus Christ. Yes, folks, a Jesus-shaped peanut." Jesse could scarcely contain his excitement. "And how much did Farmer Felder get for the Jesus-shaped peanut, you ask?"

The announcer paused dramatically, and it must have worked because all three of them sat in perfect silence until he answered his own question: "More than thirty-seven thousand dollars."

"Yes!" Jesse exclaimed, nearly dancing in the back seat.

The questions began. "For a peanut?" asked O'Shea. "Why are you so excited?" asked Berkshire.

The announcer continued: "And maybe the best part

of the story is this ..." Jesse shooshed his new friends to hear the rest. "The purchaser of the Jesus nut was none other than Steve Drain, leader of the famous ... or dare we say notorious ... Westboro Baptist Church."

"Atta boy, Silas!" said Jesse. He then proceeded to tell the fantastic story of the Westboro Baptist Church van in Oklahoma City, and Silas Felder, and the magic peanut which just saved Silas' farm.

"You know what?" said O'Shea. "I think maybe I believe in God after all, too."

Eighteen
PHINEAS

Με τον ίδιο τρόπο ο Γέννηση του Ιησού ήταν προφητεμένος, είναι πολύ γνωστός από λίγους αλλά διαθέσιμο σε όποιον το ρωτάει.

The counsel of prophets and sages is made available to any who have the faith to ask and to believe.

(The Gospel According to Trevor, chapter 2, verse 34)

The Trio of Reprobates woke Wednesday morning in their Trenton hotel rooms. The parishioners of Saint Helen of Mercy treated O'Shea and Jesse to one room, although half of it technically went unused. When O'Shea woke, he turned and noticed the other bed was not only empty but also undisturbed.

"Oh, damn," he said. He had long believed that, in a world full of equal measures kindness and wickedness, he would one day meet his demise when he bestowed his charity upon the wrong person. But he never believed he would be left stranded at a two-star motel in Trenton, New Jersey with only a few pairs of clean underwear and eleven payments still to be made on his Camry. "Damn, damn,

damn. I can't believe—"

"You can't believe what?" asked a voice. O'Shea's heart jolted, nearly replicating the chest-burster scene in the movie *Alien*. As he calmed himself with deep breaths, he realized it was Jesse's voice, even though the man was nowhere visible. *Is the homeless guy a practical joker?* wondered O'Shea. *Or did he transfigure into an angel of the Lord, come to harass me for my wickedness?*

"I can't believe ... wait, where are you?" asked O'Shea.

Jesse's head and shoulders appeared from the space between the undisturbed bed and the window.

"What are you doing on the floor?" O'Shea's thoughts were still muddled, running through myriad possibilities.

Jesse explained, "For the past week I've slept in pickup trucks, eighteen wheelers, trains, and even an actual bed." He ran his fingers through his hair, pushing it back from his face. "Do you have any idea how strange a bed feels when you've been sleeping in an alley for as long as you can remember?"

This was an unimaginable premise to O'Shea, now finally back to normal breathing. "I guess that makes sense," he said, "but I wish you would have told me. Might have saved me a heart attack."

"Sorry." Jesse stood and stretched, then continued. "The best night's sleep I got was in a park in New Mexico. After that, I didn't want to complain, but every morning my back was sore, or my neck was stiff, or something else hurt. I'm not a young man anymore. But this morning, I feel great."

O'Shea rolled out of bed, considering his own melancholy truth. With the exception of his college dorm, his stay at the monastery, and seven years with a foster pitbull named Trixie, he always had a room to himself. Yet he already missed the sparkle of Simone in the morning, which made bearable the exhilarating torment of her seductive efforts throughout the day.

"You can shower first," O'Shea said. "I'm going for a walk, so take as much time as you'd like. Then we'll get some breakfast."

He dressed, grabbed his room key, and ventured into the unsightly urban Trenton morning, made even gloomier by the storm clouds which now seemed to be his constant companion.

Once O'Shea departed, Jesse discovered a multitude of bathroom treasures–among the best of them, a tiny unopened bottle of shampoo and a new bar of soap, still wrapped in paper. The water in the shower was hot and the soap smelled of peppermint, and soon the bathroom was engulfed by steam. The length of Jesse's shower likely eclipsed the hotel's record while bringing the water level of the Delaware River down a couple of feet.

In the meantime, O'Shea walked through the Trenton Transit Center, where he paused to watch the frenzy of businessmen and women scurrying to or arriving on their trains. As he ducked away from the bustle, he grieved for those who pursued a mundane existence of wordless, ant-like commutes for nothing more than a paycheck and the company's bottom line. He slipped into a small gift shop for a few moments before he exited the station, circled Columbus Park, and journeyed back along Assunpink Creek. Always blessed with greater clarity when he walked, he used this time to consider the essential questions which presented themselves in the station: *Who am I? What is the purpose of life? What is the true nature of God? Will I still have a job when I get home?*

After being gone an hour, he knocked on Berkshire's hotel room door, then waited interminably for a response.

"Who is it?" she said, finally, from the other side of the closed door. She did not sound particularly chipper.

"Father O'Shea," he responded. "Brian."

She cracked the door until the chain stopped it, revealing a startling sight. Her hair went in more directions than the Paris Metro system, her eyes seemed the color of burnt cooking oil, and her dull, expressionless face looked a lot like a pint of tapioca pudding dropped on the sidewalk. O'Shea recoiled; after a week of Simone's flawless morning radiance, he had no idea this was how women looked before ten a.m.

"Good morning," he managed to say. "We'll be ready to leave as soon as I shower. Will you want breakfast?"

"Just coffee," she replied. "I can be ready in half an hour."

For the second time this trip, she took a quick shower and, as the warm water streamed onto her head, considered the task ahead. Her family was now a memory and her travel on the verge of completion, sweet validation nearly at hand.

O'Shea handed Jesse a new T-shirt he purchased from the gift shop at the train station. Across the chest was printed "Trenton: The Jewel of Jersey," with colorful graphics of a vibrant city splashed onto the black fabric. "It's beautiful," said Jesse. "It's more ironic, I think," answered O'Shea. "You haven't seen Trenton in the daylight."

He showered quickly as well, and once again sported his priest's collar for this final leg of the trip. Although he would still be Brian to his two companions, he surmised there might be value in presenting himself as Father O'Shea when they arrived in New York and began their work. Jesse, meanwhile, positively shined. Even though his pants needed a few cycles through an industrial washing machine, he could not recall ever being this clean. And the anticipation made even the ache in his groin bearable. Berkshire, her internal clock completely haywire after a week of train travel and the long night in New Orleans, crawled into the back seat.

They hit a Starbucks drive-through and then slid eastward, reengaging with the I-95 northbound. They passed New Brunswick and Metuchen, and all the while O'Shea and Jesse chattered like excited schoolchildren on their first field trip to the local zoo. Berkshire slept intermittently, waking to join the conversation before nodding off again.

The questions were endless, and important, and most were left unanswered for the time being. Many were procedural: How will we know what to do once we get to the Chess and Checkers House? What exactly are we looking for? Who should we talk to? What should we ask?

Others were more metaphysical: What if we misread the text? What if we fail to prove anything? What if our conclusion is wrong?

And still others were entirely practical: Since the Chess and Checkers House is equidistant from Central Park West, Central Park South, and Central Park East, where do we want to stay? How much can we afford? Does anyone know how to use the subway? Where the hell are we going to park?

Somewhere near Woodbridge Township, while

Berkshire snored softly in back, O'Shea said, "I gotta tell you, Jesse, I'm dubious that you're the actual Second Coming of Christ."

"So is everyone else," Jesse replied with a gentle smile. "True conviction is difficult sometimes. But you took a chance on me, and I appreciate that much faith." O'Shea acknowledged him with a nod, and Jesse added, "Maybe this is an epistemological quest for you, too."

They crawled past Newark Liberty Airport, crossed the Passaic and Hackensack Rivers, and made a right turn just before Secaucus. Ahead was the legendary Lincoln Tunnel and the process of merging into an ever-diminishing roadway. It was like trying to shove a gallon of LEGOs into a funnel in hopes that all the blue ones would come out together on the other end, but it was something one-hundred thousand cars managed to accomplish every day.

Now awake in the back seat, and seeing the apparently random jumble of vehicles ahead, Berkshire closed her eyes and said "Om."

Consistent with the kindness and patience one might expect from a man of the cloth, O'Shea occasionally waved drivers in front of him. O'Shea thought it odd that none thanked him, but they were too busy making sure nobody cut in front of *them*. It was a cacophonous, snarling frenzy of metal and middle fingers which fed on the weakest of the herd. And O'Shea was most definitely it.

"Father, we're gonna be in this same spot all day long unless you get a little more aggressive," Jesse finally suggested. O'Shea took a deep breath, gripped the steering wheel tightly at nine and three, and accelerated to shut down the next driver attempting to merge. The driver's strident honk jolted Berkshire from her yogic tranquility.

"Same to you, buddy!" she shouted, flipping a bird through the rear window.

"Now we're getting somewhere," laughed Jesse.

O'Shea snickered and pressed ahead, and eventually they were underneath the Hudson River. A few minutes later, the tunnel spit them out in Manhattan and, although the blue LEGOs were not all together, somehow none were damaged. It had taken them an hour to drive from Trenton and another hour to approach and pass through a mile-long tube, but they were finally here.

They drove slowly uptown, engulfed by the colossal buildings and surrounded by yellow taxis darting to and fro like giant wasps on amphetamines. They solved one of their mysteries when they found a parking garage near Lincoln Center. At thirty-eight dollars a day, it was absurdly expensive, but it was only a few blocks from Central Park and they were excited to begin their mission.

"Which way is Central Park?" Jesse asked when they stepped onto the sidewalk. Both Berkshire and O'Shea looked at their phones for directions, but since they could not agree which side of the street they were on, they also could not agree on the directions to the park. "It's this way," Jesse finally decided, pointing to his right, and the others followed obediently. Along the way, they stopped to book two rooms at the West Side YMCA, thus solving another of their conundrums.

"Can I get one of those big pretzels?" Jesse asked when they gathered in the lobby.

"Are you serious?" said O'Shea. "You had breakfast this morning, and then you ate your leftover sandwich in the car."

"It was only half a sandwich. Besides, I've eaten so well

this trip, I think my stomach expanded."

"Well, contract it," Berkshire said, pointing toward the YMCA's front doors. "We've got work to do."

The sun shone directly overhead when they arrived at the Chess and Checkers House, a handsome octagonal red-brick building shaded by elm trees. It was one of the most beautiful settings in the iconic park—surrounded by lush greenery, adjacent to a graceful arched stone bridge, almost close enough to touch the magnificent high-rises of Central Park South which pushed up the sky. But they were not here for the views.

"Thoughts?" invited Berkshire. "Anyone have anything?"

"We talked about it in the car," said O'Shea, "but no, not really."

"I think you were asleep then," added Jesse.

Since the important tactical questions were unresolved, Berkshire continued, "Well, let's give it some thought. We can't just do this haphazardly. We need some sort of methodology. Any clues from the text?"

They pondered for a while, Jesse occasionally rattling off a verse, Berkshire offering historical and anthropological angles while O'Shea provided religious perspective. But no insight jumped out at them, or even peeked around a corner.

After a long, frustrated silence, Jesse posed, "Maybe we should we explore the place. Get the lay of the land. The treasures of the Lord are not always made evident."

"Sure," said Berkshire, and they divided up the territory.

O'Shea wandered around the interior, checking out the faces of the players, looking underneath the plastic tables and at pictures on the wall, browsing the chess books illuminated by light filtering through a window, even thumbing through the sign-up sheet until the attendant snatched it away. Berkshire and Jesse conducted a similar inspection around the exterior of the building. On such a pleasant afternoon, most of the twenty-four outside tables were busy with plastic chessmen clattering on game boards inlaid into the concrete tabletops. Few players looked up from their games, and most who did made it clear they did not appreciate the inquiring eyes.

Fifteen minutes later, they came back together and arrived at their conclusion.

"I have no fucking idea," said Berkshire, and the others agreed.

"Wait," said Jesse, his hands upraised to grasp the obvious. "Why don't we see if there's anyone here named Trevor?"

"That's a pretty good idea," O'Shea said, shrugging.

"Not really," answered Berkshire, "but it's better than anything else we have."

Before they could begin their survey, an elderly black man emerged from the Chess and Checkers House. He carried a box of chess pieces and a chess clock, unsteadily. "Phineas," someone greeted from a nearby table, and the old man waved back.

O'Shea stopped and pointed. "Him."

"The old man?" Berkshire shook her head dismissively. "What can he possibly tell us?"

"Did you hear his name?" O'Shea asked, leaning in close.

"It was Phineas, right?" said Jesse.

"It was. And does either of you happen to know what

Phineas means?" When they met O'Shea's question with blank stares, he continued. "From the Hebrew name Pinchas, it means 'Oracle.'"

"I'm gonna need *a lot* more proof than that," Berkshire said, "but sure, we can at least check it out."

They decided the priest's collar might be intimidating and the professor's skeptical assertiveness too threatening, so Jesse approached first.

Phineas was dressed in a thin, faded long-sleeve button-down shirt, tan cargo shorts, a blue bathrobe, and brown suede bedroom slippers. A New York Yankees cap tilted down to cover his right eye, and his gray stubble suggested he was a few days overdue for a shave. Jesse estimated him at seventy, and the bedroom slippers at sixty-five.

"Hi, sir, begging your pardon, my name's Jesse and I'm visiting New York. These are my friends Brian and Haley."

"You play chess?" Phineas asked, setting the pieces on the board.

"I used to, I think."

"Then sit." Phineas waved toward the opposite chair and, as Jesse sat, the old man opened with pawn to king four and punched the chess clock.

"This might sound a little strange," O'Shea said to Phineas, "but I was hoping we could read something to you and get your reaction."

"Shush!" he answered. "If you're gonna watch, watch with your eyes and not your mouth."

Jesse mirrored white's pawn to king four opening and punched the clock. Phineas developed his knight and punched the clock again, his entire move taking one second. Seventeen moves later, after a brilliant rook sacrifice which left Jesse's right flank exposed, Phineas pronounced "Checkmate."

"Amazing," Jesse said.

Phineas leaned back in his chair and interlaced his fingers behind his head. "I can tell you haven't played much speed chess. It's a different game. I'm not even very good." He pointed at another player. "That guy six tables away, in the blue shirt, he's the champ."

"Listen," interjected Berkshire. "Could we buy you lunch?"

"Sure, I can let you do that." He turned to Jesse. "Have you had a New York pretzel yet?"

"No, not yet," Jesse responded, sneaking a look at Berkshire. She averted her eyes and redirected the conversation by pointing at something in the distance. "How about the hot dog cart?"

Once Phineas unwrapped the foil and took a bite of his hot dog, Berkshire summarized the Gospel According to Trevor for him. Phineas seemed intrigued but also somewhat perplexed, and when she finished, he said, "I don't know much about that. I'm just a former advertising man here in New York."

"Are you retired now?" asked O'Shea.

"You're a priest," Phineas observed, and O'Shea nodded.

The old man leaned in close, as if confessing, and whispered, "They fired me a couple of years ago. Told me I didn't have it anymore. They said at the end all I did was tell stories about the old days and eat their donuts."

Phineas sat back and assumed a cloudy, faraway look, eyes like the windows on a Manhattan skyscraper the day before cleaning. His voice rose, "If you've never felt the pleasure of eating a delicious fluffy original glazed donut hot off the line and, heaven forbid, you get struck by lightning, well surely that would be really bad."

"I suppose it would," said Berkshire. She touched him gently on the hand. "But can we talk about the Gospel According to Trevor? It could be something of tremendous historical significance."

"Historical significance, you say? That's very interesting," Phineas said, using the sleeve of his bathrobe to wipe mustard from his lip.

Now, maybe, some progress, Berkshire thought. O'Shea leaned forward while Jesse crossed his arms attentively.

"But you need to be more patient," Phineas continued, washing down the last of his hot dog with a last gulp of his chocolate YooHoo.

"That's very difficult right now," Berkshire explained, her leg bouncing. "I traveled across the country for this. We all did, just for this moment."

With the same faraway look, Phineas said, "If you hate waiting, raise your hand," and all three of them did so.

Phineas rubbed his chin and appeared deep in thought, finally asking, "Have you ever been to Rome?"

Jesse sighed and glanced warily at the others. This conversation was remarkably confusing to him, but maybe they were following it.

Phineas continued, "Should we also flood the Sistine Chapel so tourists can get nearer the ceiling?"

"That's an interesting philosophical question, Phineas," Berkshire said, wadding up her trash. "But let's focus here. Can you help us? Are you the oracle?" Phineas did not respond.

Berkshire looked at her friends and shook her head emphatically. This man was definitely not their answer.

"Please, Phineas," interjected O'Shea. "We've been on the road for a long time. We—"

"The road, you say?" Phineas interrupted. He turned to look at each of them, stopping to gaze deeply into Berkshire's eyes. He wagged his finger at her for emphasis, and the compelling gesture froze her. "Utah," he proclaimed, his stare fixed upon hers. "The road to mighty."

Berkshire flinched. "Wait a minute. How did you know I'm from Utah?"

"I'll be back day after tomorrow," Phineas said. "We can talk more then." He stood and headed toward the Central Park Zoo, his blue bathrobe fluttering behind him like the cape of a superhero named Captain Senility.

"Well?" asked O'Shea.

"That's our guy," Berkshire affirmed.

Jesse and Berkshire headed back to the West Side YMCA while O'Shea took a longer route so he could visit Strawberry Fields and the John Lennon memorial. As he ventured down Central Park West on his way back to the YMCA, it began to rain. He passed a bus stop near Seventieth Street where two teenagers tried to stay dry as they waited for the next bus. One, a pretty girl dressed in leggings and an extra-large T-shirt, looked up and smiled at him. He noticed her and smiled back.

What he failed to notice, though, was the advertisement on the outside of the bus stop structure. The ad, for New York City Taxi, read: "If you hate waiting, raise your hand."

Nineteen
ENLIGHTENED

Οι μαθητές βγήκαν στην πόλη, ο καθένας μόνος του. Και όταν επέστρεψαν, ο καθένας κατανόησε τις υποχρεώσεις του προς τον Κύριο.

The Disciples went out into the city, each on his own. And when they returned, each understood his obligations to the Lord.

(The Gospel According to Trevor, chapter 10, verse 32)

"Let's recap," said Berkshire when they sat down for dinner. They had figured out how to use the subway—another dilemma resolved—and now shared a basket of Italian bread at Carmine's.

"It was a very strange experience," said O'Shea.

"You can say that again," agreed Jesse. "'Should we also flood the Sistine Chapel so tourists can get nearer the ceiling?'" He held up his hands in exasperation. "What does that even mean?"

"Not so fast, you guys," Berkshire said. "Let's think about this. Who is the most famous oracle in the history of the world?"

O'Shea dipped his bread in oil. "The Oracle of Delphi," he responded, then took a bite. "Pythia."

"Correct," Berkshire said. She carefully poured cream into her coffee. "And for a pilgrim to gain audience with the Oracle of Delphi, they were required to offer a donation and were instructed by a priest on how to ask their questions."

"We took him to lunch," said Jesse. "Isn't that like a donation? And we've got a priest."

Berkshire shook her head. "Not the same. Pythia's priest worked for her."

Jesse's curious expression begged for more, so Berkshire explained. "According to some accounts, the Oracle answered in incomprehensible words and phrases. *Glossolalia*, we call this."

"I think we can all agree he was incomprehensible," said O'Shea.

"And the priest, then, would be called upon to interpret," Berkshire continued.

"I can speak Greek and Latin," O'Shea said, scratching his beard, "but I'm not sure I can interpret this guy."

Berkshire tapped her temple with her index finger. "Picture how he looked when he was at his most incomprehensible." She paused to allow O'Shea and Jesse to visualize. "He got that glassy, faraway look in his eyes, and then when he spoke he even sounded a little different. The Oracle of Delphi was said to do the same thing."

They recalled Phineas' empty, distant countenance, like a train's dim headlight in a dark, foggy tunnel.

She continued, "An oracle is supposed to be mystical, right? They don't just give straight answers. That's not 'oracly' enough. He's given us our first clues, and there are more to come. It's up to us to figure them out."

"But how?" asked O'Shea.

"We've got the skills to do this," said Berkshire, examining her fork. "I've dealt with historical, anthropological, and religious texts, and you're an expert on both the history and philosophy of Christianity. So it's fair to say we've both interpreted our fair share of metaphor and mythology."

"I suppose," shrugged O'Shea.

"And Jesse has such a gift for memorization, we can be as thorough as necessary. C'mon, guys, we've got this."

"I hope you're right," said O'Shea, as their pasta arrived.

They continued the discussion through dinner, and by the time the check arrived, they were still baffled. Berkshire paid the check and they ventured into the New York night.

O'Shea looked at the sky and turned to his new friends. "I need some personal time," he said. "I think we should each do our own thing tomorrow. Explore the city. Do more research in the library. Drop into a church. Visit a museum. All of the above. Then we can come back together on Friday morning with fresh perspectives. I hope so, anyway."

"Sounds good," said Jesse, nodding.

"Then I'm going shopping," said Berkshire by way of agreement, and they split up for the evening.

Berkshire strolled a few blocks south on Broadway, looking in all the different windows. New York was still far too busy for her, but she decided summer nights on the Upper West Side were altogether rather pleasant. She spent the next hour at the Victoria's Secret store, purchasing intimates she would not have considered buying before this trip, and of the sort she had not owned since her last marriage. Later that night, as she tried them on in her room at the YMCA, she felt pretty for the first time in forever.

Jesse crossed the street, walked a block down Broadway, and stopped in front of Murray's Sturgeon Shop. Even after closing, the pungency smelled much like Jesse's alleyway in Venice Beach, so he lingered for a while and reminisced about home. He then headed west along Eighty-ninth Street and arrived at the Soldiers' and Sailors' Monument in Riverside Park. Here he studied the Greek columns and the ornamental eagles for perhaps fifteen minutes before walking back to the YMCA along Riverside Drive. *Why did that speak to me?* he wondered.

O'Shea took the subway to Times Square, emerging into the more frenetic midtown at Fiftieth Street. At street level, someone handed him a card, good for one free admission to the Platinum Dolls Gentlemen's Club on Seventh Avenue. *Why not?* he thought. Two hours and four beers later, he concluded there could never possibly be another girl as stunning as Simone, and perhaps he should leave it at that—her perfection etched indelibly, untarnishable in his memory.

They continued their individual explorations on Thursday.

Jesse selected a street corner and set up shop like back in Venice. By noon, he had accumulated a sizeable return from the generous people of New York. It certainly helped, in what was essentially a volume business, to have hundreds of people walk past him every minute. He bought a new pair of boxer shorts and sat wearing only those while he washed and dried the rest of his clothes at a local laundromat. Fortunately, he checked his pants pockets before they ended up in the washer, discovering his eleven dollars and change still left from the Wendy's in Philadelphia. Afterwards, he purchased a slice of pizza and a Coke next door. His clothes cleaner and his stomach happier than they had been in years, he decided to explore the city like a native.

He walked to Columbus Circle and hopped an A train to Fourteenth Street, then transferred to Union Square. The trains were packed, so he pressed up against a man who smelled of curry while he watched a small child crawling around the car to chew on commuters' shoelaces. Next he went to Times Square, where he was entertained by a talented musician playing a Plexiglas violin which looked like some sort of clear medieval axe. *My friend Jimi would love that violin*, he thought. Jesse came to street level only to be engulfed by the mass of humanity which lived in, worked in, or simply explored New York's most gaudy district. The people, the noise, the smell, and the neon were all too much for Jesse, and he retreated to the sanctuary of underground. From a different platform, he crossed town to Grand Central Station, the grandeur of which caused him to gasp while indifferent New Yorkers jostled past in all directions. After that, he took the 6 train north to 116th Street and braved the outside once again.

He found himself in an enchanted place, where residents looked very much like him. Wonderful smells tickled his brain, and the sounds of a language he used to know frolicked in his ears. He began to roam, no agenda except immersing himself more deeply in this fairy tale.

Before long he arrived at Wagner Playground, where

activity swirled in every corner while children played soccer on the field in the center of the park. He watched quietly for maybe twenty minutes, his interest finally broken by the sound of positively joyful music, its lure impossible to ignore.

The next thing he knew, Jesse was learning to salsa dance. "Me llamo Rosa," said his partner. "Me llamo Jesse," he replied automatically, and then the music took over. He danced with most of the women there—old or young, beautiful or not, he did not care. All of them said he was pretty good, that he had *ritmo* and *estilo*, and this could not possibly be his first time.

The Ramirez family kindly invited Jesse to dinner in their home, eight people plus himself eating tamales around a small table in a cramped apartment. He stayed until well after dark, reluctant to leave the emotional warmth of this *familia contenta*. But tomorrow's meeting with Phineas beckoned, so he excused himself, thanked his hosts for their abundant graciousness, and set out for the station.

He soon discovered that Spanish Harlem, like the human soul, is a dichotomy in action, and Jesse's optimism turned when two men dragged him into an alley. "We gonna fuck you up, homeboy," said one, and when the other punched him, Jesse reacted instinctively and with great force. *How did I do that?* he wondered, his two assailants moaning in pain on the ground. He only hoped they would carry enough residual soreness to remember this day and, perhaps, to reconsider their future conduct. Jessie hurried to the 116th Street station and scraped together the last of his funds, only to discover he fell twenty-five cents short. A kind commuter rescued him with a quarter, he plugged the money into the machine, and with his fourth MetroCard of the day, boarded a 6 train downtown. He retraced his entire route (minus the above-ground excursions) and arrived back at the West Side YMCA about eleven o'clock.

O'Shea rose earlier than his roommate, and his morning walk took him around the Lake in Central Park, all the way to Fifth Avenue, south around the Pond, and back to the YMCA. By the time he finished, he was clear about what needed to be done. He showered, donned his clerical collar, and did a Google search. He then hurried one-quarter mile to The Church of Saint Paul the Apostle on West Sixtieth and, upon entering, found himself alone in the dim light under a magnificent high ceiling meant to convey the grandeur of the Lord. Only now did he realize how remiss he had been with his "Our Fathers" and "Hail Marys" during this journey.

He dipped his fingers into the holy water, crossed himself, and whispered, "Forgive me, Father," then slipped into one of the rear pews, pulled down the kneeler, and bent in supplication.

"Holy Father, Creator of all, I find myself in a difficult position. My spirit is tested and my faith is on the precipice. I welcome this time to be alone with you, to pour out my heart in search of your grace and your will ..."

But he was, in fact, not alone. Two maintenance workers, performing basic repairs in a wing of the cavernous church, were no more aware of O'Shea's presence than he was of theirs.

"Pass me the crescent wrench," said Stan, the older of the two. The younger worker, Steve, reached for his tool belt and came up empty. Puzzled, he surveyed the area in search of the absent tool.

"Bad news, Stan," Steve said. "I can't find it."

"You lost the crescent wrench?" asked Stan, sharply.

"I wouldn't say I lost it," Steve replied. "Lost implies it's gone forever, but I'm sure it's someplace."

"Of course it's someplace," said Stan. "It's always someplace. Everything is someplace. But the question right now is, where is this particular someplace where it's at?"

"I, uh, I don't know."

"In other words, you lost the crescent wrench," Stan pushed.

"I had it five minutes ago, so I know I didn't lose it. I just misplaced it, that's all."

Oblivious to this exchange, O'Shea was now deep into his prayerful penance.

"Lord, I have been the worst possible example of a Christian man, let alone priest. I have brought shame to myself and my parish and, worst of all, to You. I drink too much beer. I enjoy visiting immoral places and looking at women in a sexual way, in violation of the deadly sin of *luxuria*. It could be argued that I have disregarded the ninth commandment with my dishonesty. And definitely the fourth. You know this already, Lord God, but in your mercy, hear my prayers ..."

Stan and Steve continued their discussion of the missing tool.

"Can't you just use pliers?" Steve asked.

"If I could use pliers, I wouldn't have asked for the crescent wrench," Stan replied. "Which you lost."

"I'm telling you, I only misplaced it. I bet you as soon as we walk away, we'll find it."

"That's all fine and dandy," said Stan, "except for the fact that when we walk away, we won't need it anymore. We need it right now. Right here."

O'Shea continued to pray: "And now, I don't know, Lord, I find myself deeply confused. I am on a quest for a remarkable Christian relic that I am unworthy of finding. My sin only taints this quest, and I cannot help but wonder whether this should be left to holier men ..."

"I tell you what," said Stan. "Why don't *you* walk away and find the lost crescent wrench—"

"Misplaced."

"Whatever. You walk away and find the crescent wrench, and I'll stay here and wait for you."

O'Shea slumped over now, barely composed. It is not an easy to thing to admit our greatest failures, even in the quiet of The Church of Saint Paul the Apostle, but O'Shea was now fully vulnerable, his soul bared to the Lord.

"I leave it to you, Lord God, ruler of all. I ask Your holy guidance. What should I do, Lord? What should I do?" And, with this entreaty, he broke down in tears.

Meanwhile, Steve stood and walked a few steps away, then stopped and turned around. "Hey Stan, what should we do if I don't find the crescent wrench?"

At his breaking point, Stan stood and boomed, "Go find the goddamn thing!" Steve turned and scuffled away as Stan's sharp words echoed throughout the vastness of the church.

"Go find the goddamn thing ... Go find the goddamn thing ... Go find the goddamn thing ..." Each time the words were softer, but the message was unmistakable.

O'Shea looked heavenward and said, "Thank you, Lord. I will." Teeming with resolve, he stood, replaced the kneeler, and emerged onto Sixtieth Street ready for whatever danger, whatever mystery, whatever *glossolalia* was thrown at him. His mission was clear—the unequivocal command of God.

Berkshire began her day at a bagel place, where she noshed on a pumpernickel bagel with double cream cheese and tolerated a mediocre cup of coffee. As she had never tried a pumpernickel bagel before, she congratulated herself on her boldness. After breakfast, she spent more time shopping (this time, buying earrings and a souvenir T-shirt), then went to the Riverside Library and spent an hour lost in its variety of exhibits. By early afternoon, she logged on to one of the library's computers to research oracles, hoping for clues which would enable her team to decipher Phineas' veiled wisdom.

She worked until late in the afternoon, lost in her research, and was now famished. When she Googled "restaurants near me," it seemed there were two restaurants for every inhabitant of Manhattan, the choices nearly blotting out the map. *How do they all stay in business?* she wondered. She decided to try Hell's Kitchen, which she heard was becoming one of the city's best dining areas and provided virtually infinite options. Plus, in light of her current objective, she appreciated the irony of the neighborhood's name.

She hailed a cab and a yellow wasp buzzed across three lanes to pick her up. The cabbie dropped her on Ninth Avenue and Forty-fifth, which would allow her to work her way uptown as she searched for the perfect dining experience.

Eventually, she was attracted to a hip-looking Mexican place on Fifty-first. "One, please," she told the hostess. It was Thursday-night busy, but they had an open two-top and were able to seat her immediately.

Once the waitress introduced herself, Berkshire excused herself to wash her hands, which carried the grime of a New York library and the inside of a cab last disinfected during the Reagan presidency. As she returned to her table, she heard her name being called. "Dr. Berkshire!" She knew nobody in New York, and her scan of the restaurant left her stumped.

"Dr. Berkshire, over here!" This time she located the source, a wizened man she had seen before but could not yet place, and went over to his table.

"I'm sorry, do I know you?"

"Dr. Horace Gardiner, New York University."

"Of course," she said, less than enthusiastically.

He continued, "What brings you to the Big Apple?"

"My research. I'm on sabbatical."

He cut a piece from his burrito. "And how goes said research?"

"It's been an adventure, without a doubt, but it's going pretty well now. We're excited about some of the things we've discovered here."

"We?" asked Gardiner, his fork hovering in front of his face. "You and your students?"

"As a matter of fact," she responded, "I have some new research partners on this part of the process, and they've been extremely helpful."

"More helpful than Home Depot guy?" asked Gardiner, shoving the forkful of burrito into his mouth.

Berkshire winced. "Robbie," she said.

"Excuse me?"

"Home Depot guy's name is Robbie," she explained,

"and, if you must know, he's actually a very gifted researcher."

"Which explains why he sells nails and screws," Gardiner mumbled as he swallowed. "Or has he been promoted to plumbing supplies?" His dining companion snickered.

"Oh, pardon my manners." Gardiner indicated his tablemate, a man with a bad haircut, a broad nose, a conspicuous mole, and glasses thicker than Kansas storm windows, sitting across from him. "I believe you've heard of James X. Shaver."

"Of course I have," Berkshire said. "One of my biggest fans."

Shaver chuckled insincerely, and she continued, "I need to get back to my table." But as she walked away, she glanced back and noticed Shaver whispering to Gardiner before they shared a hearty laugh.

She stopped in her tracks, spun around, and returned to their table.

"Mister Shaver," she said, her tone no longer solicitous, "a good friend of mine called you ... what were his words exactly? Oh, yes ... an 'unenlightened and repugnant Neanderthal.' But I don't agree." Shaver nodded his appreciation, and she continued, "Because I think his characterization is far too kind."

Then she turned to Gardiner. "And as for you, Dr. Gardiner, I remember when I was working on my Ph.D., and I referenced some of your research in my dissertation. That made me proud, because I thought you were a big deal. I even hoped to meet you someday. Well, now I've finally met you." Gardiner responded with a haughty, self-congratulatory smirk.

"And you know what? I don't really care if you respect my work–"

"Good," he interrupted, "because I don't."

"I know. But you don't have to be a fucking asshole about it." Several heads turned in a nearly audible swoosh, but the room remained silent until Berkshire's meal was served.

She dined with rare contentment, and her steamed lobster tacos tasted as good as any meal she had ever eaten. When the check came, the only charge was for a bottle of sparkling water, six dollars, so she beckoned her waitress.

"I think you gave me the wrong check," Berkshire said.

"No, I gave you the right check," the waitress responded. "Every time those pricks come in here," she said, indicating Gardiner and Shaver, "they insult someone, and they take up a table for hours. And when it comes time to tip, you'd think they were being asked to give away their favorite child."

"As if they would even have a favorite child," said Berkshire.

The waitress chuckled. "The way you told them off, we all wish we could do that. So your meal is on the house."

Berkshire smiled at her, took a deep, satisfied breath, and inserted two twenties into the folder. "Keep the change," she said. And during her stroll back she was lost in joyous reverie.

As she waited to cross Fifty-sixth, she noticed the largest cat she ever saw. It was the size of a badger, or so she estimated, having never actually seen a badger. She approached the animal and, as she bent down, it scurried into the sewer and disappeared. She gasped in surprise, then heard a man's laughter and turned to him.

"I just wanted to pet the cat," she explained.

"Lady, that wasn't no cat. That was a fucking sewer rat. Where are you from, Utah or something?"

He strode away, laughing at her foolishness, and she could only laugh, too. That night she fell asleep with a rare tranquility and slept more soundly than she had in years.

Twenty
THE LAST SUPPER

Ή αγάπη είναι υπομονετική καί εμπιστευτική, επομένως εμπιστοσύνη καί υπομονή πρέπει είναι σημάδια αγάπης.

Love is patient and trusting, so it follows that trust and patience must be signs of love.

(The Gospel According to Trevor, chapter 5, verse 11)

I have a feeling today is the day, thought Dr. Haley Berkshire as she woke on Friday. The dust swirled in sunbeams filtering through metal blinds mangled over time, and a cockroach scooted for safety in the corner. But none of that mattered when compared with the excitement of the day. Lady Luck granted her the best shower in the shared women's bathroom facilities, and her new Victoria's Secret underwear looked particularly good against her hips this morning. She tugged her favorite jeans over them, topped the outfit with a perky blue pullover, and selected her most stylish comfortable shoes. Objectively, there was no telling what would happen today, but if it was to be a brush with Lord, she wanted to look her best.

She joined O'Shea and Jesse in the YMCA lobby, where they described their own tingles of anticipation. They, too, were dressed as smartly as their respective occupational and economic conditions permitted.

Morning breakfast was chatterful, as each shared their experiences of the previous day. Jesse told of the good people he met in Spanish Harlem, and the bad, and the kind and the eccentric individuals who used the subway. Berkshire told of meeting Gardiner and Shaver at the restaurant, and the audacity of her comments. "Am I a bad person for saying that?" she asked, and the vote was swift and unanimous in upholding her virtue. O'Shea recounted his visit to the church. "What do you make of it?" asked Berkshire. "That we absolutely must find the Testicle of Christ," he affirmed. "And, once we do, I have a lot more stuff to sort out."

When they finished breakfast, Berkshire recommended one more trip to the Riverside Library, where they completed a brief refresher course on oracles: Pythia, Dodona, Trophonius, Menestheus, as well as those of the Celts, Chinese, Pacific Islanders, Africans, and pre-Columbian Americans. They set off for Central Park assured in their knowledge; in fact, had "Oracles" been the Final Jeopardy category, any of them would have confidently bet everything.

They arrived at the Chess and Checkers House about 11:30. Berkshire staked out a table near the door while O'Shea checked out pieces, and he and Jesse started a game to pass the time. And pass it did, like a glacier.

With Phineas still absent at one o'clock, Berkshire visited the hot dog cart to buy lunch for everyone, including an extra pretzel for Jesse. Many of the chess players drifted away, soon to be replaced by new faces, none of whom was Phineas.

"How long do we wait?" asked O'Shea, who, for all his merits, had never been a patient man.

"All day," said Jesse. They were now on their sixth game, although neither was particularly attentive to the board so mistakes were plentiful. "He didn't say what time he was coming."

"All day," agreed Berkshire. "Absolutely."

"I sure hope he makes more sense than two days ago," O'Shea said, looking around at the various players. "But even at their best, we need to remember that oracles are notoriously ambiguous. You know the story about the Oracle of Delphi and King Croesus, right?"

"Of course," Berkshire said.

Jesse took his hand off his queen and looked up. "I don't," he said.

O'Shea elaborated, "According to legend, the King asked if he should attack Persia, and the Oracle's response was 'If you cross the river, a great empire will be destroyed.' The king thought this was a clear message, a guarantee of success, so he attacked Persia and was routed. Turned out the great empire was his own."

"Then I guess we'd better be smarter than King Croesus," Jesse acknowledged.

By three o'clock, O'Shea's priest's garb was soaked with sweat, and perspiration rolled down Berkshire's temple. Jesse pulled the Venice Beach bandana from his purple backpack and offered it to Berkshire, who used it to dab the moisture off her cheek.

"Don't you ever sweat?" O'Shea asked him.

"I sweat, sometimes," Jesse replied, "but only in much

more extreme conditions than this."

For the first time, Berkshire noticed the scar behind Jesse's left ear. It seemed to disappear into the hair on the back of his head, exactly how far it went she could not determine. She wondered what it would be like to have a roommate, and not a bad-looking one once he got cleaned up. Or maybe living with a man convinced he was the Son of God would be too burdensome, especially in Utah. What would the crazy widow across the street think? Fortunately, she did not have to decide these things today.

He looked up and caught her smiling at him. "What?" he asked.

"Nothing," she answered, and now O'Shea smiled as well.

The two men returned their attention to the game in an unconscious effort to avoid any awkwardness. After they exchanged bishops, O'Shea said, "Can I ask you guys something?" When Berkshire nodded, he continued, "Do you think I'm abnormal?"

"What do you mean?" asked Berkshire. "Why would you ask that?"

"The girl I was traveling with ... the woman, I mean ... said something—"

"Father, if you move your pawn up, you'll control the center of the board," said a voice, and they all turned at once. It was Phineas, dressed in the same shorts, slippers, hat, and bathrobe as Wednesday. He had changed his shirt.

Phineas insisted they finish their game, and his exaggerated gestures and facial expressions in response to their moves provided such interesting commentary that Berkshire studied him instead of watching the game itself.

O'Shea finally won, Phineas slapped him on the back, and they returned the board and pieces before adjourning to the comfort of a nearby shady tree.

"Any luck on finding his nut?" Phineas asked, pointing at Jesse.

"None yet," said Jesse.

"We wanted to talk to you some more," added Berkshire.

"I'll talk some more. Buy me a meal and I'll talk all night," Phineas said. "I know a place."

Phineas led them to a steakhouse just off Fifth Avenue, currently at a lull between lunch and dinner. He entered first and laid his bathrobe on the hostess stand. "Coat check," he announced.

They were seated at a booth, served water, and the waiter appeared with menus. This would be an expensive consultation, but with a priceless payoff. While Phineas glanced at a menu, Berkshire examined the restaurant impatiently. O'Shea turned to see the hostess lifting Phineas' robe with a broom handle and navigating it onto the coat rack near the front door. Jesse, meanwhile, focused his attention on this most unusual mystic with whom they shared a table.

When a basket of bread arrived, Phineas took the first piece. Berkshire noticed his eyes were once again glazing over, so she leaned closer. Struggling to break the bread, Phineas said, "Somewhere on an airplane, a man is trying to rip open a small bag of peanuts."

"I'm sorry," said O'Shea. "Are peanuts meant to be metaphorical?"

"Wake up to the adventure inside you," Phineas answered.

Berkshire sighed noticeably. "Trust me, Phineas, we're ready for—"

They were interrupted when the waiter reappeared. "We're not eating," explained Berkshire. "Just him."

The waiter frowned, but turned to Phineas and asked, "For you, sir?"

"Top sirloin, medium rare, with a baked potato and a beer. A large one."

"We have Pilsner Urquell, Heineken—"

"John Boston Beer tastes amazing," responded Phineas. "According to cannibals, so did John Boston."

"We don't carry, um, John Boston," said the waiter, obviously confused.

O'Shea turned to the waiter and whispered, "Just bring him a beer in a tall glass. Doesn't matter what kind."

When the waiter left, Berkshire turned to Phineas. "You were saying? About peanuts?"

"What about peanuts?" Phineas replied. O'Shea shook his head, burying his face in his hands with a sigh.

Phineas looked around the restaurant, then removed his right slipper, set it on the table, and picked at his pinkie toe. "After about age two, there's no such thing as having too much energy."

"That's true," said Berkshire, eyeing the slipper apprehensively. "Now, about the artifact."

"The Testicle of Christ?" asked Phineas. O'Shea looked up from his hands.

"That's the one," she affirmed. "We're trying to understand what you mean. What should we do?"

"Don't leave home without it," Phineas said as he replaced his slipper.

"But we don't have it," Jesse replied.

"Ohhhh. You want me to help you find it."

"Yes, we do," said Berkshire, sensing a breakthrough. "We want your wisdom to guide us."

"It's perfectly alright to be incompetent for hours on end," Phineas responded. "I am. And so is everyone I know."

"But we don't believe that," said O'Shea.

"Is your life more interesting than a squirrel's?" continued Phineas.

"I certainly hope it is," O'Shea replied.

The waiter delivered Phineas' glass of beer. "Thank you," O'Shea said to the waiter. The old man took a sip and licked his lips.

"Soup is good food," he said matter-of-factly.

"You ordered steak," Berkshire reminded him. "Remember?"

"It's what's for dinner," Phineas replied with a nod.

"Yes, it is," she confirmed.

Phineas eyed the television over the bar, now broadcasting the local weather report. On the electronic map, large swaths of red sliced across Pennsylvania and up into the Northeast—the very storm which chased O'Shea since Cleveland. The old man appeared deep in thought, as if trying to solve the unsolvable puzzle of the Seven Bridges of Königsberg in his head. Everyone else waited impatiently, not even daring to breathe. Perhaps this could be their answer.

"Without a TV, how would you know where to put the sofa?" Phineas finally asked, and all three exhaled in desperation.

"I gotta use the facilities," Phineas said, smiling. They slid out to let him pass, then huddled together.

"We've got peanuts, cannibals, and squirrels," summarized Jesse. "Too much energy. Incompetence. Soup and beef. TVs and sofas."

"I think the energy one might have been meaningful," said Berkshire. "Oracles often talk about energy vortexes and whatnot. I was watching him when he said that—"

"We really need to ask more direct questions," O'Shea interrupted. "There's absolutely no coherence here." Neither Berkshire nor Jesse disagreed.

Phineas returned and slid back into the booth just as his meal arrived. Once he enjoyed a few bites of his steak, his eyes seemed much clearer.

"Phineas, let's make this as simple and straightforward as possible," said Berkshire. "Can you tell us where we can find the Testicle of Christ?"

"The Testicle of Christ?" he repeated.

"That's right," O'Shea affirmed.

Waving his steak knife for emphasis, Phineas explained, "You can find whatever you're looking for by looking to the heavens."

"You mean through a telescope?" asked Berkshire.

"No, you need to go get it, just like anything of value. Love, fame, salvation, it doesn't matter." He turned to O'Shea. "Am I right, Father?"

"Great point," said O'Shea.

"Free your mind and your spirit," Phineas continued. "Be bold. Have wings. Seek the flame of liberty."

"Do you mean the Statue of Liberty?" asked Jesse.

Phineas nodded slowly, profoundly.

"When should we do this?" pushed Berkshire.

"As soon as you can," Phineas said, turning toward her slowly. She quivered with anticipation as he continued,

"Tonight. Don't wait. You cannot wait. He who hesitates ..."

O'Shea recoiled from the phrase, leaned back against the booth's black vinyl, and threw up his hands. "But that's impossible."

Phineas' eyes glazed over once again. "Impossible is nothing," he said. "Just do it."

"Can you tell us what, exactly, we're looking for?" asked Berkshire. "Is it in a box? Maybe in a secret compartment? Is there some sort of riddle? Phineas?" But the old man's mind had run to the edge of his world and jumped into the pit of monsters. He did not respond to another question for the rest of dinner. Berkshire glumly paid the tab while Phineas recovered his bathrobe from the coat rack and put it on with fanfare suitable for a prince boasting a garment woven with golden yarn.

When they walked him outside, he turned and wandered off, mumbling so incoherently that other pedestrians gave him the widest berth New York sidewalks would allow.

"Let's follow him," O'Shea suggested, and they did, a discreet distance behind as he rambled uptown on Third Avenue. Just past Sixty-sixth, Phineas passed the Nike store, thrust his fist into the air, and yelled "Just do it!"

Then he started to run, his blue bathrobe flowing behind, and they lost him. "How in the world do you run that fast in slippers?" O'Shea asked, and none could offer an answer.

They crossed through Central Park and stopped at a bench to gain clarity and consensus.

"He said the Statue of Liberty," Berkshire began. "We know that for sure."

"The flame of liberty, to be exact," corrected Jesse.

"The torch, then."

"And tonight," said O'Shea. "He definitely said tonight."

Jesse added, "He said we cannot wait. And I think I know why." Their looks begged for elaboration, and he continued. "The thing about the peanuts. 'Somewhere on an airplane, a man is trying to rip open a small bag of peanuts.' He's telling us that other people are trying to find it, too."

"You know, that makes sense," said Berkshire.

"So we've got to get to the Statue of Liberty's torch, tonight," summarized O'Shea. "And we need to fly there, right? He told us to have wings."

"That's right," Berkshire agreed.

"That leaves me with only one more question," O'Shea continued. "But it's a big one."

"How are we going to do it?" answered Berkshire.

O'Shea bobbed his head earnestly. "Exactly."

"I have an idea," said Jesse. "I need to do some reconnaissance, but I think I know what we have to do."

Twenty-one
THE JESUS NUT

Πηγαίνετε τολμηρά, χωρίς φόβο ή δισταγμό, καί σίγουρα βρείσετε τόν Θεόν.

Go boldly, without fear or hesitation, and you will most certainly find God.

(The Gospel According to Trevor, chapter 11, verse 15)

A blast of thunder hurried them through Central Park, but they managed to return to the YMCA before getting wet. Jesse said, "Give me four hours. I need to wait until after dark, but if I am who I think I am, we can do this thing tonight."

"Where are you going?" asked O'Shea.

"Just give me four hours, okay?"

"Be careful, Jesse," said Berkshire. He smiled, touched her hand, and slipped away.

O'Shea went to his room and pulled out his Bible. The Good Book had not been out of his suitcase since Seattle and was overdue for some attention. He opened to the book of Matthew and began to read.

Berkshire went to her room, found a pen in her purse,

and tore a sheet of paper from the spiral notebook she brought from Utah. "Dear Aunt Sally," she began writing.

Jesse took the 1 train to Penn Station, having decided the subway was great fun, and spent an hour at a Starbucks waiting for dusk. Many times he had waited like this, often longer, always in more austere conditions. Once satisfied with the light outside, he left the Starbucks and trudged toward the Hudson River through the growing drizzle. By the time he reached the Javits Center, his clothes were damp and the sky was black. He made a left turn and walked four blocks south to arrive at his destination: the West Thirtieth Street Heliport.

The area was safeguarded by tall fencing topped with razor wire, all gates secured electronically. He whistled and listened for guard dogs, but none responded to his call. He shook the fence and listened again, with the same result. As he surveilled the perimeter, he found nothing out of the ordinary. Through the fence, he saw more than a dozen aircraft, and although he guessed more were parked out of sight, he was still hopeful for visual confirmation of his target. Most of the birds were sleek newer helicopters, many adorned with corporate logos. But then he saw it: a Bell UH-1 Iroquois helicopter. A Huey. She was a comfortable sight, perfect in fact. "Hello, beautiful," he purred.

As he continued his reconnoiter around the perimeter, he was unexpectedly blinded by headlights and he heard the single blast of a siren. He thought momentarily of running, but that probably would have been the end of it all, so he froze and put his hands behind his head while two of New York's Finest pulled up, turned off their engine, and approached.

"Whatcha doin', buddy?" asked one of the cops.

"Just looking at the helicopters," Jesse said.

"We can see that," said the other, who was taller than his partner. "Why?"

"I used to fly when I was in the army. I just like looking now."

"Looking time is over," said the tall cop. "Move along."

"Yessir," said Jesse. "Sorry for the bother."

The police car drove away and he turned uptown, thankful his story worked. He performed the last of his reconnaissance before heading back to the YMCA in the rain.

"I've got this," Jesse told them when he returned, drying his hair with a towel while he spoke. "We move out in one hour. Dark clothes, quiet shoes. No fragrances. No cell phones. And bring anything you have that's made of metal."

"Are you going to tell us the plan?" asked Berkshire.

"The less you know, the better," he responded, partly because he was still working out the details in his head.

"Sounds very mysterious," she said.

"Is it legal?" added O'Shea.

"No questions ... please," insisted Jesse. "Haley, can you go to the store and buy two screwdrivers? One flat and one Phillips. And a box of paper clips." She nodded.

Jesse turned to O'Shea and continued, "Brian, find some metal pop-tops, you know, from soda cans. Half a dozen is fine."

This was Jesse's show now, or dare we say the Son of God's. Each of them spent the next hour in a frenzy of preparation. Fortunately, Jesse's Trenton T-shirt was black, easily turned inside out to hide its graphics. He lay down in bed and closed his eyes, trying to visualize every step of the mission, every contingency, every possible complication. His hands moved and his eyes flitted behind dark eyelids as he saw the plan in three-dimensional vividness, stopping only when O'Shea, still wearing his all-black priest outfit, returned with the pop-top requisition and offered them to Jesse. "Perfect," Jesse said, slipping them into the small pocket of his purple backpack. Meanwhile, Berkshire visited a local drugstore and purchased the supplies, along with a navy blue long-sleeved T-shirt since she brought only cute colorful clothes. At the appointed hour, they mustered in the lobby of the West Side YMCA. Jesse's purple backpack contained, among other items, a woolen blanket appropriated from the small closet in their room.

They took the subway to Penn Station, each on a different car lest suspicion be raised. Then, for the second time that night, Jesse walked toward the Heliport, this time with the professor and the priest paralleling him on the opposite side of the street. The buildings offered little cover from the rainfall, and they regathered at the Twelfth Avenue bus stop just north of Thirtieth Street with squishy shoes and glistening skin.

"Now I can tell you the plan. I'm going in there," Jesse said, pointing at the Heliport through a break in the trees which ran down the center of Twelfth.

Berkshire spoke first. "You're doing *what*? How are you going to—"

Jesse raised his hand to cut her off. "I'm going in there. I need approximately fifteen minutes. Haley, you stay here at the bus stop. Brian, you go to the corner and hang out. There's not much to look at, but find something. Most important, both of you need to listen. If you hear a whistle like this ..." He softly whistled "whee-ah-wee," then continued, "meet me at that gate." He pointed at a gate thirty meters up the street.

"But if I whistle like this ..." He softly whistled "wheet-wheet-wheet-wheet." "If you hear that whistle, then we are aborting the mission, without delay. Brian, you immediately head two blocks east on Thirtieth Street, take the stairs up to that park ... the High Line ... and walk back in this direction. Haley, you go up to Thirty-fourth, turn right, and get on the High Line there. You'll cross paths soon enough, and you can evaluate the situation."

"What if a bus comes and we miss your whistle?" she asked.

"Or what if a bunch of people get off and it's too noisy?" added O'Shea.

"Last bus on this route came at 10:35," Jesse explained. "Should be quiet the rest of the night. Now, worst-case scenario, if you don't hear either of those whistles, that's also an abort."

"I don't like that one," Berkshire said. "What would happen to you?"

"Don't worry about me," he answered, yet her concern was obvious in the way she chewed her lower lip. "While I'm gone, watch for cops, but please be casual about it. Not like the restaurant in Philadelphia."

"Jesse," Berkshire said, "I know why you're doing this, and I hope it works out for you."

"Thank you."

"But Brian, you never told me exactly why you got involved in this whole crazy scheme. Was it just the fact that everyone hated me? In that case, I could have published my carrot cake recipe, which really isn't very good."

"Nah, the fact that everyone hated you just sealed the deal."

"Then what was it?" Berkshire continued.

"*Agape.*"

"What do you mean?"

"It's all there at the very beginning," O'Shea explained. "The Gospel According to Trevor, chapter one, verse one, where Jesus says, 'God is love ...'"

Jesse joined in, "'To love God, you must love all others: greater or lesser, woman or man, native or immigrant. Love all ...'"

Now Berkshire joined in, too, and they recited in unison, "'... No matter who they love, where they live, or what they believe.'"

O'Shea finished the passage on his own. "'This is the message,' said Christ. 'Everything else is merely elaboration.'"

Both Berkshire and Jesse smiled.

"Trevor got it right," O'Shea said. "That's religion in a nutshell ... or, at least, it should be. And nobody ever said it better."

"Okay, give me all your metal items," said Jesse.

Berkshire handed him the two screwdrivers and the paper clips, a lipstick tube, a hair barrette, and a ballpoint pen. O'Shea offered a bottle opener and his room key. Jesse added them to the pop-tops and the Venice Beach keychain in his purple backpack, along with an aluminum can plucked from the trash.

"Anything else?"

Berkshire blushed as she reached into her purse and

withdrew her "friend," her DiddleBang DeluXX, and offered it to Jesse.

"Please don't judge," she said.

"Who am I to judge?" he replied. "I sleep behind a dumpster."

She smiled as he took the DiddleBang DeluXX and zipped it up in his backpack.

"Here we go," Jesse said. "See you guys in a few minutes. I hope."

Berkshire stopped him and kissed him delicately on the cheek. He paused for a moment to consider it, then dashed across Twelfth Avenue while his two partners assumed their respective posts. Berkshire's bus stop kept her somewhat dry, while O'Shea rummaged through a trash can until he found a newspaper to shield himself from the downpour.

Jesse acquired the location he scouted a few hours prior, checked up and down Twelfth for traffic, and scaled the chain link fence in mere seconds. At the top, he laid the purloined blanket over the razor wire and adroitly rolled over the top, snatching the blanket on his way down. He was in, with no sign of breach.

He moved silently across the heliport toward a singular objective: the Bell UH-1 Iroquois helicopter. His beautiful Huey. Although this one bore an NYC logo on its side, it was otherwise as familiar as a favorite pair of shoes might be to a more prosperous man.

The copter's skids were chained to a thick iron ring embedded in the pavement, and its hatch featured a lock with what appeared to be a one-inch cam. Both were easy. Jesse released the padlock on the chain with one of the pop-tops (a trick he remembered learning from a friend, long ago), slid the chain off the skids, and jimmied the hatch with the flathead screwdriver. He entered the cockpit to find the power switch safeguarded by a retrofitted security device, which he was uncertain he could penetrate within his time constraints. Undaunted, he dumped the contents of his purple backpack onto the seat and sifted through the various metal items in front of him, then utilized the Phillips screwdriver to disassemble the dashboard. Moments later, his Venice Beach keychain, two more pop-tops, a paper clip, O'Shea's bottle opener, and parts from Berkshire's vibrator brought the engine to life.

After shutting down the Huey and cleaning the unused items off its seat, he jumped back onto the tarmac, whistled "whee-ah-wee," and double-timed toward the rendezvous point. He had been gone for twelve minutes.

When they heard the whistle, O'Shea and Berkshire crossed the soggy street and hurried to the gate as instructed. Twelfth Avenue was deserted by now, and both considered this a fortuitous circumstance. But they said nothing of it; in fact, they said nothing at all.

Jesse had already disabled the lock when they arrived at the gate, and they slipped through before he relatched it. He waved for them to follow as he darted across the heliport. Within moments, they stood before the helicopter.

"Hop aboard," Jesse said with a welcoming sweep of his hand.

"How did you do that?" asked Berkshire.

"Wait a minute," said O'Shea. "We're going to steal a helicopter?"

"No, we're going to *borrow* a helicopter," Jesse

responded. "And only for a few hours." Then he turned to Berkshire. "To answer your question, I flew one of these in Afghanistan."

"You served in Afghanistan?" she asked.

"I saw it all last night in a dream. Operation Eagle Fury. I was a helicopter pilot with the Special Forces. We engaged the enemy in the Bahgran Valley for forty-three straight hours. I was a damn fine pilot, and my guys were badass. But so were the Taliban."

"What happened?" O'Shea asked.

"On one of my airdrops, they hit my Huey with an RPG-7. Funny thing, they got those weapons from us when they were fighting the Soviets. Anyway, we went down. Two of my men sustained serious burns. And I was never the same, obviously."

Berkshire gasped. "Oh my God, that's horrible."

"They gave me a Purple Heart in the hospital. I must have lost it, though." He laughed at his inability to remember, adding, "Now I just have a purple backpack."

Rain dripping from her hair, Berkshire pointed at the helicopter. "So we're supposed to go up in that thing? In this weather?" There was a loud clang as the wind bounced the metal halyard cable against a steel flagpole fifty feet away. Their wet clothes stuck to them.

"I've flown in worse conditions," Jesse reassured. "Compared to when the enemy is shooting at you, rain is nothing."

"But I'm terrified of flying!" Berkshire blurted.

Jesse grasped her shoulders and looked into her eyes. "No you're not," he said gently. "You're not terrified of anything anymore."

She deliberated for a moment, then announced, "You

are absolutely right. Let's get this thing up in the air."

Jesse bade her be patient. "Father," Jesse said, "before we go, could you please offer a blessing?"

"Of course," he said, and they all bowed their heads.

"God of love, power, and all understanding, we stand now prepared to cross the Rubicon, but we do it with new friends for whom we are eternally thankful. We humbly ask that each of us might gain from tonight's quest what we seek, and what we have long sought, and most of all what You desire for us to achieve. Please show us mercy through the mystery of faith, so that we each find God in our own way. Amen."

"Amen," the others echoed, then climbed into the Huey. Jesse, entering last, took the driver's seat, placed his Venice Beach postcard on the dash, and shut the door behind him.

"Home?" Berkshire said, and he nodded.

Once again he fired up the engine, and Berkshire gasped at the immensity of its roar. "Hold on tight," Jesse said as he pulled the collective pitch control and worked the torque pedals and throttle to get airborne. The Statue of Liberty was a five-mile trip down the Hudson River and, at a maximum airspeed of 110 knots, they would be there in three or four minutes.

"Look at all the lights of the city. It's so beautiful up here," Berkshire said.

O'Shea was equally impressed with the views, but as the rain continued to grow in its ferocity, his trepidation grew along with it. "Hard to see out the window in this storm," he said, hoping for some sort of reassurance.

"Not a problem," answered Jesse. "Just look for the big lady with her arm sticking up in the sky."

As they approached Battery Park on the south end of Manhattan, they spotted Ellis Island in the distance with Lady Liberty just beyond. The rain and wind were beginning to jerk the Huey around, but nevertheless they could not contain their excitement. The statue was now within reach, and Jesse maneuvered the chopper for his approach. The Testicle of Christ would soon be theirs.

Suddenly, a lightning bolt flashed through the sky, striking the top of the helicopter. The craft shuddered, the engine sputtered, and the Bell UH-1 Iroquois plunged violently into the Hudson River.

Twenty-two
RESURRECTION

Όταν όλα φαίνονται πλέον χαμένα, τότε βρεθήσοιο.

When all seems most lost, that is when you shall be found.

(The Gospel According to Trevor, chapter 6, verse 3)

Residents of both Manhattan and Jersey City, across the river, called police to report a stunning flash of light in the stormy night sky. Some described it as being like an arc welding project or a giant sparkler, while others wondered if someone was shooting a Hollywood movie. One woman in the West Village swore it must be the beginning of a terrorist attack, while a man in Tribeca theorized Ellis Island erupted. The stories offered a fascinating diversity of descriptions, and perhaps an intriguing window into the psyches of the various callers had Sigmund Freud been available to interpret. The watch commander from Lower Manhattan's First Precinct was soon convinced to send out a patrol boat to investigate. It took two hours from the time of the first call before they located the site of the accident.

The cranes eventually extracted three large pieces

from the water: the front half of the Huey, the back half, and the rotor and propeller. Miscellaneous debris still floated nearby and countless smaller pieces of metal sunk to the river bottom, where they would join centuries of Hudson River refuse among the fish, never to be found. One diver located a pair of shoes, badly worn, while another found a soggy picture postcard from Venice Beach, California.

Around daybreak, recovery crews dragged the helicopter's carcass onto the Incident Command Post at Battery Park Slip 6. Authorities now began the process of tracing the helicopter's serial numbers, with the objective of figuring out who owned it, where it came from, who was flying it, and what in God's name they were thinking going up in such nasty weather. Investigators soon determined it was a city-owned helicopter, parked until last night at the Thirtieth Street Heliport. But that finding only scraped the surface. Their curiosity demanded more, as did the requirements of official New York Metropolitan Form 87/14A, the report mandated in cases of lost or damaged city property. Unfortunately, as the form was designed primarily to account for damaged office equipment, filling it out would prove challenging even if they knew all the answers. Which they did not.

The most pressing of unanswered questions was what exactly happened to the helicopter, because that determination would establish bureaucratic jurisdiction, chain of command, and rates of overtime pay. In the same way a hammer sees every problem as a nail, each investigator considered the event from his or her own unique skill set and field of expertise. This meant some worked in opposition to others, but since none of the callers' hypotheses or descriptions comported with any realistic scenario, this shotgun approach would have to suffice. So while the police spent their time trying to figure out why the helicopter went up in the air, state aviation investigators tried to figure out how it came back down.

Toward this objective, a mechanic inspected the wreckage, with a state investigator following like a hungry puppy.

"Never seen that before in my whole livin' life," the mechanic said. As a city employee and longtime member of New York City Local 246, he had witnessed exploding cars, runaway garbage trucks, cranes with minds of their own, fire hydrants which didn't work when there was a fire and worked when there wasn't, and all other mechanical oddities and improbabilities which are part of the weird fabric of daily life in New York City. Yet he still scratched his head over this one.

"I think maybe it hit the Jesus nut," the mechanic finally theorized. "The lightning did."

"The lightning hit the what?" asked the investigator. He was new to his position with the New York State Aviation Bureau, recently transferred there after making a crucial math error while working at the New York Workers Compensation Board. He was assigned to this particular crash only because a single-craft incident in the river did not warrant calling any of the veteran investigators in the middle of the night and making them drive all the way into the city from Great Neck on a Saturday morning. Even if it did involve a stolen helicopter.

The investigator had been on scene four hours and counting, and he desperately wanted French toast and coffee.

"The Jesus nut," continued the mechanic. "The retaining nut that transfers the entire weight of the helicopter from the main rotor shaft to the rotor itself."

One look at the investigator established he was no less confused, so the mechanic simplified, "The nut that holds the main rotor in place."

"Okaayyy," said the investigator, drawing out the word as he struggled to make sense of it all. "I think I get it. The thing that the other thing goes into." He illustrated with hand gestures which, from a distance, looked like a third-grader explaining sexual intercourse to his friends on the playground. "But I don't understand the name. Why is it called the Jesus nut?"

"When somethin' happens to it," said the mechanic, "it's bad."

"What do you mean, bad?"

"Fucking catastrophic. All you can do is scream 'Oh, Jesus!'"

But even as they pieced together a tapestry of ideas about the helicopter, investigators and police were both stymied by one elusive yet vital piece of information: Where were the bodies of the pilot and of any passengers?

"Keep looking," ordered the officer in charge of the Incident Command Post. "That chopper sure as hell didn't fly itself."

Half a mile away, anchored just north of Ellis Island, sits the Honorable William Wall—a floating barge, home to the Manhattan Yacht Club and the finest selection of top-shelf scotch in New York. With the sun peeking above the Atlantic and filtering through the skyscrapers of Lower Manhattan, security guards and morning prep cooks arrived for the early shift at the Honorable William Wall. If they noticed the salvage operation at work just off the bow, they chose not to mention it. This being New York, after all, the divers could have been searching for almost anything—from the mayor's wallet to the lost continent of Atlantis.

As their ferry dropped them and they boarded the barge, the early shift was startled to discover three people already on deck. A priest sat in a deck chair, his arm twisted grotesquely. Blood trickled from a deep gash above a woman's eye. Her head rested in the lap of a barefoot man wearing an inside-out T-shirt and clutching a purple backpack.

"What the fuck?" said a security guard as he drew his service revolver. Jesse, his eyelids fighting to stay open, raised his hands to ask for calm but said nothing.

"Oh, Jesus," said O'Shea. "Thank God you're here." He pointed weakly at his arm. "I think it's broken."

"It sure is," said the security guard. "That's nasty looking. And I'm gonna break your other arm if you don't tell me what's going on. How'd you get here?"

"We had an accident last night," O'Shea said. "Went down in the river." Then, pointing at Jesse, added, "He saved our lives."

"Is this true?" asked the security guard, and Berkshire nodded feebly.

"Are you guys stupid or what? You went boating last night? In that crazy weather?"

"Yeah, we know," is all O'Shea offered. "Look, we really need a doctor right now."

The United States Coast Guard, NYPD, and the Honorable William Wall's assistant bar manager all arrived at the barge at about the same time. The three intruders were read their Miranda rights and taken into custody while the bar manager checked to make sure nobody stole any liquor. The City of New York paid for emergency room physicians to set O'Shea's arm and sew thirteen stitches into Berkshire's head. Even though Jesse insisted he was fine, the doctors checked him out anyway, and discovered nothing unusual except for an old scar which ran from behind his left ear to the top of his skull. And then they were transported to the First Precinct, fingerprinted, and shoved into holding cells.

They appeared in city court two days later, first case on the Monday morning docket, to that point still legally disconnected from the mystery of the helicopter whose pieces now resided in the parking lot behind the inventory room at the station house.

Each defendant sat beside their own court-appointed lawyer. Berkshire's legal counsel was a young woman, probably fresh out of law school, who gnawed incessantly on her pencil. A middle-aged man wearing a blue paisley tie and brown suit represented Jesse. O'Shea drew a younger man, flashy, hair slicked back like his day job might be with the Corleone family. With six people at the defendants' table, things were cozy.

"All rise," said the bailiff as the judge entered the courtroom. When everyone was seated, the judge began, "This is an arraignment on the charge of criminal trespassing against Haley Berkshire, Jesse Morales, and Brian William Callum Robert O'Shea."

"That's quite a mouthful," said O'Shea's lawyer. The priest replied wanly, "So I've heard."

"I see you're all represented by counsel," said the

judge. "You understand, I trust, that each of you has a different lawyer to avoid any potential conflict of interest." The defendants nodded.

"Very well, let's get started." The judge shuffled through some papers. "In addition to the aforementioned trespassing charge," he said, "we now have another issue of far greater significance." The three defendants sighed and slumped in resignation.

The judge continued, "There seems to have been no recovery of any watercraft in the vicinity of the Honorable William Wall. However, the recovery of items from the wreckage of a certain helicopter ... I'm sure you're familiar with the situation, since the *Post* still has it on their front page ... has led the District Attorney to file additional charges against the defendants. These charges are another count of criminal trespassing, third-degree burglary, second-degree grand larceny, reckless endangerment, and operating an aircraft without a valid license."

The court-appointed lawyers, surprised by this new development, looked at their clients. The best response any received was a shrug from O'Shea, who then hoisted his arm cast onto the table with a thud.

"Defendant Haley Berkshire," continued the judge. "How do you plead?"

She stood and said, "Not guilty, your honor, I guess."

"Defendant Jesse Morales, how do you plead?"

Jesse began to stand, wearily.

"If it please the court ...," came a voice from behind them. Recognizing the voice, Jesse spun to see a man in full Army Service Uniform: navy blue coat with two stars on his epaulets, tie, service ribbons, aviator wings, the whole nine yards of military splendor. Jesse snapped to attention and saluted as the general stepped forward, his hat tucked underneath his arm.

"At ease, son," he said to Jesse, then turned toward the judge. "If it please the court, I would like to speak on Mister Morales' behalf."

"That's not standard procedure at an arraignment, General," said the judge.

"I understand, Your Honor," the general replied. "But I hope you'll agree this whole case is not exactly standard, either. If the court would indulge me for two minutes ..." The judge motioned for him to proceed, and the defendants sat down to listen.

"Your honor, I am General Angelo Metcalf, currently assigned to the United States Pentagon. I do not presume to know all the facts of the case, as we only learned about this situation last night. However, I believe that if anyone else was flying that bird, we would not be here today because all three of them would have bought the farm." He indicated the three defendants, all still very much alive, while Berkshire reached past her lawyer and tenderly placed her hand on Jesse's arm.

"What I do know beyond any reasonable doubt is that Mister Morales is a war hero. During Operation Eagle Fury, nine February 2003, Warrant Officer Jesse Morales flew eleven helicopter sorties without rest, each time delivering personnel and supplies and then extracting wounded from one of the fiercest battles in the history of our engagement in Afghanistan. On the third sortie, his aircraft sustained significant damage, yet he continued flying for another twelve hours, always in the face of enemy fire. On sortie number eleven, his aircraft was hit by a rocket-propelled grenade and went down in flames.

Disregarding his own safety and injuries to both his head and groin, and under assault from the enemy, Warrant Officer Morales rescued his two crew members from the wreckage and dragged them to safety."

"Very impressive, General," said the judge. "How do you know all this?"

"I was commanding officer," replied General Metcalf, "and that's more or less what it says on the citation." He turned to Jesse and added, "I've been lugging a Distinguished Service Cross all over the world for the past sixteen years. Right now it's sitting in my desk drawer at the Pentagon. I really wish you'd come pick it up."

"Yes, sir," Jesse whispered.

"That's all well and good," said the judge, "but what about our helicopter?"

General Metcalf assumed his most assertive pose. "Your honor, this man belongs in college, not in prison. Per that appraisal, I have been authorized by the United States Army to offer the City of New York two decommissioned Bell UH-1 Iroquois helicopters in exchange for the dismissal of all charges against this particular defendant."

Jesse shook his head, emphatically indicating Berkshire and O'Shea as well.

"Against all three defendants," Metcalf corrected. "You will have one more Huey than you started with, plus Mister Morales has identified an important municipal security breach you can now resolve."

The judge looked at the District Attorney. "How about it?"

No one dared breathe as they awaited response.

"Without prejudice," the DA bristled. His right

eyebrow twitched. "If they ever get so much as a ticket for littering, we will immediately refile all charges."

"Sounds reasonable to me," said the judge, who turned to face the defendants. "My recommendation ... which I strongly urge you to follow ... is that you leave New York. As expeditiously, and permanently, as possible. Until that time, don't even think about throwing anything on the ground." He passed the case file to his clerk. "I hope I make myself clear," the judge added before banging his gavel. "Case dismissed."

"Oh, thank you Jesus!" cried Berkshire, who then gasped, put her hand over her mouth, and cast a worried glance toward Jesse. O'Shea, too, looked for Jesse's reaction.

"Yes, thank you Jesus," Jesse replied quietly.

He stood and hugged General Metcalf before stepping back to indicate the others. "Sir, these are my friends, Haley and Brian."

"Pleasure to meet you both," Metcalf said as he shook their hands.

"Excuse me," interrupted the paisley tie attorney, pointing toward the door at the back of the courtroom, "but we need to vacate."

"By all means," said the general, who stood aside for the others to pass. As they exited the court, O'Shea could not help looking back to see if the judge, realizing his grievous judicial error, was now dispatching security to corral the three felons. But no guards rushed toward them, so O'Shea rejoined the others. The male lawyers' expensive wingtips, the woman's pumps, and the general's shiny oxfords clacked down the impressive hallway to the elevator, and they rode together to the first floor.

As they stepped into the lobby, the pencil gnawer and the Corleone lawyer discreetly slipped away, while General Metcalf placed his hand on paisley tie's shoulder. "Nice work, counselor," he said.

The attorney responded with an uneasy chuckle, followed by a huge sigh of relief. "To be perfectly honest, I had no idea what I was going to do."

"I know," said General Metcalf, and there was a discomforting pause.

"It was, um, it was nice to meet all of you," the attorney finally said, before scampering back into the solace of an open elevator.

The general led the others outside, where they were treated to a crystal blue sky.

"If you don't mind me asking, sir," said Jesse, "how did you find me?"

"You got yourself arrested," replied Metcalf, adjusting his coat to achieve full military crispness. "The police lifted your fingerprints off some of the items you used to hotwire the helicopter. Damn clever improvisation on that, by the way. Last night the Pentagon got a fingerprint request, an alert technician called me, and an hour later I jumped on a transport."

"Please thank the technician," Jesse said.

The general shook his head. "Negative. You can thank him yourself. And then you can tell me the whole story. Just don't make me regret this."

Metcalf placed his hat on his head and turned to the others. "Thank you for finding Morales. He's a good man."

"Yes he is," affirmed Berkshire.

"And if there's anything I can do for either of you ..."

O'Shea answered, "As a matter of fact, my car's been in a parking garage since Wednesday, at thirty-eight bucks a day. You think maybe you can get some sort of special military discount?"

The others laughed as the General, who hated waiting, stepped forward to hail a cab.

"I was completely serious about that," O'Shea protested to his friends while a yellow bullet zipped across two lanes to pull up in front of them.

"You want this one?" Metcalf asked as he reached for the door. When he opened it, horrible techno music flooded out.

Berkshire cringed. "No thanks. We'll take the subway."

The uptown 1 train was so packed they could not even speak to one another. Jesse found himself pushed against a young man carrying a trumpet case. Berkshire squirmed to avoid a cat carrier jabbing her in the ribs and its occupant, a twelve-pound Siamese, hissing at her while its owner read a novel, oblivious. O'Shea, smashed against one of the vertical railings, endeavored to keep from whacking anyone with his arm cast. The trip lasted half an hour and it seemed like they were forced to hold their breath the entire time, as each stop added even more passengers to the underground sardine can on wheels. When the train pulled into the Fifty-ninth Street/Columbus Circle station, they were barely able to disentangle themselves in time to jump onto the platform before it took off again.

A short while later, the three not-quite felons walked into the West Side YMCA, causing the desk clerk to look up from his newspaper. "Haven't seen you guys in a few days," he said. "We were beginning to wonder."

"We were at the Yacht Club," Berkshire replied, and Jesse suppressed a laugh. "We'll be checking out in an hour."

"It's after noon," said the clerk, looking over his glasses at Jesse's footwear, orange flip-flops courtesy of the New York penal system. "We'll have to charge you for another night."

Berkshire grunted her assent before she hurried upstairs to take her third quick shower of the trip. Her hair still damp, she packed her luggage and rolled it downstairs to handle payment. As she signed her credit card receipt, the clerk asked, "You hear what happened?"

"What happened when?" Berkshire replied, disinterested.

"Friday night," the clerk explained. "Someone stole a helicopter and crashed it in the river. Can you believe it? A freakin' helicopter?"

"Amazing what people will do," she said. Finding a seat in the lobby, she began reading a stray copy of the *New York Post*.

Jesse enjoyed what he knew could be his final shower for a very long time. He shook his hair dry as he filed down the austere hallway, reflecting on the simple dignity of having a closing door and a bed. Back in his room, he pulled on his only pair of pants—which still smelled faintly of the Hudson River—and his Venice Beach T-shirt. Needing little time to gather his own meager belongings, he helped pack O'Shea's bags before joining Berkshire downstairs.

O'Shea changed into civilian clothes, then retrieved his Toyota Camry from the parking garage—six days at thirty-eight dollars a day plus a ten-dollar tip for the attendant, which was apparently fair compensation for the extraordinary skill of hanging a set of car keys on a hook. In total, it was more than his monthly car payment, but he had little choice.

He double-parked in front of the YMCA and they quickly loaded the luggage into the Camry's trunk while enduring the honking of impatient Manhattanites. Jesse noticed a cop observing them from across Sixty-third.

"Hang on a minute," Jesse said to the others, chasing down a candy bar wrapper that danced along a gentle breeze. Once he deposited the offending litter into a nearby garbage can, he scuttled into the back seat. "Now we can go."

Thirty blocks passed in conflicted silence until O'Shea stopped at Penn Station just after three o'clock.

"Thank you for everything, Father," Jesse said. He stepped onto the pavement and opened the passenger door for Berkshire, who turned to O'Shea and asked, "What are you going to do?"

O'Shea shifted into park. "Head west, back to Seattle. After that, I really don't know."

"Me, neither," she answered, and looked at Jesse.

"I'm supposed to go to D.C., I guess," Jesse said, shouldering his purple backpack. "And then ..." He trailed off and shrugged.

"This really threw me for a loop," the priest added.

"Me, too," Berkshire agreed as she got out of the car. A horn jolted her, and she looked toward it but responded with only a sigh. While Jesse hauled Berkshire's suitcase from the trunk, she turned back toward O'Shea. "Have a safe trip, Brian," she said.

O'Shea watched them disappear into the crush of

humanity surrounding Penn Station. When he could no longer see them, he battled his way back into Manhattan traffic and towards the LEGO funnel which would convey him into New Jersey and on his way home.

EPILOGUE

Dr. Haley Berkshire took the Lake Shore Limited back to Chicago, then the California Zephyr home to Salt Lake City. Except for occasional incognito trips to Jitterbug Coffee, she spent most of the next three weeks inside her house, trying to reconcile her failed quest and figure out what she would be able to produce in support of her sabbatical. Although unsure of the exact requirements, she assumed a scar on her forehead would be considered insufficient.

In October, Robbie the Home Depot guy informed her that a faculty member of Salt Lake Community College's Religious Studies Department would be retiring in the spring, thereby opening a teaching position for the next academic year. Realizing how badly she missed her interactions with students, Berkshire applied, nailed the interview, and was offered the position and, with it, an even better salary than she earned at the University. Better still, no research agenda was required or even expected. She accepted on the spot.

Saying goodbye to Dr. Ronald S. Wexford was enjoyable. Saying goodbye to his secretary Roxanne was particularly satisfying.

Freed from the demands of academic research and with months before her new appointment was to begin, Berkshire devoted herself to becoming the best teacher possible, beginning with an overhaul of her lecture notes and tests. She joined the local gym, at first limiting her workouts to late nights when few could witness her painful efforts on the StairMaster. As her fitness improved, she supplemented her training with yoga classes and even became friends with one of the instructors. Otherwise, she mostly spent her days reading, gardening, and learning to play the accordion, a pursuit her mother vetoed when Haley was a child. Her hydrangeas flourished under her more regular care, and she often tended them while wearing yoga pants.

"For a dentist," the widow across the street mumbled to herself, "she's got a cute little ass."

Jesse Morales traveled by train to Washington, D.C.—this trip with a ticket, courtesy of Dr. Haley Berkshire—and spent his first night sleeping in Potomac Park, which he found far more restful than the holding cells at the First Precinct in New York.

In the morning, Pentagon security detained him for more than an hour, then took another thirty minutes to escort him to General Metcalf's office in the cavernous building. The Department of Veterans Affairs helped him land a two-day-a-week job shuttling roughnecks via helicopter to and from an offshore oil rig located a hundred miles off the coast of Houston in the Gulf of Mexico, so he packed his Distinguished Service Cross and a new pile of official-looking papers into his purple backpack and headed nervously for Texas.

Once he arrived, Jesse slowly furnished an apartment and, from his small dining table, sent thank-you cards to his friends Tommy and Jeong in Venice Beach and to General Metcalf at the Pentagon. In October, finally confident this was not merely some fantastic dream, he splurged on a bed and a set of dishes, bought a used Mustang with enough quirks to keep him tinkering, and celebrated with a box of Red Vines.

With the assistance of the GI Bill and a phone call from the Pentagon attesting to his aptitude, Jesse began classes at Rice University in the spring. Although his academic advisor suggested he start slowly, he jumped in with both feet: a major in Mechanical Engineering, to engage his passion for creating, building, and fixing; and a minor in Poverty, Justice and Human Capabilities, which provided him with the tools and the opportunity to help homeless veterans. As much as he loved helicopters, he could think of nothing to inspire him more.

Jesse gave away hundreds of dollars to Houston's homeless veterans, plus shepherded them to medical care, shelters, rehab, and counseling appointments. He served as gracious host when Berkshire visited her family in March—fetching her from the airport, calming her with a double latte, and sleeping on his floor so she could have the bed. She spent a day tagging along to Jesse's classes at Rice, but refused his offer to purchase a Groupon for a nighttime helicopter tour of the city. Once was enough of that.

Father Brian William Callum Robert O'Shea was, not surprisingly, relieved of his pastoral duties at Saint Helen of Mercy in Seattle. It was just as well, because he knew somewhere around Indiana that he must resign his position anyway. He now understood he was a man of God but also merely a man, human and flawed, unable to live up to the unrealistic expectations of the priesthood.

For the time being, he worked at the Fred Meyer grocery store in Boise, Idaho and lived with his mother while his arm healed and he reassessed his options. Delighted to have him home, his mother allowed him to live rent-free, enabling him to send twice-monthly checks to the North Seattle Diocese marked "reimbursement to discretionary fund." On a grocery store wage, it took until Christmastime before they were square. With that weight finally off his mind and with snowy walks along the Boise River providing clarity, he arrived at his answer just in time for the new year.

O'Shea pulled his Toyota Camry into the parking lot of Savior of the Hills Lutheran Church in northwest Boise. The four-person hiring committee introduced themselves, and the interview began cordially enough until they pressed him about his reasons for leaving the Catholic Church and the unusual availability of a pastor with such remarkable qualifications. Having already decided he could not obfuscate, would not tell half-truths or lie by omission, O'Shea closed his eyes, took a deep breath, and unlatched the gates.

He related the story of his neighbor, Dolores Anderson, and her recovery from cancer. He discussed his work at Saint Helen and his infatuation with Simone which, for the first time, made his shortcomings abundantly clear. He described the trip to New York in detail, the theft of the helicopter, and his arrest. Through it all, he spoke convincingly of purpose and redemption and salvation. A church custodian entered the room, saw five adults crying, and ducked out. And on the first Sunday following Ash Wednesday, Brian William Callum Robert O'Shea was introduced to the Savior of the Hills congregation as their new Associate Pastor.

O'Shea invited his two reprobate friends to join him

for Easter sunrise service. “I haven’t set foot in a Lutheran Church since the day I married my first husband,” Berkshire objected. “And, for the record, I’m still a nullifidian.” Nevertheless, on Easter morning she sipped her coffee in the front row alongside Jesse, who flew in the night before. Pastor O’Shea’s sermon, “Precipitation and Resurrection,” mixed witty observations and funny stories with a description of quixotic religious pilgrimages and one man’s personal struggle with faith. The congregation agreed it was the best Easter sermon they ever heard.

In late May, one year after Berkshire’s stunning presentation at the 2019 North American Society of Religious Scholars conference, researchers from Heidelberg University published their own paper about the Gospel According to Trevor. They argued that Trevor, for all his spiritual inspiration and lofty intention, was not particularly good at spelling.

Among Trevor’s many errors, perhaps the most egregious was the phrase *ό όρχις του Χριστού*, translated as “the testicle of Christ.” The Germans’ analysis of Trevor’s linguistic inadequacy was often contentious (there are rumors one academic attacked another with a lute), but the team ultimately concluded he actually meant *ό ὀρχήσις του Χριστού*—“the dance of Christ”—as a metaphorical reference to Jesus’ life.

A footnote praised one unfortunate American academic for her accurate translation of the curiously erroneous phrase, and hoped she was not too inconvenienced by Trevor’s mistake.

So there it was. A scholar, a preacher, and the Messiah all found God. Not quite the way they planned, mind you. But one must never forget chapter 13, verse 37—the final six words of the Gospel According to Trevor, appropriate here in all their profundity: *Ό κύριος δουλεύει έν μυστηριώδοσι τρόποις.*

Or, for those of you who do not understand ancient Greek: The Lord works in mysterious ways.

Amen.

Appendix

THE GOSPEL ACCORDING TO TREVOR

(selected verses, translated from the original Greek)

Chapter 1 (which describes who is Jesus)

[1] "God is love. To love God, you must love all others: [2] man or woman, greater or lesser, native or immigrant. [3] Love all, no matter who they love, where they live, or what they believe. [4] This is the message," said Christ. "Everything else is merely elaboration."

[28] Those who believe will be ridiculed and tormented by the unbelievers. They will be confronted with mockery and scorn, and will find solace only among the outcasts. [29] Yea, verily I say unto thee, their unkempt appearance hides their true splendor.

Chapter 2 (which describes Jesus' birth)

[29] And so shall be revealed great truths, which few are prepared to hear.

[34] The counsel of prophets and sages is made available to any who have the faith to ask and to believe.

Chapter 3 (which describes Jesus' life and teaching)

[7] Be not above the temptations of the world, but go amongst the sinners so that you may understand the many sufferings of man.

[40] Bind together as God's beloved pilgrims. Your differences are of no matter.

Chapter 4 (which describes Jesus' life and teaching)
[16] Many things are done in a kind and good spirit; all are a reflection of the grace of God.

[22] Accept all gifts, then, as they are intended—as gifts from the Lord to be used when the time is right.

Chapter 5 (which describes Jesus' life and teaching)
[11] Love is patient and trusting, so it follows that trust and patience must be signs of love.

[48] The moneychangers and the charlatans were challenged by Jesus. He flipped their tables and called out their vice for all to witness.

Chapter 6 (which describes Jesus being called to Jerusalem)
[3] When all seems most lost, that is when you shall be found.

[17] Those near to you may fall away, and those distant may again grow near. [18] Your plans may go astray; your straight path may become crooked.

Chapter 7 (which describes Jesus entering the city)
[36] The Lord entered the city and began to teach, yet none would hear Him because His thoughts were unusual to the authorities. [37] The women made themselves busy with chores and the men became diligent with their work, and all were contemptuous of His words.

Chapter 8 (which describes Jesus' teaching)
[19] Jesus embraced the child, which some said was a sinner, but He told them all were good in the eyes of God.

Chapter 9 (which describes Jesus' teaching)
[4] Be always the watchman, prepared to do good works.

[23] While the glory of the rising sun may bid you hurry, let it also draw you to the Lord.

Chapter 10 (which describes the betrayal of Jesus)
[14] Not all will see clearly, but God will take them to task in His own way.

[32] The Disciples went out into the city, each on his own. And when they returned, each understood his obligations to the Lord.

Chapter 11 (which describes Jesus' forgiveness)
[3] Even as you revere those who lived before, give your heart to those nearest you. They are your greatest treasures.

[15] Go boldly, without fear or hesitation, and you will most certainly find God.

Chapter 12 (which describes the mortality of Jesus)
[7] People shift like wind across the fields or rainclouds in the sky. Only God is unwavering.

[20] God offers us abundant possibilities in the same way a servant brings platters of food at a feast, allowing us to choose which to eat.

Chapter 13 (which describes the time after Jesus' death)

[5] In the great metropolis of the modern world, a place both west and east, in a gathering place used by many.

[6] Look to the strategizers, who tarry at games but know much more.

[26] Live with wisdom and humility, proclaiming joy for the immeasurable beauty of this world.

[37] The Lord works in mysterious ways.

BOOK CLUB QUESTIONS

1. Why would Dr. Haley Berkshire choose Religious Studies as a career? Is a nullifidian even qualified to teach Religious Studies? Why or why not?

2. *The Jesus Nut* attempts to convey the scourge of homelessness, focusing on Jesse, a homeless veteran. Does the novel portray homelessness accurately? What can communities and governments do to address this problem?

3. Are the challenges of the clergy (especially Catholic clergy, who must take a vow of celibacy) within the ability of fallible humans? How does Simone's character force Father O'Shea to confront this question, and how does he respond?

4. Berkshire hurls numerous criticisms at the evangelical leaders during the rally at Temple University. Are her criticisms valid? Why or why not?

5. Berkshire, O'Shea, and Jesse all have issues with the hypocrisy of evangelical Christian leaders and their followers. Yet oracles were the ancient world's version of the same idea. Why don't our characters make this connection? Why do they so willingly follow Phineas?

6. Does each of the three characters "find God" in some way? Are they better off at the end of the novel because of their journeys?

7. Who/what are the various "Jesus nuts" contained in the novel? Why is each important?

8. Are the excerpts from the fictional Gospel According to Trevor consistent with other Biblical tenets? Specifically, consider Trevor 1:1-4, which O'Shea cites as the fundamental principle of the entire Gospel. Would everyone agree with this passage? Why or why not?

9. Is *The Jesus Nut* successful at using irony or subverting expectations in any way? If so, how?

10. What is faith? How do the characters struggle with it, and how do they embody it?

11. Religious topics aren't often treated with humor, and when they are, many people get offended. Was the novel's use of humor and satire effective? Why or why not?

12. What is the impact—both historically and present-day—of a Bible compiled only by men?

ACKNOWLEDGMENTS

This book lay dormant in my brain for more than ten years, until it finally *needed* to be written. Still, my first draft was a hodgepodge of ideas both old and new, finally reconciled thanks to the wisdom of beta readers Tom Dugan, Sarah Armistead, and Jerry MacNeil (himself an author of considerable chops and a lantern for me during a particularly dark August). Thanks to each of you for devoting your time and offering your thoughtful critique to shape this crazy story into a far better novel.

Forced to listen to my peculiar and oft-disjointed narrative as we walked our dog Noodle, my wife Fran maintained enough trust and patience to allow me to talk things through. Thank you. Love you. Our son Daniel thought my premise was funny, an initial push which cannot be overlooked. Neither can Noodle's supervisory efforts from underneath my desk.

Thanks to fellow authors in my San Diego writers Meetup (especially David Larson, Mike Gibbs, Brian Hogan, and Henry Herz) for their insights, Dr. Chad Day for his Koine translations, and my wonderful and inspiring Write My Wrongs editors Chrissy and Becca. Dr. Travis Ritt provided clarity about Nicaea, Tom Droze automotive expertise, John Snider helicopter wisdom, Karen Knappenberger and Seongjin Park foreign language help, Dan Ballecer assistance with legal procedure, and Stuart Calderwood textual punctiliousness. All were incredibly valuable. As was Google.

I am beyond grateful for the support of Nick Courtright and Kyle McCord of Atmosphere Press, who saw enough merit in this book (and this writer) to shepherd it into print. They, along with Kevin Stone, Sarah van Hoose, Cammie Finch, and Kelleen Cullison, demonstrated both enthusiastic professionalism and unflappable grace. I trust this end product proves worthy.

Before we moved to California, my wife and I spent two years attending First Church UCC in Phoenix, Arizona. The love, compassion, and diversity of that community are, I hope, reflected in this story.

Finally, I must not neglect the impact of Rob Hall, moderator of a long-ago *How to Write a Novel* workshop. Rob still lives in my head, always pushing for better. If this book is any good, my debt is to you.

ABOUT ATMOSPHERE PRESS

Atmosphere Press is an independent, full-service publisher for excellent books in all genres and for all audiences. Learn more about what we do at atmospherepress.com.

We encourage you to check out some of Atmosphere's latest releases, which are available at Amazon.com and via order from your local bookstore:

Madeleine: Last French Casquette Bride in New Orleans, a novel by Wanda Maureen Miller
Ignite, a novel by Marie A. Wishert
Adam's Roads, a novel by Edwin Litts
Heir to the Silver Cross, a novel by Chris Perry
Letters I'll Never Send, a novel by Nicole Zelniker
Somebody's Watching You, a novel by Robin D'Amato
A Gang of Outsiders, a novel by Bobby Williams
The First Great American Novel: Where Parallel Lines Meet (A Story of Non-Sequiturs), a novel by Mathew Serback
No Way Out, a novel by Betty R. Wall
The Saint of Lost Causes, by Carly Schorman
Monking Around, a novel by Keith Howchi Kilburn
The Cuckoo of Awareness, a novel by Andrew Brush
Falling Into The Light, a novel by M. J. Wiley
The Regular, a novel by Dave Buckhout

ABOUT THE AUTHOR

John Prather is a baseball fan, satire aficionado, mustard enthusiast, and film noir devotee. Now retired from teaching and coaching, he lives in Carlsbad, California with his long-suffering wife, extraordinary teenage son, and neurotic Bichon/Poodle mix. He once ran, a lot. His favorite color is orange. He has broken his nose 15 times. Visit him at JohnPratherWriter.com.

CPSIA information can be obtained
at www.ICGtesting.com
Printed in the USA
LVHW040919090621
689682LV00006B/245

9 781637 528891